The Roots Beneath Us

Gina,

Merry Christmas!!!
2024

Joey Jones (signature)

A Novel by
JOEY JONES

ISBN: 978-1-948978-22-4 (PRINT)

ISBN: 978-1-948978-23-1 (EPUB)

ISBN: 978-1-948978-24-8 (MOBI)

For Meredith Walsh:
You have designed eight of the most
beautiful book covers in existence.
I appreciate your dedication to bringing
each of my stories to life in one image.

Also by Joey Jones

ALONG THE DUSTY ROAD

" *'Life is about love. About giving love and receiving love.'* This is my favorite line from Joey Jones's new book, Along the Dusty Road. Written with a poetic honesty, Joey brings Luke to life on every page and carries us through Luke's conflicting search for his happy ever after. Sometimes sweet and sometimes intensely emotional, this story hits every mark." —Lacey Baker, USA Today Bestselling Author

WHERE THE RAINBOW FALLS
(The Rivers Series, Book 2)

"A riveting story with an ending sure to make your heart swell, WHERE THE RAINBOW FALLS is a novel that leaves you feeling satisfied and accomplished." —Brittany Curry, Librarian

WHEN THE RIVERS RISE
(The Rivers Series, Book 1)

"A threatening hurricane is on the horizon and love is on the line . . . this captivating story of love and loss will keep you turning the pages and wishing for more. This is Joey Jones delivering what his fans have come to expect!" —Riley Costello, Author of *Waiting at Hayden's,* a shopfiction™ novel

THE DATE NIGHT JAR

"A beautiful love story, capturing the poignancy of both new affection and the power of deep, lasting devotion. Readers of Nicholas Sparks, Debbie Macomber, and Nicholas Evans should add THE DATE NIGHT JAR to their reading list." —Jeff Gunhus, *USA TODAY* Bestselling Author

A FIELD OF FIREFLIES

"This is a tale of tragedy, romance, heartbreak and, ultimately, redemption. With lyrical writing and strong character development, Joey Jones effortlessly pulls readers in." —Kristy Woodson Harvey, *NEW YORK TIMES* Bestselling Author

LOSING LONDON

"I read the entire book in one day... I could not put it down! WOW!! LOSING LONDON was incredible; I laughed, I cried, and I'm still in shock." —Erica Latrice, TV Host, Be Inspired

A BRIDGE APART

"Filled with romance, suspense, heartbreak, and a tense plot line, Joey Jones's first novel is a must-read. It is the kind of book you can lend to your mom and best friend." —Suzanne Lucey, Page 158 Books

Acknowledgments

It's hard to believe I have written eight novels. I am incredibly grateful to have one of the most amazing supporting casts an author could imagine. So many people have stood behind me, beside me, and led me through every step of this journey. First and foremost, I would like to thank God for giving me the ability to write and planting that passion within my soul. Branden, my oldest son, is an amazing father to a two-year old girl. Parker, who I can't believe is starting second grade, is full of energy, love, and laughter. I cherish our adventures together, making memories that will live forever.

I would also like to thank my wonderful family. My parents Joe and Patsy Jones taught me how to become a responsible adult, and I hope to leave a legacy that makes them proud. My dad now resides in Heaven, and I miss him dearly. My mom, my breakfast partner and one of my best friends, is the most humble person I know. My brothers and sisters DeAnn, Judy, Lee, Penny, and Richard are some of my closest friends. In many ways, their support is my foundation.

My editor Donna Matthews is incredibly talented at polishing my writing. My graphics designer Meredith Walsh did a fantastic job with each of my novel covers and supporting pieces. Polgarus Studio made the intricate process of formatting the interior of this novel a breeze. Once again, Deborah Dove worked her magic in creating the book blurb. Mashal Smith, who travels the world photographing mesmerizing landscapes, captured my author photo gracefully.

Lastly, I want to thank some people who have been influential throughout my life: some for a season but each for a reason. Thank you to Alan & Kathy Hammer, Andrew Haywood, BJ Horne, Billy Nobles, Bob Peele, Cathy Errick, Courtney Haywood, Diane Tyndall, Erin Haywood, Jan Raynor, Jeanette Towne, Josh Haywood, Josh Towne, Kenny Ford, Kim Jones, Mitch Fortescue, Nicholas Sparks, Ray White, Rebekah Jones, Richard Banks, Steve Cobb, Steven Harrell, and Steve Haywood. It is a privilege to call each of you my friend.

The Roots Beneath Us

1

Piper Luck glanced at her rearview mirror. Her whole life was behind her, and that was where she chose to leave the past all of it. When her caramel brown eyes returned to the road beyond the front windshield of her bright blue Jeep Wrangler, she realized the rest of her life lay ahead. The time to write a new story was here. Today, the first of May, marked her fortieth birthday, and she left the excitement of Miami for a slower pace.

With Duck, North Carolina, plugged into her GPS, she didn't know much about the place nor a soul there and had never visited. These and a thousand other things made this trip unique.

Having the top down let her long jet-black hair blow in the wind as free as a kite as she cruised north on I-95. One of the positives of living on the Outer Banks would be not losing her tan although Italian roots guaranteed a dark complexion year round. She never used a tanning bed, even when she lived in Boston, Bismarck, or Juneau. One of her goals was to live in all fifty state capitals plus DC—she checked off the last city on the list earlier this year.

She and a friend came up with that idea in their mid-twenties which somehow felt like yesterday and a lifetime ago all at once.

There were moments she never wanted to forget and others she wished she didn't remember. She saw things she never imagined and did many she regretted. Who hadn't, but the career she chose lent itself to danger and secrets.

Now, with all that over, Piper hoped never to hurt or deceive another human being again. Over the years she and her coworkers made up stories that people believed rather than ones people didn't, which was what they often heard in their line of work. She lived in all kinds of locations with some of those same people. They faced death on more than one occasion. She once hopped off a moving train, but the time she jumped out of a helicopter into the Pacific Ocean probably topped that story.

Staying in tip-top shape was necessary. Although she couldn't wait to eat a burger and fries, she didn't want to lose the flat stomach taking in the breeze between the loose-fitting knit tank top and pink leggings she chose for this trip. Subconsciously, she raked her fingers across her abs as another exit sign became a blur. All the fresh-caught seafood sure to abound in her new environment should help keep her healthy. Plus there was certain to be runs on the beach, swims in the ocean, and loads of other outdoor activities. Now it would all be for her and not the powers that be holding clipboards or at least manifesting eyes that resembled checklists.

Nobody would be breathing down her neck about toned biceps, quick hands, scissor grips, and flawless moves. With that life behind her, she hoped to settle down, grow roots, build a new life, and hopefully, find someone to share it with. Until now she pretty much gave up on the possibility of a relationship, at least one with genuine depth. Maybe starting a family would be on the table. She always wanted kids. All these ideas seemed surreal, but at the same time, they suddenly felt within reach.

2

oone Winters, wearing gray jogging pants and a short-sleeved, red dri-fit shirt, paced around the house like a precision madman all morning. Two rugged suitcases laid open on the queen-sized bed where the memories made were both good and bad. For weeks he slowly accumulated the items he wanted to take with him but had been careful about how and where he placed them. He prayed not to forget anything important like the glasses on his face. That thought led him to touch the frame again to make sure they were there.

The planning allowed him to pack quicker now. In so many ways he dreamed of this day his whole life but never imagined having the guts to follow through. This thought reminded him that he hadn't left yet. He ran away a few times during his teenage years but always returned. On the first attempt his parents found him before dark, and he paid a price for leaving. Another time, he disappeared for a few nights but quickly ran out of food and money. An abandoned house that gave him the creeps was the best place he found to stay, and living there proved worse than with his parents. At least they fed and clothed him.

As Boone darted from one room to another, he found himself stopping to look at the pictures one last time and even moved a couple to a suitcase. He stared at a variety of knickknacks placed neatly on shelves and tables. Even though forgetting the whole house seemed like the best idea, each room filled with memories grabbed his attention. He was leaving so much behind, most of it on purpose, and would miss the familiarity and the comfort.

Boone packed about two weeks' worth of clothes but had no idea where he would wash the outfits. An envelope stuffed beneath a stack of shorts contained several hundred dollars. Another hundred in twenties filled his front pocket. He wasn't used to having much cash and didn't own a credit card. That would probably work in his favor. He would need more money soon though because what he had now would barely cover the trip across the country.

His boss, who happened to be the only true adult friend he ever had in this world, encouraged him to leave for a while now. He hated that cancer had recently taken Claude away from him, but in a way the loss pushed him to this point. On his deathbed, Claude promised Boone a job would be waiting at his destination. The limited details and the fact that he was gone made it scary, but he trusted Claude. Upon arrival Boone needed to contact a man who would explain everything.

Although relieved to know he would soon be about as far from Oakland, California, as possible without needing a passport, Boone didn't know if Beth would come looking for him. If that happened he wanted to make sure she didn't find him. Not leaving clues behind had been paramount. He thought through every step hoping not to leave a trail. It helped that he didn't have a cell phone—another tracking device like a credit card or driver's license. Shockingly, he didn't have the latter either although legally he could have been behind the steering wheel over twenty years ago.

Boone zipped the second suitcase shut and headed to the front door with a strap over each of his bony shoulders as well as a bookbag on his back. Physical strength wasn't an attribute he could claim. As he stretched a hand toward the knob that led to freedom, Boone felt weighed down physically, mentally, and emotionally. An image of Beth standing on the front porch staring at him when the door opened popped into his mind. The thought caused him to shiver as if snow piled up outside, and he pulled in a deep breath before twisting his wrist.

Boone jumped when the hinges screamed at him but not because of the typical noise. He froze as a black cat darted across the sidewalk nearly making him drop everything.

"Bad luck," he scoffed. He wasn't superstitious anymore. How could things get worse? He wasn't stupid; life could still go downhill, but as the soles of his tightly tied tennis shoes touched the concrete, he knew he wouldn't turn and walk back through that doorway if a thousand black cats ran across the front yard.

Boone sighed and trudged down the brick steps. This would be easier if a car waited in the driveway for him to hop into and drive east until the gas needle begged for a refill. He felt confident he could figure out how to operate a vehicle. For nearly eighteen years he watched his parents, and he had been riding in the passenger seat beside Beth longer than that.

The sidewalk leading to the neighborhood entrance never looked so long. Boone's legs paced as fast as his body allowed while his head swiveled, watching for cars and people, technically one vehicle and one person—Beth. He nearly panicked when the first car turned onto their street. Same color as theirs but a different model. His heart seemed to beat faster with every step.

When Boone reached the main road, he held out his thumb but didn't stop or slow his gait. He figured the chances of someone picking up a grown man carrying two suitcases were slim. Who hitchhiked these days, anyway? He thought of a commercial where a guy on the side of the road held a case of beer in one hand and an ax in the other. A man driving by with a woman in the passenger seat beside him wanted to pick up the stranger, but the lady quickly pointed out the obvious while the guy's focus remained on the alcohol.

The only weapon Boone carried was a pocket knife tucked away in the backpack's zipper pouch. He kept it nearby in case of trouble. Hopefully no issues would arise, he thought as a white pickup truck passed. To Boone's surprise the taillights suddenly lit up, and he watched the vehicle ease onto the shoulder of the road up ahead.

As Boone approached urgently, the driver slid across to the passenger side and manually rolled down the window.

"Where are you headed, young man?" the fellow asked when Boone stopped at the window.

"The train station," Boone murmured to a burly man with gray hair and a snow-white beard.

"The police station?" the guy asked while touching his ear.

"Train," Boone clarified.

"Hop on in," he invited, motioning with a hand gesture.

When Boone reached for the silver handle, he noticed a black vehicle come to a halt behind the truck.

3

nce Piper exited the interstate, the scenery shifted as the route led her to the Historic Albemarle Highway. She passed antique stores in the middle of nowhere featuring aged signage, dated gas pumps, and random memorabilia from yesteryear. Open fields abounded, and she loved the old tattered barns, some still in use and others falling apart yet somehow resembling a piece of art rather than a condemned building.

Canals that looked like perfect kayaking trails lined a long stretch of the roadway. She crossed several lengthy bridges with magnificent views of open water, and at the end of one she raised her hands victoriously at the sight of the sign that read, "Welcome to the Outer Banks."

When she reached Nags Head, she found the NC 12 split. The southern route led to Hatteras, Ocracoke, and other places she never heard of while the northern stretch went to Kill Devil Hills, Kitty Hawk, Southern Shores, Duck, and Corolla. The road took her past Jockey's Ridge State Park, the Wright Brothers National Memorial, and other popular tourist attractions. Many of the license plates showcased the "First in Flight" tagline and background image of Orville and Wilbur Wright's iconic airplane, and the OBX identifying letters made picking out the locals easy.

From there, it didn't take long to find the "Duck Town Limits" sign followed by another with a tennis court for the backdrop that read, "Welcome to Duck, North Carolina." A wide sidewalk on the right side of the street looked like a wonderful place to walk, run, or ride a bicycle.

Piper quickly reached the quaint village area which seemed to start at the Aqua Restaurant & Spa where she noticed a path on either side of the road as she slowly meandered her Jeep through the winding street while taking in her surroundings.

Piper excitedly took mental notes of places she wanted to visit like Scarborough Faire Shops, Roadside Bar & Grill, Kellogg Supply, Sweet T's Coffee, and Wee Winks Market & Deli. She loved the many gravel parking lots and how the town appeared nestled amongst a plethora of live oak trees providing unique charm.

A mile later, at the northern end of the village, a spectacular roadside view of the Currituck Sound became visible between The Waterfront Shops and Sunset Grille & Raw Bar. Piper pulled over to marvel in the beauty, and that is when she realized Duck had no stoplights and only one gas station. However, the town seemingly offered everything a local or tourist could want or need, setting it apart from many other small places she visited.

After snapping a few photos with her phone, Piper reached her destination. The leather flip-flops beneath her feet made a crunching sound in a bed of rocks when she climbed out of her Jeep onto the driveway of the cutest little yellow beach cottage she ever saw. When she found this place online a few weeks ago, she wondered if it would live up to the photos and reviews. At first glance from the outside, it instantly earned the nearly five-star rating, and she closed her eyes to take in something the words on the website failed to capture. The unmistakable aroma of salty air filled her lungs as the faint sound of waves crashing in the distance tickled her ears.

This place where she would live for the next week while wandering the island in search of something permanent wasn't oceanfront or even oceanview but nestled in a small neighborhood across the street from a stretch of land that mirrored the beach. She considered a home overlooking the Atlantic Ocean when searching for a temporary dwelling. Knowing she couldn't afford that lifestyle long term, Piper decided against the idea, thinking the place where she eventually settled might then seem like a downgrade.

Clusters of live oaks like the ones she spotted on the drive in filled the neighborhood, separating one house from the next making each relatively secluded. Most of the yards, including the one she walked across now, were a mixture of grass and the kind of sandy dirt kids often wore on bare feet in the summertime. The environment looked more natural than any from her travels.

Piper snapped a photo to commemorate the occasion then let down her ponytail. The breeze gently kissed her hair as she keyed in the code at the front door. A cast-iron table flanked by two chairs sat on the porch. It looked like the perfect breakfast spot which she added to her mental notes. A potted plant sat beneath each of the front windows, framed with bright blue shutters. Stepping inside, she only carried her purse to hold her phone and keys. The rest of her belongings would have to wait until after the self-guided tour.

Hardwood floors connected the shotgun-style home's open living room and kitchen floor plan. From the front door Piper could see the back door tucked away in a small area housing a washer and dryer. On her right a door opened to a small bedroom, and when she drifted into the kitchen another doorway on the same side of the house led to the master bedroom where she found a bathroom with a claw foot tub. She immediately made plans for a bubble bath at some point this evening.

Piper loved how it felt to smile naturally, and she could not remember the last day she smiled this much. Usually on her birthday she would have drinks with friends, likely leading to other shenanigans. Not tonight. She didn't want to go out and not because she didn't know anyone here. If Piper learned one thing from moving all over the country these past twenty years, it was how to make friends. She could start a conversation with nearly anyone, and complete strangers would share details about their lives that shocked her even though nothing much surprised her these days.

One of her friends was the reason she came here. Although their relationship was strictly work related initially, he became a friend, a good friend, and she missed him dearly. Over twice her age, Hardy Turner modeled the adult father figure she needed. Her biological father still existed, but the two of them didn't have much of a relationship. Piper sometimes saw her parents around the holidays, but everyone wore masks although they never gathered for Halloween.

With Hardy she was herself. He accepted her for who she was, where she had been, and where she desired to go. The two of them talked about hopes and dreams, mistakes and failures. She shared how she wanted to start over, and he told her he knew the perfect place. The man traveled the world. He owned homes and businesses in a handful of countries and across the United States. His material possessions were basically unlimited. That was why it shocked Piper when he revealed he lived most of his life unhappy. She vividly remembered the day when the two of them sat on the bow of his yacht in the South Pacific, and he shared the pivotal time that changed everything.

It broke her heart when Hardy passed away. He seemed to have so much good left in him.

After testing out the bed where she would lay her head later tonight, Piper retrieved her luggage and pulled a trifold brochure from one of the suitcases. In bold lettering the title read: THE ROOTS BENEATH US.

Hardy swore by this journey, a course local to Duck. The group met once a week. "Transformative" was the word his unmistakable gravelly voice used to describe the experience.

Piper believed him because she watched his life transform. He went from a selfish, hedonistic prude to one of the most humble and giving people she ever met. She witnessed the bad habits he stopped and the positive ones formed. She saw the joy it brought him to give away more money than he spent. He thought the program fit perfectly into her goals, and she planned to attend the next session.

In the meantime a seashell magnet held the brochure, featuring the silhouette of a live oak tree and the elaborate root system beneath, securely on the black refrigerator. Almost all the décor in the house carried a beach theme from the throw pillows to the backsplash in the kitchen to the random driftwood-framed quotes on the walls. The one above the bed where Piper placed her pillow read: All who stay here are found. She wasn't exactly sure how to decipher the message but thought she liked it.

It took at least a half dozen trips to lug everything packed tightly in her vehicle hundreds of miles ago into the house. Before leaving Florida she sold most of her belongings because she didn't want to rent a truck or trailer. She had been there and done that, and it sucked. After a few moves she cut back on buying material possessions and spent most of her discretionary income on experiences.

The final item she retrieved came off an attached bike rack. When she hopped on the tan seat of her mint green retro beach cruiser bicycle, she felt as free as the dozen or so birds soaring effortlessly above the tree line.

Time to explore the island, Piper decided as her feet began to draw circles with the pedals.

4

eneath a brown hoodie Boone stared out a train window and felt thankful the black vehicle that stopped behind the pickup wasn't Beth's. Having to look twice sent fear rushing through his veins, and he didn't know what he or she would have done had it been her. *Keep going,* he imagined any logical human being shouting if they knew why he ran.

Boone barely noticed the frantic pace at the station as passengers boarded; he only focused on the faces of every single person within a relatively close distance of the train. He kept expecting Beth to show up, and the image in his mind of her glaring at him on the other side of the window caused his shoulders to shudder. He wouldn't rest easy until the doors slid shut and the train started rolling on the track.

If Beth showed up at the house or pickup truck or found him here, he knew she wouldn't let him leave without a fight. The first time he mentioned leaving, she threatened to take her life. The next time, she claimed if he ever went through with it, he would never breathe again. Serious threats haunted him, but the other consequences left emotional and physical scars.

A man wasn't supposed to end up in an abusive relationship. Not that a woman was either, but no one ever talked about a man being beaten by his significant other. All the bruises and cuts Boone accumulated over the years to prove it made for better stories if they "happened" on a construction site, in the garage while fixing something, or from a fight with another man.

The guys at the job sites already teased him enough because he didn't fit the mold of a construction worker. He wasn't strong or rough or loud. In fact, he was the opposite. These things happened to a person like him who grew up in a verbally, physically, and sexually abusive home.

Only one person knew that as a teenager Boone's parents took money from strangers, friends, or anyone with cash in exchange for him to engage in a wide array of sexual acts. He experienced situations many teenagers and young adults fantasized about, but none of them voluntarily. Beth basically bought him from his parents at age sixteen because she liked the things he did to and for her in the bedroom. He cohabitated with her ever since.

Like his parents she provided for him. When he graduated, she made him get a job to help pay the bills. College wasn't an option, and honestly, it still surprised him that neither his parents nor Beth forced him to drop out of school to work so they would have more money to fund their bad habits. Boone figured if people knew his story, they would probably wonder why he didn't choose to quit. School offered a breath of fresh air, an open window into the real world. Without the reprieve he would have likely gone crazy.

If Boone hadn't worked as an adult, he imagined he might be dead or in an asylum by now. Beth would only agree to let him work with other males, so he built fences, sheds, swimming pools, houses, and many other things over the years. She dropped him off and picked him up. All the guys called her his sugar mama or a cougar.

When Beth broke him free of the bondage at his parent's house, he fell in love with her for the wrong reasons. One of the best things about her was she didn't make him have sex with anyone besides her even though he knew she had other partners. When forced to be intimate with someone, no matter how attractive they were or how good they were in bed, it felt like torture. Most people Boone encountered in that environment were unattractive for an array of reasons usually connected to drugs and alcohol. His parents mainly used the money they made off him to support their addictions. Beth didn't battle substance abuse; she just had twisted sexual desires and the money and looks to get almost anything she wanted.

The doors collapsed, the train breathed, and the sound of heavy wheels rolling on the track echoed throughout the narrow railcar. They started slowly and then moved a little faster. Boone's eyes darted inside and outside. This was really happening.

When the train exited the station and reached cruising speed, Boone's shoulders relaxed for the first time today, and it felt like a weighted vest dropped from his body. Then something uncontrollable happened. The thoughts in Boone's mind began to fall from his eyes one drop at a time, each landing on the backpack in his lap.

He was safe.

Free.

Ironically, Boone knew he would miss Beth. Although unpredictable and controlling, she was loving, comforting, and adventurous. He wondered if she would take her life when she gave up on finding him. In a way he suddenly felt responsible if that happened, but going back wasn't an option. He would never go back and never get into another abusive relationship. *Ever.* Somehow, someway, he would defy the odds and make it on his own.

5

Piper pedaled around Duck as the final hours of daylight expired. She loved the proximity of her place to the local shops and restaurants which quickly led her to realize she could get used to this lifestyle. Living near the center of town wasn't a new experience. In most places she sought an apartment downtown with all the necessities within walking distance.

Duck was similar in that regard, yet the atmosphere felt completely different. The calm streets and sidewalks made riding her bicycle relaxing rather than chaotic. This evening she didn't have to dodge a single person or vehicle. Although several people waved, no one honked or yelled at her to get out of the way. These folks seemed polite, so she smiled and waved back. Pedestrians on the walkways said hello and random strangers held doors open at the shops.

In some cities Piper lived, she didn't have a vehicle. She walked, took public transportation such as the subway or a bus, and used ride sharing services. A moped served as her ride in a handful of other places. Piper stopped pedaling momentarily when she happened upon the local dance studio. The sign out front featuring the silhouette of little dancers caught her eye. She always wanted to work with kids in that environment but never found the time. Maybe she would check in soon to see if they needed another instructor. Teaching dance would be fun. If they didn't have an opening, volunteering might be an option. While a steady income in the near future would be beneficial, she saved up for this life transition.

In a way Piper felt prepared for this new adventure but at the same time clueless regarding what came next. Although her career took her all over the place, she always lined up a job. Life somewhat revolved around the awkward itinerary it brought along. She wondered if sleeping on a normal schedule here would be possible. It would be nice if her internal body clock would adjust but only time would tell, she figured. Maybe she would work from eight to five like most people.

Piper wondered if a fresh face like hers stood out to the locals. The Outer Banks was a popular tourist area, so she imagined she didn't look like a sore thumb although the prime season still lay ahead, so she might. She wondered if the streets would be congested then.

A plate of freshly caught and cooked fish occupied the bottom of the basket beyond the handlebars on Piper's bicycle. Once settled she might grill her own but for now these from Sunset Grille & Raw Bar smelled delicious. The server at the counter recommended the roasted parmesan green beans and hushpuppies too. Hopefully, she burned enough calories pedaling to deserve the latter as well as the slice of red velvet cake she picked out at Tullio's Bakery. Everything behind the glass case looked nearly as sweet as the little old lady who boxed her birthday dessert. The woman wore a chain on her large, framed glasses, and her gray hair took the shape of the curlers that molded it.

Piper smiled when parking her bicycle next to the back porch. After pushing the kickstand with her foot, she filled her arms with all the goodies collected during the first of many anticipated excursions. When picking out her birthday dinner, she contemplated whether to eat at the kitchen table or on the couch while watching television. However, when she reached the end of the gravel driveway and spotted sporadic little yellow twinkles dancing amongst the cluster of dangling branches in her new backyard, she decided to eat with the fireflies.

Piper set her dinner plate on the outdoor patio table and carried everything else inside. She opened a few cabinet doors in search of a wine glass for the bottle of pinot noir she carefully selected earlier. The nice gentleman at Sweet T's Coffee, Beer, & Wine eloquently described a variety of favorites from the local vineyards and then carefully wrapped the bottle with packaging paper after her mode of transportation came up in conversation.

"Just remember there is no drinking and driving on the island," he chuckled when handing her the bag, including a complimentary corkscrew, in case her place didn't have one.

"Are you second guessing the gift?" Piper giggled, and the man twenty years her elder laughed out loud.

"Not at all," he ascertained. "I trust your judgment."

"I just hope my bicycle's tires don't find any bumps on the way home and send this bottle flying out of the basket."

"Be safe," he uttered with a grin. "And happy birthday, young lady."

On her fortieth, Piper contemplated how many more years people would call her *young lady*. Maybe the trick rests in spending time with the older generations. They were wiser too, or at least most of them. She met a few who never grew up. Her friend Hardy Turner fell into each camp at different stages of the life in which she knew him.

The first bite of blackened Mahi tasted so wonderful Piper immediately forked another before trying the veggies.

"Mmm," she announced to the fireflies.

The branches beyond the porch swayed with the breeze. It felt just cool enough for Piper to grab a light sweater when inside earlier. The wine paired well with the fish as she sipped slowly, taking in everything her five senses allowed. After tasting the green beans and hushpuppies, Piper decided this might be the best birthday dinner ever.

She appreciated the quiet of the night and the serenity offered in this backyard. The fireflies reminded her of string lights draped from the low-hanging branches although not quite bright enough to illuminate the space around them, providing a somewhat mysterious appeal to the setting.

Piper took her time eating. Having nowhere to be and nothing to say or do relaxed her. Although she imagined having a friend or a group of people to share this with would be fabulous in its own way, this was her night. She deserved a birthday alone. No colossal party like most people received on this momentous occasion. She didn't feel forty; she felt happy and refreshed. Most of all she felt free.

After the last bite of dinner, Piper poured another glass of wine and fetched the slice of red velvet cake. This time while sitting on the patio, she heard the faint sound of music somewhere in the distance; something soft, maybe jazz or blues. She imagined someone like herself sitting alone on their back porch taking in the night with the beautiful dark sky filled with more stars than her pointer finger could count. She attempted that feat many times over the years and never found a better math problem.

Piper celebrated every minute of the remainder of her birthday, literally resting her head on the pillow when the clock struck midnight. There would be plenty to do over the next few days, but the only thing she did tonight other than enjoy the outdoors was pull out her toiletry bag and pajamas. While brushing her teeth, she smiled at the bathtub.

"Another night," Piper whispered as if it had ears.

She loved it when a wonderful surprise trumped a great plan. Visions of sipping wine while relaxing in a hot bath, maybe reading a book with the flicker of candlelight dancing all around her, previously filled her birthday self-care thoughts.

Piper woke the following day around eight to rays of bright sunshine spilling through the window. The soft flannel pajama pants wrapped around the legs she stretched beneath the covers warmed her. She gently tugged the bottom of the matching top to cover her stomach when she sat up on the edge of the bed. Her bare feet barely touched the cold hardwood.

Piper spent the next few days settling in although unsure how long she would be in this house. The thought of renting it for a second week or even a month or more crossed her mind. She grocery shopped at Wee Winks Market, enjoyed breakfast on the front porch a couple of times, rode her bicycle all over town, and visited the dance studio. Unfortunately, they didn't have an opening but the owner agreed to let her help the instructors.

"We can always use an extra set of hands especially with the littlest ones," she chirped.

The woman, tall and thin with modest curves, looked the part. Her bubbly voice energized the room surrounded by mirrors and accessorized with barres, turn boards, and other equipment positioned neatly on the glossy parquet-style hardwood floor. Piper was glad she stopped and asked although part of her felt a twinge of sadness that a paid position wasn't available. She would look for something else to pay the bills and let dance be for fun. Dancing should be the primary goal anyway, not making money, she concluded.

While riding around town on her bicycle and in her Jeep, Piper looked for houses with for sale or rent signs in the front yards. The options appeared limited, but she discovered a few that might work although she hadn't found *the one* yet. A real estate agent showed her around her top choices and a few others beyond her price range.

Piper walked to the ocean one day with a bag over her shoulder and a chair in her hand, and sunbathed for a couple of hours. The water wasn't warm enough to jump in yet, but she looked forward to swimming once the temperature rose to her liking. The following morning she went for a beach walk and collected shells, and that same night wandered a similar trek but spent most of her time looking out or up rather than down. She cherished the sound of the waves rolling, the mystery in the darkness, and the coolness of the sand under her bare feet. Most of all she loved that the beach was within walking distance.

When Thursday rolled around, Piper pulled the brochure from the refrigerator and reread the words: *THE ROOTS BENEATH US. The group meets on Thursday evenings at seven o'clock.*

"Let's do this," she whispered encouragingly to herself.

6

The trip from Oakland to Duck took eighty-one hours and eight minutes. When Boone first mapped out the route with Claude, he knew he wanted to travel the cheapest way possible outside of hitchhiking across the country. That meant trains and buses as well as nonstop travel to avoid hotel room expenses sure to cut into his limited budget. Flying never existed as an option for several reasons. Booking a flight left a paper trail and required identification beyond what he possessed; plus the airline companies made paying by cash nearly impossible.

The first and longest leg from Oakland to Chicago by train lasted almost fifty-two hours. Boone slept in the small cabin, or at least tried. Not having Beth in the bed next to him felt awkward. All these years he shared body heat with another human being. He woke once and put his arm around someone who wasn't even there. When reality struck at that moment, tears flooded his eyes. He doubted anyone in the adjacent rooms or hallway heard him crying, not that it mattered; they were all strangers.

Being around people seemed helpful although he barely talked to anyone. Watching them occupied more of his time than anything else. The scenery in some areas had been quite beautiful. The hills and mountains offered the most spectacular views. He loved the old farmhouses and the animals that roamed the land, some tamed and others wild. He saw a bear, cows, deer, goats, chickens, and all kinds of birds. Seeing the children's faces light up for these animals proved to be the best part of the trip.

Boone dreamed of having kids and wondered what life would be like with children and how having a family would have affected his relationship with Beth. However, as the miles between them increased, he was grateful she never got pregnant. With kids in the picture, leaving would have been impossible. Maybe that was one of the only perks of her having sex with other men; she remained on birth control out of fear of having a child with a random person. The downsides were countless including the times Boone ended up with sexually transmitted diseases. Of course there was never a question about where it came from, and when he asked early on in their relationship, he paid a price for inquiring. Beth accused him of cheating on her every time it came up, but they both knew the truth. He never experienced consensual relations with a woman other than Beth, not that their intimacy could be categorized in that regard. Although he grew to enjoy their lovemaking at times, he despised her for how their relationship started. There was nothing consensual about it.

Boone noticed attractive women on the train but found no interest in them. The thought of approaching a woman made him cringe for multiple reasons. What if she turned out to be like Beth and all the other women before her? What if he didn't even know how to have a real relationship? He became so good at taking orders in the bedroom and everywhere else that he doubted the possibility of a healthy relationship.

Far more important things occupied his mind, like where he would live after arriving at his destination. What would this job Claude lined up for him be like? He promised Boone he possessed all the skills necessary to handle the project; it was construction but different. Claude calling it a project also concerned him. How long would it last? Would he eventually need to search for a different job? Doing anything other than what he knew seemed scary. "If you make it to the Outer Banks, you will realize you can do anything you want." That line spoken by his boss remained etched in his mind.

The train ride from Chicago to Charlottesville totaled twenty hours and forty minutes. The passengers' faces changed, the seats felt softer, and the cabin smelled different. Most of the sounds remained the same. Boone peered out the windows during the daylight hours and tried to sleep at night. Several times he stared at one of the photos he brought of him and Beth. She was pretty—green eyes, light brown wavy hair, a pale face due more to makeup than skin tone, and one more earring than a person could count on all their fingers. Her physical strength amazed Boone. She pinned him down with ease anytime she wanted. Regular aerial training with fabric, hoops, trapezes, and so forth built muscles throughout her body, making her strong and easy on the eyes. Beth appeared so sweet in the photos, and Boone remembered that some days the title fit her.

A night bus ran from Charlottesville to Richmond, an hour and fifteen minute drive. Boone dozed off but jumped the first time he saw his reflection in the window. Unfortunately, there were no cabins on buses, not that the relatively short ride allowed time for true sleep. The passengers seemed rougher around the edges, and Boone tried to ignore them although some of their outfits and looks screamed for attention. He accidentally made eye contact with one man who then glared at him off and on for the rest of the trip.

When Boone switched buses in Richmond to head for Elizabeth City, he was grateful the crazy-looking guy didn't follow him. In a way the man reminded him of some people he worked with over the years, and Boone randomly wondered if he would miss them. Acquaintances would be the best word to describe his coworkers although he knew quite a bit about their lives. He listened way more than he talked.

Approximately three hours after boarding the bus to Elizabeth City, Boone walked down the steps he climbed earlier. This marked his first time in North Carolina; he even saw the sign a ways back on the road to confirm it. Now the final destination was less than sixty miles away. However, no trains or buses—other than tour buses which would undoubtedly exceed budget—traveled to the Outer Banks.

Boone decided to finish the last leg of the journey across the United States the way he started it—hitchhiking.

7

iper stood on the sidewalk outside the building where the schedule said the class met. Upon arriving she tugged at the handle only to find the door locked. She knocked, but no one answered. Then she cupped her hands around her eyes and held them to the glass. The inside of the space appeared completely dark, almost as if vacant, so she checked the address on her phone. This seemed to be the right place.

Glancing at the time, she realized she was ten minutes early. Maybe the others would show up soon.

While waiting, Piper decided to read the brochure again:

THE ROOTS BENEATH US is a simple journey that helps solve life's complex obstacles. Some of the roots beneath us keep us grounded in truth, love, and a plethora of positive experiences while others hold us down, tangle up our lives, and keep us from flying. One of the first steps is to figure out the difference: Which roots are positive and which are negative? Which are too large and which are too small?

Life is largely about balance. We need healthy roots in order to grow wings. A well-balanced life equally nourishes spiritual, emotional, mental, physical, social, occupational, and financial health. We need balance in everything: relationships, family, work, children, volunteering, exercising, etc. Often the single thing that keeps us from a well-balanced life is fear. On this journey we establish our fears and goals (often related), prioritize the list, and tackle them one by one through bravery. Fear doesn't necessarily go away, but as we overcome our fears, we realize we are stronger than them.

The brochure mentioned being paired up with an accountability partner who would walk through the journey alongside you. When seven o'clock rolled around with not a soul in sight, Piper presumed she wouldn't be matched up with anyone tonight. What were the chances everyone was late? Doubtful. Maybe the time or the day of the week changed? Who knew how long this brochure had been around? She concluded that the website address at the bottom might offer more information.

She hopped on her bicycle seat and balanced herself while pulling out her phone to check the online site. Before she could scroll through the options on the homepage, she noticed a person walking hurriedly across the parking lot. She found it odd that they didn't drive but then glanced down at her mode of transportation smiled, and shrugged her shoulders. On this small island a lot of people walked too.

As the person drew closer, Piper noticed him glancing around as if unsure of his whereabouts. Instinctively, she reached into her bag and placed a hand on a small bottle of pepper spray attached to her keychain just in case. They were the only two people in a dimly lit parking lot. However, at this point she wondered if he even saw her, and the moment when she realized he did, he jumped a little, stopped short of her, and stood within talking distance.

"I am sorry if I startled you," Piper announced.

"That's okay," he replied shyly. "I didn't see you standing there."

He glanced around to see if anyone else might be waiting near the building.

"Are you here for The Roots Beneath Us class?" Piper inquired.

"Yes," he answered, looking at his feet while speaking. "Are you the teacher?"

Piper chuckled. "Me? No way," she proclaimed. "I thought maybe you were."

"No," he answered, shaking his head.

"This is my first time," Piper announced.

"Me too."

"I guess everyone else including the instructor is late," Piper pointed out glancing at her watch which showed five after.

"Yeah."

"How did you hear about the course?" Piper asked. "Is it a course?" she contemplated out loud. "The brochure doesn't specifically say; I think it's called a journey," she acknowledged.

"A friend."

Piper waited to see if the man would respond to the second question. When he didn't she furrowed her brow slightly but figured he assumed the question to be rhetorical. She also thought he might ask how she heard about the class but he didn't.

"How long have you lived on the island?" Piper asked, making small talk and hoping one person showing up meant more would trickle in soon.

The guy shuffled his feet. "I don't live here," he revealed. "Well, I might live here."

Piper didn't hide her confusion. "Are you saying you're not sure if you live here, or that you are considering living here, but you don't right now?" she questioned. She wondered if he was homeless. He wore a dingy brown hoodie and jeans with holes which could be anything from a fashion statement to a sign of poverty. She noticed how he avoided eye contact, but when she caught a glimpse of his eyes, they looked kind yet gave the appearance that he hadn't slept much lately. It seemed unlikely for there to be a homeless population here like in many of the cities she lived, but she guessed people everywhere happened on hard times.

"I think I am going to live here," he clarified.

The man looked intelligent, but the glasses could be misleading. "Are you vacationing here to see if you like it?"

"Not really," he mumbled. "I plan to stay."

"Me too; this place is magical."

"Good," he said, pushing his hands into his pockets and glancing around as if hoping someone else would show up to interrupt their conversation.

Something about this man intrigued Piper. "How long have you been in town?" she inquired.

He glanced at his watch. "Only long enough to find a place to stay and walk here," he shared.

"Geez," Piper responded. "I guess that means I am no longer the newest resident on the island." She laughed but he didn't.

"How long have you been here?"

Piper thought that might be his first question since the mostly one-sided conversation started. "A few days, and I already love it."

"Are you on vacation?"

Wow, another question. Maybe they were making progress. Perhaps she should be the instructor of this course, or journey, or whatever the title. "I feel like I am on vacation; however, I just moved here from Miami."

"Nice."

Back to a one word response. Maybe she should stick with being a student if the teacher ever showed.

"My name is Piper," she offered, reaching out her right hand.

"I'm Boone."

Boone's hands felt as rough as sandpaper yet timid.

"It's a pleasure to meet you, Boone."

"Thanks," he replied, sharing a sideways grin.

"Where are you from?"

"Um, I would rather not say." When the words slipped out, he wished he said something different. He had to find a better way to avoid direct answers.

"Oh, are you like a secret agent or something?" she teased. Piper met enough of those over the years to know he wasn't one.

"No," Boone answered. He didn't want Beth to find him, so the less information divulged, the better. He wondered if he should have even shared his real name but knew he didn't want to start this new phase of life lying to people.

"I have lived all over the country," Piper proclaimed.

"Nice." Boone wondered if she ever lived in California but didn't dare ask.

"I probably lived somewhere close to where you're from," she presumed.

Boone didn't like the sound of that. What if she had? What if she met Beth? Knew Beth? What if they worked together? Worked out at the same gym? This woman looked very fit. The purple leggings she wore highlighted every muscle from her thighs down. A loose-fitting black top hid most of her upper body, but he imagined it matched the lower half.

"Maybe," Boone responded.

"Are you shy?"

Boone pondered the question although he knew the answer; he had been called shy his whole life. "Kind of," he answered. For some reason the way she asked didn't embarrass him like many others had.

"I am quite the extrovert myself," Piper claimed. "I like meeting new people and making friends."

"That's cool."

"The brochure says we will be paired up with an accountability partner," Piper revealed. "Did you see that?"

"I haven't seen a brochure." The only things Boone knew about the course were what his boss shared. Claude took the class and highly recommended it.

"I think that will be awesome. Being new to the area, I love the idea of getting to know someone through working together on this project."

Boone wasn't sure how he felt about an accountability partner. On the one hand, it would be nice to meet and get to know someone. Unlike this woman, meeting people didn't come easy to him; it never had. In fact he wouldn't have talked to her if she hadn't initiated the conversation. If in Oakland, he would have already walked away because Beth wouldn't want him talking to a pretty lady.

"Yeah," Boone finally uttered because he couldn't articulate a better response.

Piper looked at the empty parking lot. A few cars passed by on the street and she kept expecting some to turn in, but they hadn't.

"Do you think anyone is coming?"

"It doesn't look like it," Boone answered. "I was afraid of being the last one here and almost didn't come because I didn't want to look stupid walking into a class that already started."

Piper smirked. She understood but personally never had trouble making an entrance.

"What will we do if no one shows?" she wondered out loud.

"Go home, I guess."

"I didn't quit my career, pack up everything I own, and drive all the way here from Miami to give up on this journey." The more Piper said *this journey* the more she liked the sound of the words.

"You did all that for this class?" Boone asked.

"Yeah, kind of," she answered. "Well, I did it for me."

"Oh."

"Why did you move here?" Piper inquired. "Or why *are* you moving here?" she rephrased.

Realizing the eerie similarity of the paths that led them here, Boone furrowed his brow. "I kind of moved here for this class too," he divulged although he didn't want to share much more.

"Really? What a coincidence," Piper contemplated. "If this class attracts people from all over the place, I wonder why no one else is here."

"Maybe the class was canceled this week," Boone suggested. "I guess we could try coming back next week."

Piper glanced at the phone still resting in her left hand. "I pulled up the website just before you walked up. Let me see if I can find any further information."

"Good idea," Boone acknowledged as he watched Piper's finger move on the screen.

"I guess I should have looked at this sooner," she revealed.

"What?"

Piper tilted the screen where Boone could read the words. "It says the class no longer meets because the founder passed away."

"That's terrible." Boone suddenly felt like he traveled all this way for nothing. However, he knew better. A toxic relationship was the main reason he left. Still he depended on this course to help him navigate this new life. Claude promised that. Suddenly, he felt alone.

"I know, it makes me sad. My friend Hardy talked so highly of this program." She wondered when the founder passed. Obviously Hardy didn't know about it but she wasn't sure if he would have. This journey was something he did in the past when he lived here, so he probably lost contact.

"My boss did too," Boone shared but then wondered if he should have.

"Wait, your boss took the journey as well?"

"Yeah, he said it transformed his life."

"That's wonderful. Hardy said the same thing." Piper scrolled down on the screen a little further. "The website encourages people to find an accountability partner and use the online course material." She sure wished Hardy were around to be her accountability partner. However, it sounded like the program was designed to go through with someone else involved in the journey simultaneously.

"Like an online accountability partner?"

Piper read a little further. "It doesn't specify, and I don't see an option to connect with someone else registered in the course but that's a pretty good idea," she professed.

"Yeah, thanks," Boone conveyed. "I guess I'll figure out something." His preference would be to do it alone anyway. Regardless he didn't have any friends let alone someone he could ask to commit to a class like this. For some reason the thought of asking Beth slid across his mind, but he knew she would laugh at him. He once suggested counseling. She proceeded to slam him against the wall in their bedroom and told him their relationship was fine. A few bruises later, he agreed.

Piper's shoulders dropped. "Me too."

"It was nice to meet you," Boone declared and then turned to walk away.

"You too, Boone. I hope you find joy through this journey."

"Thanks," Boone responded over his shoulder.

Piper pushed her phone into the leg pocket on her pants explicitly designed for the device and then folded and buried the brochure in her shoulder bag on the basket. When she steadied herself on her bicycle, an idea struck. She glanced up and located Boone at the other side of the parking lot about to disappear beyond the bushes from where he must have emerged earlier.

Boone walked quickly. Not having the class tonight allowed more time to look for a tent. He previously assumed the campground where he left his belongings might have one for sale or rent but they didn't. In fact, the place, which he and Claude found online when they planned this trip, wasn't really a campground. It turned out to be the backyard of a man who divided the area into small campsites and it seemed unofficial—no sign out front, just a mailbox with a street number.

When Boone first knocked on the front door, the epitome of a hippie—a man with long braided gray hair wearing a headband, tie-dye shirt, baggy pants, and a peace necklace—stepped onto the screened porch and invited him to sit in one of the rocking chairs as he went over the loose ground rules which included providing your own tent. Boone hoped he could find one. The overly friendly guy told him a couple places to check and let him leave his bags on the porch. Boone figured that option seemed safer than hiding his things in the far corner of the campsite behind some thick underbrush, his initial plan when the barefooted man walked him to his spot. Before leaving, he paid for what the guy labeled "the experience," in a severely mellow tone because it was the last available of a handful of sites. Thankfully, Boone only had cash because credit cards weren't accepted.

Boone was about to walk through a small opening in a line of hedge bushes when he heard a bell ring. Startled, he turned and saw Piper pedaling in his direction.

"Hey," she called out.

He stopped and waited for her to roll closer.

"I have an idea," she declared as the wheels halted. "We are both brand new to Duck, and neither of us knows anyone here, but this journey we wish to embark on is obviously significant to both of us." Piper paused momentarily to catch her breath, and it surprised her to find Boone's warm green eyes locked onto hers. "What I am getting at is, would you like to be each other's accountability partner?"

8

Boone sat at the campsite on a log a few feet from a warm campfire, thinking about Piper and what she asked, considering Beth and what she would do if she saw him talking to that woman. How could he say yes to being Piper's accountability partner? He didn't know her. In all honesty he didn't really want to know her. Sure, she was attractive. More than attractive. The woman was possibly the most beautiful person he ever met.

Boone shook his head as if it would bring him back to reality, but it didn't. The most beautiful woman he ever met just asked him to be her accountability partner. These things didn't happen in real life; encounters like the one he experienced this evening only occurred in the movies.

All Boone could think about were the what-ifs. What if Beth showed up in Duck and found him talking to Piper? Piper seemed nice; he didn't want to take any chance of dragging her into his nightmare. What if he decided leaving Beth was a mistake? Then he would have to tell her about Piper being his accountability partner. Beth would ask if Piper was pretty and then question which of them was prettier. Of course he would say what she wanted to hear, but he would have to tell her about Piper. He wasn't a liar, and he never wanted to be. He guessed the bit about who was prettier would be a little white lie but beauty was more than skin deep. Maybe underneath, Piper wasn't all that beautiful. Perhaps she had an ugly side . . . like Beth.

Maybe neither of them was pretty. Boone shook his head again and stared into the flames as if the answers flickered within their dancing. He felt so conflicted. Here he was trying to start this new life, yet Beth still controlled his decisions. How could someone on the other side of the country whom he left have this much power over him? That's why he needed this program and this place. He had to overcome his fears. Out of all the scary things on this earth, he feared Beth the most.

Boone didn't expect nor want to meet another woman so soon. Even if Piper held no interest in him beyond this course, and why would she, he didn't want to spend time with someone of the opposite sex right now. Too many emotions would become involved. He didn't want to reveal personal information to her. He hadn't even thought much about this accountability partner stuff before now, but somewhere in the back of his mind he assumed a man would fill that role. Preferably someone going through a similar situation. All he and Piper had in common was moving here for this course. And their age. He didn't ask but figured she was most likely born in the 80s like him.

With the dark of the night bearing down all around, Boone wished Claude was here. He wanted his friend to be the accountability partner he needed as he held a photo of Beth between him and the fire. Would his accountability partner encourage throwing it in like the dry sticks he tossed on top each time the flames dwindled? Should he drop it in right now?

Boone stood to his feet and held the picture near the smoke. His finger pinched the corner tightly, and then his grip loosened. He stared at the stars and then back down but couldn't let go. Physically, he could, sure. Mentally? Emotionally? That was a different story. Other than the clothes in his suitcases, the photographs were all he had left of the only life he knew.

Boone glanced at the tattered sleeping bag given to him by the considerate owner of the house he could see in the distance. After walking around town only to find all the stores closed for the evening, he confessed to the man that he didn't have a tent.

"You paid money to rent the campsite, so I won't turn you away just because you don't have a tent," the man declared as they stood on the screened porch. "But you do need to get one tomorrow because the policy requires an enclosure for sleeping," he explained. "I don't think other campers will complain as long as you don't mention it or draw attention to yourself."

"You don't have to worry about that happening," Boone promised. The last thing he wanted was attention.

"Do you at least have something to sleep on?"

Boone shook his head from side to side. He didn't own a sleeping bag, not that he would have had room to bring it. He didn't pack blankets either or even a pillow. Why hadn't he thought of these things?

"You are welcome to the bag and pillow over there in the corner that someone recently left behind. At this point I don't think they are coming back for them."

Boone glanced at the items sitting in a pile near a trash can on the dusty and evenly floorboards. He imagined they were only still there because the trash hadn't been taken out yet.

As the fire warmed Boone's hands, he hoped the bedding didn't have lice or bedbugs although he already thought about shaving his head to change his appearance. The way social media worked these days he feared a picture of him might somehow pop up on one of Beth's pages. He didn't have social media; she wouldn't allow it. Double standards, the story of his life.

Boone thought about his response to Piper's idea.

"Let me think about it," he had answered.

"Fair enough," she responded.

"I will give you my phone number, and you can call if you decide to take me up on the offer."

"I don't have a phone," Boone explained.

Piper cocked her head. "Did you lose it?"

"No."

"Break it?"

"No."

"Then what happened to your phone?"

"I don't own one," he admitted sheepishly.

"What? How do you function without a phone?" Piper quizzed. Maybe he *was* homeless. "I don't think I ever met an adult who doesn't have a phone."

"Now you have."

"There's a first for everything, I guess," she chimed. "Well, I can't think of another way for you to contact me. You seem harmless, but I am uncomfortable giving a stranger my address."

Boone couldn't imagine what it would feel like to walk into another woman's home. The thought of that alone scared him to death.

"I wouldn't expect you to," he disclosed. "And for the record I didn't ask for your address."

"I know you didn't, but you said you would think about whether you wanted to be accountability partners, and I assumed we need a way for you to let me know since you are the only adult in the United States who doesn't have a phone," she reminded him while explaining her train of thought. "Where are you staying?" she asked.

Boone cringed. "I'm not telling you where I'm staying." Not only did he not know her but he also didn't want to tell the most attractive female he ever laid eyes on that starting tonight he lived at a campsite in someone's backyard and didn't even have a tent, sleeping bag, and pillow.

"Fair enough," Piper smirkingly replied. Now this man intrigued her even more. Usually men begged for her phone number and for her to come to their place even though this circumstance seemed a bit unique. She wondered if Boone was married although his ring finger didn't point to that conclusion. No ring, no tan line. She noticed such things. However, plenty of married men with and without rings invited her to their home but she proudly never took a single one up on the offer.

"Maybe the accountability partner thing just isn't a good idea," Boone suggested. Did all women practice double standards? He realized men usually took the leap of faith although he never asked a girl out, even when he lived with his parents. *If they aren't paying, you're not wasting your time with them*, he vividly remembered his dad saying on multiple occasions. They may have paid money, but he paid the price.

"You might be right," Piper affirmed, and then she pulled a pen and a small piece of paper from her bag. "I am not sure why I am doing this, but you seem different than any—" She almost said *man* but it went beyond that, and she didn't want to give him the impression that she was interested in him romantically. "—human I have ever met. Here is my number. If you change your mind, I am sure someone will let you borrow their phone."

9

Piper stretched on a pair of royal blue leggings. She never counted but figured she owned a pair for every day of the month, making her smile as she struck several poses in the mirror while dressing. She wore a dressy white tank top and layered her outfit with a black kimono. It seemed like the perfect look for the dance studio where she planned to complete paperwork.

When Piper climbed into the Jeep, she double-checked her hair and makeup then figured she probably better leave the top on so the ocean air wouldn't blow her hair all over the place. The conversation with Boone last night popped into her mind off and on since their parting. The guy seemed awkward. He came across as shy yet blunt and definitely put up walls. She guessed everyone did. She didn't want to date him; she simply thought it would be helpful to have someone with which to work through the journey, and he was kind of her only option since the class didn't meet anymore. The idea seemed to make more sense than standing outside the door every Thursday evening waiting for someone new to show up who will agree to be an accountability partner.

"Hello, Piper," the studio owner greeted when Piper waltzed in the door where floor-to-ceiling windows lined the front of the building.

"Hello, Kelly," Piper replied, thankful she remembered the woman's name and vice versa.

"I am so grateful you came back," she asserted sprightly.

Piper's eyes widened thinking maybe a position opened since earlier in the week. "Thanks. You mentioned stopping by at my convenience to fill out paperwork, so I wanted to take care of that."

"Yes, I will need you to complete an application to volunteer."

It sounded like nothing changed after all. "I am happy to do that."

"I will also need to run a background check," Kelly mentioned. "We do that with all employees and volunteers for the children's safety."

Piper's mind darted through a slideshow playing some of the things she had been involved in over the years. "Of course," she agreed. She knew her record would return spotless.

"I apologize that things were a bit hectic when you came in the other day," she advocated. "We didn't get to talk much about you and your experience."

"I totally understood."

"I recall you mentioning you recently moved here. Where are you from?"

"Miami is where I moved from, but I am originally from Rochester."

"That's where the Mayo Clinic is located."

"You are right," Piper confirmed. Her father worked there, but she didn't want to get into all that.

"I have been there with my husband," she explained. "He has an autoimmune disease."

"I am sorry to hear that, but I hope the doctors at Mayo were able to help."

"They have been beneficial," Kelly shared. "It's cold there during the winter months," she remembered.

"It seems there are more cold months than warm months; that's for sure."

"Well, Duck isn't Miami, but the weather is much warmer than Minnesota," Kelly promised. "Do you have children?" she inquired.

"Unfortunately not," Piper revealed.

"Siblings?"

"I wish. I am an only child."

"Are your parents still with us?"

"Yes, they are." Piper didn't want to talk too much about them.

"That's wonderful. Do they still live in Rochester?"

"They sure do."

"Did your mother enroll you in dance when you were little?"

"Yes, I danced my way out of my mother's womb and never stopped," she stated chuckling. Her mother always said that, but Piper wasn't sure why she kept repeating it.

Kelly laughed. "I think a lot of my littles did that."

"I bet. I took ballet, tap, jazz, and a few others. I spent more time on the dance floor than anywhere else."

"It is a magical place," she insisted, pausing momentarily to take in the beauty of the dance floor in their presence. So many memories happened there. "Have you taught children?"

"Does teaching adults who act like children count?" Piper asked with a smirk.

Kelly belly laughed. "It has to count for something," she figured. "I have honestly never taught adult classes but imagine it would be more challenging in some ways than teaching children," she assumed. "I like your wit, Piper."

"Thanks. When I was a teenager, I helped teach the younger students at the studio where I grew up."

"There you go; that's helpful for the dance resume."

"I believe there is an art to dancing regardless of our age or style."

"Very true."

"Can you show me a sample of your dancing?"

Piper tried not to look surprised. "Really? Like right now?" she questioned.

"Sure. I would rather see you dance than review your resume. Words might have the power to move people emotionally but words themselves don't move. Your movements, which I believe are an expression of your heart, mind, and soul, convey everything I need to know."

Piper wouldn't argue any of that. She could create a resume, but the secretive nature of her positions would persist.

As Piper and Kelly loosely chatted, Piper slipped off her shoes then made her way to the hardwood. When she reached the center of the floor, she closed her eyes and stood as still as a concrete statue until she slowly let her body move to the music in her soul. She felt free yet secure and knew the confidence flowing from within would speak volumes. She was bravest when on the dance floor.

When Piper finished, she noticed the expression on Kelly's face and smiled.

"Piper, did you dance professionally?"

Piper chuckled. "Do weddings count?"

Kelly laughed out loud again. "They count for something," she assumed, and the two snickered in unison. "You dance marvelously. I wish I had a paid position available for you. I am a good dancer, but you could dance circles around me and any instructor at this studio," she confessed. "Please don't tell my staff I said that although it won't take them long to discern."

"That's mighty kind of you to say," Piper responded. "However, rather than comparing myself to other dancers, I view dance as an expression rather than a competition."

"You are very humble," Kelly insisted. "How have you stayed in such great dancing shape?"

"Dancing is one of my passions." In all honesty Piper possessed a love/hate relationship with dancing. "I workout a lot and eat healthy," she revealed. "But those hushpuppies from Sunset Grille might be my downfall," she teased.

"They melt in your mouth especially if you add honey butter," Kelly added before returning the conversation to the topic. "As I am sure you know, most of our classes are late afternoons and evenings since the kids are out of school then. Will you be available?"

"For now I am, but I am looking for a job, so I won't know my schedule until I figure that out."

"I sure wish I could hire you, Piper."

Kelly's excitement about having Piper around made Piper feel appreciated. She loved this woman's contagious enthusiasm. "Maybe in time it will work out," Piper mentioned.

"I like your positive outlook," Kelly shared. "Where have you applied?"

"Just here so far," Piper confessed. "I am still settling in."

"You let me know if I can help you find the type of work you are looking for or assist you in any other way since you are new to the community."

"Thanks, I really appreciate your willingness to help."

"What are your passions other than dance?"

"I have worked in physical fitness my whole life." That was the most generic way to explain her career. "I want to do something different, which is one of the reasons I moved to Duck, to figure out what comes next."

"I will keep my ears open for opportunities. A lot of the parents own or manage businesses on the island."

"Sounds wonderful."

"You will meet most of them through volunteering, and who knows where a few conversations might lead."

Piper completed the paperwork after chatting like old friends a bit longer. Kelly handed over a schedule and asked her to consider which classes interested her most.

When Piper left the studio, she drove a short ways to the real estate agent's office, once again admiring the village's relaxed vibe. On the way she decided to start asking everyone she met how they liked their job and about the pros and cons.

"I love the flexible hours," her agent stated as they sat in her office. "But the job requires a lot of night and weekend work because my clients are mostly available then to talk and walk through the homes that interest them."

Piper wasn't opposed to nights and weekends but that might interfere with volunteering at the dance studio which would be a bummer.

"What credentials are required?"

"You must pass the North Carolina real estate exam to obtain your license. The test is a bear, but the courses available prepare you well. Most people who invest adequate time to read and study the material do fine. Plus you can take the exam until you pass; you just have to pay the fee again."

"Thanks, I will keep this in mind."

"Wonderful. Let me know if I can help."

"Certainly," Piper confirmed.

"Would you like to tour a few more houses I picked for you?"

"I would love to."

"Sounds fun. I need more clients like you who are available on a whim," the agent vowed with a smile. "And during the daytime hours on top of that."

Piper enjoyed walking through the homes with her agent, one of the friendliest people she ever met. Come to think of it, everyone she crossed paths with in Duck seemed super friendly, with the possible exception of Boone. The jury was still out on him, but he wasn't from here so maybe he would be pardoned temporarily.

Unfortunately, none of the houses Piper walked through with her agent jumped out as *the one*. Maybe she was being too picky, but she wanted to find a place where she would be happy long term rather than settle.

The next stop on her agenda brought her to the local bank. She needed to open an account and figured she might as well introduce herself to the branch manager and pick his brain about banking jobs.

"We have a variety of positions that require different education and experience. We have several teller levels. The first is an entry-level position for those new to banking. Our loan officers start with general operational tasks like opening accounts and helping customers with basic questions, and then move up the loan ladder dealing with vehicle loans, mortgages, business financing, and so forth," Preston Bynum explained.

"It sounds like you offer many options," Piper acknowledged.

"If you are interested, drop off your resume, and I will see where you might fit in best."

"I might do that," Piper considered. "What are the pros and cons of working in the banking industry?"

Preston snickered. "Banker's hours."

Piper smirked. "Is that a pro or con?"

He chuckled. "I guess it depends. For me, it's a pro. I like working from nine until five Monday through Friday so I can spend time with my family on nights and weekends."

"That makes sense."

A knock came at the door, and Piper turned to see the woman who showed her to the manager's office earlier standing there.

"Sir, there is a gentleman here to see you."

"Does he have an appointment?"

"No but he says Mr. Claude James sent him to meet with you specifically."

Preston's eyes grew, and he sat up a little straighter. "What is the gentleman's name?"

"Mr. Winters."

"Please tell Mr. Winters I will be right with him."

Piper could tell Mr. Bynum seemed eager to talk to this person. He had set up her account before discussing bank positions, so she decided to get out of his hair and move on to the next part of her day.

"I have probably taken up enough of your time," Piper insisted, standing after the lady walked away.

"It was a pleasure meeting you, Ms. Luck," he vowed. "If there isn't anything else I can assist you with today, I will walk you out and check in with the gentleman in the lobby. I have expected him for quite some time," Preston explained.

"You have been very hospitable."

"Thank you and feel free to stop by anytime."

"Anytime between nine and five, right?" Piper teased.

He laughed. "You catch on quickly."

When Mr. Bynum walked Piper back into the lobby, she shockingly recognized the person waiting in the same gray leather chair where she sat earlier.

"Boone," she announced.

Boone looked up. "Hello," he responded.

"You two know each other?" the bank manager asked, seeming surprised.

"Yes," Piper replied. She couldn't help but notice Boone looked a little more put together today although like he might have had a rough night. His green eyes appeared tired. However, there were no holes in this pair of jeans, and a dark green V-neck shirt replaced the dingy hoodie; on second thought the wrinkles made her think it could have been beneath the pullover last night although it looked relatively clean. He definitely put product in his styled curly hair this morning.

"Kind of," Boone added, standing as the others stepped closer.

Preston glanced at Piper then at Boone.

"We met recently," Piper explained, attempting to clear up the confusion.

"Very well," the branch manager concluded.

"Do you work here?" Boone asked Piper.

"No, I just opened an account."

"Oh."

Piper realized Boone wasn't here to visit with her. "It was good to see you again, Boone," she admitted. The excitement of the banker to discover Boone's arrival seemed most likely to disprove the homeless theory although she noticed the same backpack he wore last night sitting on a nearby chair. This guy became more intriguing by the moment.

Boone studied his own feet for several seconds. "You too," he finally responded then glanced up at her quickly before turning his attention to the bank manager.

"Have a great day, gents," Piper said, walking away before the conversation turned more awkward. However, for some reason, she would love to know what brought Boone to the bank today.

10

oone felt nervous when he woke up this morning. Now
after running into Piper, more emotions danced through
his mind. He hadn't rested well last night. Although the
sleeping bag and pillow turned out to be relatively comfortable, he
never slept in the open air before. At first it offered a certain allure.
The breeze comforted him, the songs nature sang provided a
melody, and the stars above the tree line offered a spectacular view.

Eventually Boone grew cold; the random noises startled him;
and the distance between him and the stars reminded him how far
he was from home, from Beth. He found himself wanting to curl
up next to her and sleep in the bed where he slept for years. When
he shook those thoughts, his mind raced about the meeting with
the banker. What was this project? Would he like the work? How
much money would he make, and when would he receive his first
paycheck? How long would he have to sleep at the campground?
Once he bought a tent today, and hopefully his own sleeping bag
and pillow, his cash supply would be nearly dry.

"Mr. Winters, it is a privilege to finally meet you," the bank
manager asserted. "I am Preston Bynum."

"Thank you, you too," Boone replied with his hand shaking as
he reached for the banker's.

"Let's step into my office, and I can explain things."

A few moments later, the door shut behind them, and Boone sat in the seat Piper occupied five minutes ago.

"First, I am terribly sorry about Claude James. He was one of the finest men I ever met."

"Yeah, me too," Boone agreed. "I miss him."

"He didn't share the details about your life but told me you would eventually come to Duck for a fresh start."

Boone smirked. He appreciated the vote of confidence from Claude. "That's true."

"Mr. James wanted me to ask if you are here alone."

Boone knew what that meant. "Yes, she didn't come with me."

The banker leaned back as far as his leather executive chair allowed. "The woman who was just in here—she wasn't with you?" he asked with his brow furrowed.

"No, I just met her."

Mr. Bynum pulled himself up to the desk and clicked a few tabs on his computer to reach the needed file. "Let me pull up the documents I created for Mr. James so I can make sure we cover all the details accurately." Preston remembered documenting the name of Boone's significant other per Mr. James's request. The name Piper didn't ring a bell, but he wanted to look at the last name to be sure. Luck was Piper's last name; he remembered that from making a copy of her license for bank records. He even made a comment that he liked it.

"Beth Tingle was your significant other?" Mr. Bynum checked.

"That's right," Boone verified although the word *was* stung.

"Mr. James was a friend of mine," Preston announced. "What I am doing for him, and for you on his behalf, is outside of my normal duties. That said, I want to clarify that everything is completely legal. All the documents and arrangements he made are contractually binding and will hold up in a court of law. My asking if Ms. Tingle is with you is more of a lawyerly question but everything Claude set up is contingent on you living alone for a specified amount of time while you take the course—" he trailed off for a moment while searching for the name of the class. "—The Roots Beneath Us," he clarified, "in which you are required to have an accountability partner."

Boone's eyes widened but he didn't speak.

"Mr. James said you are familiar with the course which is one of the reasons you are moving here."

"That's correct."

"There are a number of steps to this process, and other than your arrival in Duck, the course is the first," he explained. "Have you started it, or when do you plan to?"

"I actually went to the meeting last night just after I arrived," Boone told him. If the man needed official documentation, he would have to explain the whole truth.

"Very good. You are one step ahead, and you might have already handled this second step," Preston mentioned familiarizing himself with the list again. "Do you have an accountability partner?"

Boone's eyes dropped to his shoes. "Yes, kind of," he answered looking back up at the banker.

Mr. Bynum tilted his head. "*Yes* or *kind of?*"

"Piper asked me to be her accountability partner," he explained. "We met at the class last night."

"It's a small world," Preston pointed out. "Is there a formality the two of you are awaiting?"

"Well, no, not really," Boone admitted. "It's just that I don't know Piper, so I didn't say yes."

"Did you say no?"

"I told her I would let her know."

"I see," he responded. "I am unfamiliar with this course beyond what Mr. James shared. Are you trying to decide between her and another accountability partner?"

"I think she may be my only option for the time being," Boone explained.

"Mr. Winters, I am married, and my wife is the most beautiful woman on this planet. Therefore, if I were in your shoes, it wouldn't be in my best interest to agree to be accountability partners with that lady who was just in my office because she's the second most beautiful woman on this planet, if you know what I mean," Preston admitted. "I need your accountability partner to sign the document I am looking at, so if I were you and no longer in a relationship with Ms. Tingle or anyone else, I would highly consider taking Ms. Luck up on her offer."

Boone cleared his throat. He didn't expect the project to be contingent upon him taking the course and having an accountability partner. However, he knew precisely why Claude set it up this way. His friend knew Beth was no good for him, and Boone realized Claude wanted to do everything in his power to help him not go back.

"I understand," Boone replied.

Mr. Bynum turned his chair, keyed in a handful of numbers on a small vault behind the desk, and then handed Boone an envelope.

"This is for you from Mr. James, regardless of whether this project moves forward from here," he explained. "If you would like it to continue, I need to have a conversation with you and Ms. Luck in person. If you both agree to the terms, I will need your signature as well as hers."

Boone wondered if he looked as shell-shocked as he felt. "Can you tell me what the project entails?" he asked. "Claude promised I would have a job waiting for me when I arrived, and I need the money."

"I understand. I can't tell you the details without the presence of your accountability partner, but I can tell you that the project is for you to build a house," Preston divulged. "As for money to keep you afloat in the short term, I encourage you to open the envelope."

Boone glanced at the envelope in his hand and then peeled it open. From inside he pulled out and counted ten one-hundred dollar bills. His face instantly beamed with appreciation. A thousand dollars would undoubtedly buy some time.

Although Boone experienced temporary relief, his mind ran in many directions. Was he supposed to build a whole house entirely on his own? He built plenty of homes with crews and even been an on-site project manager for the last five years or so for Mr. James's company. He had so many questions. "Whose house am I building?" he asked Preston. "Will I have a crew?"

"Mr. Winters, I am afraid I can't give you any more details until I meet with you and your accountability partner," he insisted. "It might be best for you to give all this some thought and call Ms. Luck so the two of you can discuss this opportunity."

"I don't even know what *this opportunity* is," Boone exclaimed.

"I understand it's a lot to process," the banker sympathized.

Boone knew Claude had his best interest in mind, and at this moment, *this opportunity* suddenly all seemed like fate. What were the chances he and Piper would both show up for the class last night and be the only two people standing outside a dark building? A class that no longer met, nonetheless, and that she would ask him to be her accountability partner. "May I call her from your phone?" Boone requested.

"Are you sure you don't want to think about it? Perhaps talk to her in person about being accountability partners before bringing this project into the conversation?"

"This seems to be the way Claude intended," Boone recognized knowing he wanted to be upfront with Piper. He hoped her running into him here at the bank would add validity to a request that would probably sound very strange.

"Fair enough," Preston responded. "Do you have her number?"

"Yes but I don't have a phone," Boone admitted. "May I use yours?"

A look of surprise formed on the branch manager's face. He didn't know anyone without a cell phone. "Of course you may use mine."

"I will step out if you would like to speak with Piper privately first," he offered.

"Do you have a speakerphone?" Boone asked.

"Yes, sir."

"Let's call her on speakerphone. I think we might be able to explain this best together," he admitted. Boone feared if he called Piper from a random phone later tonight, tomorrow, or whenever and tried to explain all of this, she would think he was crazy. It sure sounded crazy.

Boone pulled the sliver of paper Piper gave him from his pocket and read the number aloud. As Mr. Bynum pressed each digit on his desk phone, Boone's shoulders felt as tense as a tightrope at the circus.

Preston touched the speakerphone button, and Boone's jaw clenched when he heard the first ring.

"Hello," he heard Piper answer.

"Ms. Luck, this is Preston Bynum, the branch manager at the bank."

"Hey Preston, I didn't expect to hear from you so soon. Is everything okay?" Her voice was smooth and confident.

"Yes, everything is fine," he assured, assuming she feared an issue with her new account. "I am here with Mr. Boone Winters. I have you on speakerphone, and we need your help with something."

The line fell silent momentarily, and Boone and the banker stared at one another until Piper spoke again.

"Okay," she stalled.

"Mr. Winters moved to Duck to handle a project for our mutual friend, Mr. Claude James. In order for the project to proceed, Boone needs—." The banker stopped for a moment.

This sounded more awkward than he initially expected. He thought it would be similar to explaining it to Mr. Winters, but all of a sudden, it seemed much different because Mr. Winters knew his own situation which neither he nor Ms. Luck knew anything about.

Recognizing Preston's uncertainty, Boone chimed in. "Piper, I want you to be my accountability partner," he requested abruptly.

"Okay," Piper responded. "What does that have to do with the bank and the project?"

Preston waited to see if Boone would respond.

Boone sighed. This must be what Claude wanted, for him to share his story with someone else who could help him move forward in this course designed with that goal. He wondered if Claude would have chosen this same path if he knew the person would be Piper, a woman who could be just like Beth for all they knew.

"My friend knew I needed The Roots Beneath Us class and an accountability partner, and he wants to make sure I am committed to this journey and this project to move forward."

"Last night you didn't seem interested in being my accountability partner, but now you need me to be yours all of a sudden?"

Preston looked at Boone, and Boone could read his thoughts: *Why didn't you say yes last night?*

"Yes, I need you to be my accountability partner."

"So now you are asking me?"

"Yes," Boone replied.

"So do you *want* me to be your accountability partner, or do you *need* me to be?"

Boone remembered his vow of honesty. "I need you to be my accountability partner," he said. "And I need to want you to be my accountability partner," he admitted.

"This all sounds pretty confusing," Piper declared. This man, Boone Winters, just rose to a new level of interesting.

Mr. Bynum cut in. "Would you be able to come in for a meeting with me and Mr. Winters?" he asked. "It might make more sense if we discuss this in person."

"Sure, why not," she agreed surprisingly.

"What does your schedule look like this week?"

"Well, I just got off the phone with my realtor whom I have been talking to since I left your office," she shared. Piper was excited that the owners of the rental house agreed for her to stay the rest of the month. Thankfully the off-season allowed her realtor enough flexibility in the schedule to upgrade a few weekend guests to another home on the island. She loved that lady. "I am still in the bank parking lot; I never even cranked my car."

Three minutes later Piper sat next to Boone, who suddenly found breathing hard. Having the conversation via phone seemed difficult, but in person it felt impossible. He feared the worst. Piper would say no, and somehow he would end up back with Beth.

Mr. Bynum initiated the conversation. "Like I mentioned earlier, Boone moved here to handle a project for Mr. Claude James. The project is to build a house on the island. For Boone to build the house, he must be taking The Roots Beneath Us program, have an accountability partner, and live alone."

"Why all these stipulations?" Piper questioned as she studied Mr. Bynum's and then Boone's face.

"These are Mr. James's requests," the banker clarified.

"What am I getting involved in here, Boone?" Piper asked directly after turning her attention to him.

"You don't have to agree to be my accountability partner, but right now I am going to assume you are; otherwise, I can't reveal a secret I have kept my whole life," Boone shared. "Mr. James was the only other person who knew what I now feel like I have to tell you."

"Was?" Piper questioned.

"Mr. James recently passed away," Preston clarified.

This story kept getting deeper; maybe Boone was a secret agent after all.

"Last night I was willing to be your accountability partner, but now I can't commit to that without knowing more about what's happening here."

"Can I have a few minutes alone with Piper?" Boone asked.

"Of course," Preston agreed. "I need coffee anyway. You two want some?"

"Yes, please," Piper requested.

"No, thanks," Boone replied. If he attempted to hold a coffee mug in this state of mind, it would probably end up shattered on the floor.

When Mr. Bynum exited the office, Boone skipped the small talk and opened the floodgates. "I have been in an abusive relationship my whole adult life," he revealed, contorting his face to keep from crying in front of someone he barely knew.

"Physically or verbally?"

"Both."

"You think telling me that you beat a woman your whole adult life will convince me to be your accountability partner just because your friend wants to bribe you to change your life?" Piper asked.

"No, I would never think that."

"Good because I won't sign up for that," Piper exclaimed. "You need a therapist."

"You are probably right; I could use the help of a professional," he agreed. "However, I think you misunderstood me which is one of the reasons I never tell anyone about my life." Boone sniffed, pulled his glasses up, wiped his eyes with his hands, and paused for a moment. "I have been physically, mentally, emotionally, and verbally abused my whole life, not just in adulthood. I have been slapped, hit, kicked, and abused in ways you would never imagine. I didn't grow up like a normal child, and the older I got, the worse it became." Tears fell down Boone's cheek one right after the other, even faster than when on the train the day he left.

Piper didn't know what to say. "I am so sorry," she uttered. "Sorry that you have been abused, and sorry that I assumed you were the abuser."

Boone shook his head. "It's okay."

Piper never met a man who suffered abuse, at least not one brave enough to admit it. However, she spent much of her adult life helping women stuck in situations like Boone's. "Is that why you didn't want me to know where you are from?" she asked.

"Yes," he admitted.

"You are afraid she will find you?"

Boone shook his head north to south while all the thoughts from last night ran through it.

11

"Boone, I will be your accountability partner," Piper agreed as they sat next to each other in the bank.

"Because you want to or need to?" he asked without thinking.

"Both," she answered immediately. "Last night I needed an accountability partner. Now, I want and need you to be my accountability partner."

"Are you sure? Because if you're just feeling sorry for me, I don't need sympathy." Why was he trying to talk her out of it?

"You're not the only one with secrets," Piper promised. She couldn't imagine being as forthcoming as the man whose green eyes become even warmer when tears fell out of them. Without thinking twice, she wrapped her tanned arms around Boone's neck. "These are the moments that accountability partners are for," she whispered into his ear.

A knock came at the door, and a second later Mr. Bynum stuck his head in. "Oh, sorry," he confessed. "I can come back in a bit."

"Come on in," Piper okayed. "As long as it's alright with Boone."

Boone shook his head up and down and then wiped away the tears when Piper pulled back from their embrace; technically, her embrace, he realized he never put his arms back around her. He felt frozen. No one other than Beth hugged him since his mom hugged him as a teenager. Every now and then, when sober, she sympathized with him.

"I will be Boone's accountability partner," Piper informed Mr. Bynum. "If that is still what he wants."

"Yes," Boone uttered sniffling.

Preston walked to his chair and sat, thinking maybe he needed to ask what he was getting involved in here. If Mr. James was still living, he would have called him on his cell phone from the breakroom. "Is now a good time to continue this meeting, or should we reconvene?"

"Now is fine," Boone answered. "As long as Piper agrees."

"It's okay with me too," Piper added.

Mr. Bynum clicked a button, and a form slid out of the printer. "This document simply states that the two of you agree to be one another's accountability partners," he explained, pushing it across his desk for Piper and Boone to review. "Piper, you are not responsible for anything else, but Mr. James strongly encouraged you to attend all meetings between Boone and me moving forward."

Piper and Boone read the piece of paper together.

"That's pretty straightforward," she said. "I'll sign it."

"Yeah, me too," Boone agreed.

The banker handed each of them a pen. A minute later, he made two copies of the document. He gave one to Piper and Boone each and slid the original into an empty folder he pulled from a nearby file cabinet.

"Boone, Mr. James is hiring you to build a home on the island."

Piper furrowed her brow. "I don't want to sound disrespectful, but how can Mr. James hire someone when he is no longer alive?"

"He left a trust fund to handle everything including Boone's salary."

"Oh," Piper responded.

"The blueprints are in my file cabinet," Preston explained. He pulled a rolled-up set of plans out and handed them to Boone.

"May I spread these out on your desk?" Boone asked eager to have a look.

"Of course," Preston agreed as he pushed a few items aside to make room.

"Wow," Boone uttered after studying the plans. "This house is spectacular. The blueprints alone look like a work of art." Over the years he helped build larger houses, but the details and features this one offered mesmerized him.

Preston stared at the plans with his mouth agape as Boone pointed out the intricacies of the swimming pool, library, exercise room, and more. This marked the first time he saw them unrolled. Mr. James had been pretty secretive about everything.

"Whose house will this be?" Piper asked a moment before Boone could pose the same question.

"I wish I could tell you but as you can imagine, that information must be kept confidential for a home like this."

"Must be someone famous," Piper assumed enthusiastically.

Mr. Bynum shrugged his shoulders.

Boone pointed at some lines on the large scroll of paper. "If so, this gate and fence surrounding the property will keep out the paparazzi and overzealous fans."

Preston and Piper laughed.

"Where will this house be built?" Boone asked.

Preston pointed to an address on an attached map. "The land has already been purchased," he noted as Boone read the location out loud.

"That's on the ocean," Piper reeled off. "My realtor and I were on that street the other day."

Mr. Bynum shook his head in agreement.

"Who is the contractor?" Boone asked.

"Technically, Mr. James's company is the contractor."

"So who is in charge?" Boone asked. "Who do I report to?"

"You are in charge, Mr. Winters," Preston announced. "Mr. James wanted it that way."

"That can't be right," Boone professed.

"Why not?" Piper asked, baffled.

"I'm not a contractor. I know how to build houses, but I am not the one who meets with the owner, orders the materials, hires the crews, and does a thousand other things that contractors specialize in. I am an on-site project manager, meaning I ensure the job gets done to the contractor's specifications."

"Mr. James wanted it this way," Preston clarified. "He left a detailed list, including the materials you need. You will make all the decisions. There won't be anyone else involved in the process."

"I have never built anything quite like this," Boone admitted.

Piper chimed in. "Boone, this man, your friend, obviously believed in you enough to leave you in charge of this project after he passed. You can do this," she encouraged. "The journey we are taking together, The Roots Beneath Us, is all about stepping outside our comfort zones."

"I think she's right," Preston articulated.

"So what's next?" Boone asked Mr. Bynum.

"If you are willing to sign the document stating you agree to build the house, I believe the next step is up to you."

"Hiring crews and ordering materials," Boone said to himself more than anyone else. "The financing?" he queried.

"Everything is arranged through a trust," he reminded Boone. "Bring in the quotes for each portion of the project, and I will write the checks."

"This is unreal," Boone professed. Last night he slept on the ground, and today he became responsible for building a luxurious oceanfront home.

12

"Do you want to grab lunch and talk about the journey?" Piper asked Boone.

After walking out together, they stood outside the bank, the sun nearly directly above their heads in a sky dotted with puffy white cartoon clouds. Boone had held the door for Piper, and she appreciated the small act of chivalry.

The journey sounded odd to Boone. Why didn't Piper call it a course or class or something like that? Those options seemed more normal. His gut said to answer *no* to Piper's invitation.

A long moment passed as Piper waited for a response. Boone dug his hands into his pockets and stared at the concrete sidewalk between the building and her Jeep.

"I am not sure; I have a lot to figure out about this house project," he answered while staring at the rolled-up blueprints dangling by his side like a croquet mallet. "I don't even have a clue where to start."

"Boone, that is what the journey is about, where and how to start," she explained. "I read that last night on the website."

Boone raised his head to meet Piper's gaze. He figured the person on his shoulder with the voice telling him *no* belonged to Beth. *Start, huh?* "Can we talk about the house at lunch?" he asked, his eyes returning to the oversized scroll.

"We can talk about anything we want," Piper reeled off. "This course isn't like sitting in a high school classroom."

"I liked high school."

Piper felt her brown eyes bulge. She never expected to hear this man make that statement. His picture probably couldn't be found in the yearbook's social awards. In fact she imagined Boone sitting at a table with a few stragglers who didn't quite fit in with any of the clicks. "You must have played sports."

"No, I wasn't allowed."

"Why not?"

"My parents needed me at home," he answered simply.

"Did you grow up on a farm or something?" she inquired with a laugh. "They needed you to milk the cows or collect chicken eggs?"

Boone snickered. "I wish."

Remembering what Boone shared inside the bank, Piper's train of thought shifted. His parents must have been strict, perhaps overprotective. Kids growing up in that environment were often the most vulnerable.

"Where do you want to eat lunch?" Piper asked.

"It doesn't matter to me."

"I want to try all the local restaurants," Piper shared. "Are there any foods you don't like?"

"I can eat almost anywhere."

"That makes the choice easier. Did you drive here?"

"I walked."

"Would you like to ride with me?" Piper invited pointing to her vehicle. She almost added the *I don't bite* joke but then recollected the list of things done to him. He probably didn't trust women, maybe even people in general. "Or I am happy to walk with you if you prefer."

Boone studied the passenger door on the blue Jeep. He hadn't ridden in a vehicle alone with a woman other than Beth in over twenty years. At that moment another voice called out from his shoulder-*start*. He and Piper spoke that word a couple minutes ago; maybe the inner echo of one of their voices reminded him. Perhaps Claude? God? It didn't matter; Boone knew for sure this wasn't Beth's voice.

"I will ride with you."

Boone climbed in gingerly as if the vehicle was contaminated. He reached across his shoulder for the strap to snap in the seatbelt, and a moment later the wheels rolled just like the ones on the train a few days ago. His breaths became quick as the voices in his head battled.

"There is a restaurant I have been wanting to try, Roadside Bar & Grill. I noticed it when I first drove into town, and every time I ride by on my bicycle, it calls my name. It kind of has a fish camp vibe from the outside, so I think it might be a good place for us to eat and talk in a relaxed environment if that works for you."

Boone collapsed his eyelids when Piper touched the brake at the stop sign.

"Sounds good."

Piper studied the traffic on the road to the left and the right, and she noticed Boone's closed eyes before pulling out. "Are you praying?" she inquired. "I promise I'm a good driver; I haven't been in a wreck the whole time I've lived in Duck," she laughed, one hand guiding the steering wheel and the other resting on her inner thigh.

Boone chuckled through his nostrils, a smile easing onto his face as he opened his eyelids. "Just relaxing my eyes," he conveyed. "You have lived here less than a week."

"Yep and no tickets or accidents to report."

"That's admirable. How about in Miami?"

"I think I got a ticket in Miami, but I recall no accidents. All the cities I lived in somewhat run together. I have definitely had more tickets than wrecks."

"Oh my."

"How about you?" she asked. "How many tickets and accidents?"

"None."

Boone's answer didn't surprise her; he seemed extremely cautious about everything.

"I'm from California," he randomly offered.

That particular comment did astonish Piper.

It only took a minute to reach the eclectic cottage-style restaurant where a narrow asphalted entrance between the building and a cute little bright orange and turquoise market nestled amongst shade trees led to a parking lot made of sandy dirt, gravel, and clam shells. "We made it safe and sound," Piper pointed out.

"Thanks for driving," Boone felt relief, not because he feared an accident but because he stretched beyond his comfort zone.

On the backside of the lot, a wood-framed entrance with a hundred or so attached empty wine bottles led to an outdoor area where Boone imagined droves of people gathered on summer evenings. A dangling surfboard sign read "Backside Bar," and in the distance a stage featuring more wine bottles, in a formation resembling the shape of a Christmas tree, seemed to be the main attraction. Haphazard outdoor seating included tall homemade wooden tables, bar stools in a variety of colors, and a long white canopy covering everything. A makeshift movie screen occupied the far right corner, and a tattered barn-style bar on the left was decorated with random signs, old license plates, and more bar stools. It looked like one of those places where you could spend the whole night looking at the decorations and on the next visit still find ones you missed.

As Piper and Boone walked in the other direction toward the restaurant, Boone smirked when he spotted a sign that read: Hippies use side entrance. He instantly thought of the campground fellow.

The front of the restaurant included a relatively expansive screened porch type area; however, no roof or screens covered the exposed wooden beams above. Globe lights hung from one beam to the next; blue umbrellas sheltered each table; and overhead fans circled while tall, portable outdoor heaters awaited cold days.

The restaurant was busier than Piper expected with nearly every seat occupied, outside and inside. Still, a table became available within minutes of checking in at the hostess stand.

"Right this way y'all," the waitress with long curly locks of blonde hair instructed in the perfect Southern vernacular.

Piper noticed the indoor vibe felt similar to the outdoor style. Small rooms decorated with stained glass art, old photos and newspaper clippings, and antique books offered a unique layout, piquing her interest.

Nestled in one of three high-back booths in the bar room, Piper ordered water, and Boone asked for iced tea.

"I'll get these drinks and give y'all some time to look at the menu," she offered. "My name is Kayla; if y'all need anything just let me know."

"Thank you, Kayla," Piper responded.

"Is this your first time here?"

"Yes, can you tell?" Piper checked, noticing and loving the bright splash of blue the nearby tall bar stools offered. It contrasted well with the glossy wood decor.

"I don't recognize y'all, and I've been waitressing for twenty years ever since I turned sixteen. I know all the locals, so I figured you must be new in town. Tourists?"

"We both just moved here," Piper shared, choosing not to provide a synopsis of the situational complexity which brought them here today.

"Well then, welcome to Duck," Kayla greeted. "Y'all will love this place. I have lived in this area my whole life. As of May 1, 2002, Duck, North Carolina, is the most recently incorporated town on the Outer Banks. Less than a thousand people live here in the off-season but in the summer that number swells to around twenty thousand because of the tourists who flock here for vacation. As you might imagine, the community's name came from an earlier time when this place was mostly known for duck hunting. The hunters would stay in cottages, some built in the willow swamp and later moved inland. You are currently dining in one of the village's original cottages."

"Thank you for the warm welcome and the history lesson," Piper replied, intrigued. Boone smiled. "I might live here the rest of my life," Piper added.

The waitress giggled and performed a quick move reminiscent of a cheerleader. "You won't want to leave, especially once beach season arrives," she promised. "But honey you already got your tan."

Holding the menu like a book, Piper glanced at her arms. "Thank God for Italian skin."

"And Italian men," the waitress chimed, cracking herself up with the rhyme. "No offense, shug," she noted as she touched Boone's pale arm. "You're doing something right," she added, winking noticeably and nodding her bleached blonde curls in Piper's direction.

Piper laughed so hard at the Italian men remark she nearly snorted but then reeled it in hoping Boone wouldn't take offense to the latter part of the woman's observation. This waitress didn't know him, not that she really did either, but Piper liked that he was beginning to peel back the layers.

Boone felt the need to explain that he and Piper moved here from different places and weren't together. He then cleared that thought like the crumbs the server wiped off the tabletop before they sat. It didn't matter here; he no longer needed to explain himself.

"She's silly," Piper concluded after the waitress waltzed away.

"Yeah," Boone agreed.

Piper could sense Boone's nervousness by the way he fidgeted with the menu. "What are you thinking about getting?" she asked. Hopefully conversation and laughter would loosen him up. Laughing was the best medicine, and she was good at it as well as doing things that caused others to laugh at her.

"Maybe the hamburger and fries," he reported.

"While driving here from Miami, I kept thinking about burgers and fries," she mentioned. "Maybe I should get that too."

Before they could make a decision, the waitress popped over with their drinks and gave them dried pasta. Boone furrowed his brow.

"Are these pasta straws?" Piper asked holding one up for examination before looking through it like a telescope, drawing a laugh from Kayla.

"Sure are."

"I have eaten at restaurants all over the world, and this is my first experience drinking from a pasta straw," Piper announced, pushing hers through the ice.

"What do you think?" Kayla asked.

"Different, and a way better idea than paper straws."

"Do y'all need any recommendations?"

"Sure," Boone responded.

"The only items I don't like on the menu are things I don't even like if my granny cooks them," she chuckled. "Everything else is delicious, and everyone raves about the shrimp and grits and our burgers."

"Sold," Piper interjected. "Boone said he was probably getting a hamburger, and I have been craving one all week."

"Your name is Boone?"

"Yes."

"I love that. I ain't never met a Boone, other than Daniel Boone, and I ain't actually met him," she reported laughing at herself. "I don't think Daniel is still with us. Do you wrestle bears like he did?" she asked, shifting rapidly from one comment to the next. "Didn't he have a pet bear?"

Boone laughed louder than Piper expected but not enough to draw attention, and she didn't hold back either. Perhaps she should try to set Boone up with the waitress; this woman could probably make him laugh all day.

"I think you're thinking of Davy Crockett," Boone corrected.

"Yeah he killed a bear when he was only three."

"That's right," Piper recollected. "There's even a jingle about that."

The server sang the familiar tune out loud, and Piper joined right in while the patrons at the nearby tables halted their conversations trying to figure out what was happening. The staff smiled and kept working, making it obvious they were accustomed to such shenanigans. Boone sat wide-eyed with a smirk covering his face.

"What did Daniel Boone do?" the waitress wondered aloud.

"He was an explorer known for the settlement of Kentucky," Boone explained. "He also served as an officer for the militia in the Revolutionary War." Boone didn't know much about Duck prior to Kayla's history lesson, but he knew quite a bit about Daniel Boone because they somewhat shared the name.

"Are you one of his descendants?"

"Boone is my first name."

"Oh, yeah, that makes sense. I still like your name. It's way better than Daniel." The waitress tapped her pen to her chin. "Do you want a burger too, Mr. Boone?"

Boone chuckled. Piper nearly spit out the sip of water in her mouth.

"Yes, please, and fries."

"Believe it or not, we actually don't have a fryer because of the age of the house."

"This place gets more interesting by the minute," Piper replied.

When the comedian walked away with their order, Boone tasted his tea, and his eyes nearly bulged out of his head. "Oh my goodness, this is super sweet," he told Piper. "It tastes like syrup."

"Welcome to the South, California boy."

Boone shook the shock off his face and took another swig. "I am not sure if I love or hate it."

"If you keep drinking sweet tea the taste will grow on you, and you will be addicted in no time."

"I feel like the sugar might start oozing out of my pores at any moment," Boone declared, studying his arms.

"That won't help with your tan," Piper teased. "You will have to spend a lot of time at the beach to counter the sugar effect."

"Ha-ha."

The conversation dwindled for a moment, and Piper hoped she hadn't offended Boone. She would be careful about making comments that might trigger her new friend's past, but she couldn't stop being her silly self.

"This is fun; I'm glad we came here," Piper commented.

"Me too."

Piper glanced at the papers Boone brought in from the bank. He left the blueprints in the Jeep because of the size, plus he didn't want to risk spilling food or drink on them.

"Do you want to discuss the house project first or The Roots Beneath Us journey?" Piper inquired.

"Either is fine."

"I read quite a bit of material on the website last night, so I recommend discussing the journey and then the house. I believe the course guide might help point you in the right direction with planning the construction project."

"Okay."

"I promise we will talk about the house; I know that is important to you."

Piper opened her phone and went to the tab she saved last night. She read out loud the overview she discovered yesterday while waiting for the class meeting, which never happened.

"What do you think?"

"I remember Claude reading a statement like that to me."

"I think we both started the journey before we even got here," she surmised.

"What do you mean?"

"I don't know the specifics, but it appears you walked away from an abusive relationship," she reminded him. "That's beyond brave."

"I did," he said somewhat proudly.

"You shared a delicate part of your story with me in the bank," she recollected. "I imagine you didn't expect to face that fear today."

Boone shook his head. "Not at all."

Piper pulled a spiral notebook from her bag. "We are supposed to list our fears and goals, including things we avoided doing in the past and present," Piper explained. "I think we need to write down these accomplishments as reminders that we already started."

Boone took a sip of tea. "Okay."

Piper wrote her name on the left of the first blank page and Boone's on the right. Then she jotted down the two things she pointed out to him followed by a third. "You also told me where you are from."

"You told me where you are from too," he reminded her.

"I did but I would tell anyone that," she laughed.

"You moved here, that's brave."

"I have moved more than fifty times," she noted with a snicker. "I don't think moving counts for me. Each of our lists is going to look different."

"Holy cow, why have you moved so much?"

"I wanted to travel."

"It sounds like you accomplished that."

"Definitely. I have lived in every state capital in the United States."

"Are you serious?" Boone felt fear rinse through his body. This news meant Piper lived in Sacramento, where he was born and raised, which was only slightly over an hour from Oakland.

13

oone fought to flush the emotions from his system reminding himself Piper lived in forty-nine other state capitals. If they were close to the same age, that meant she spent less than six months in each city on average. Math was one of his strengths, which came in handy for construction work.

"Living in each state capital and Washington, D.C. was one of my goals."

"Wow," Boone replied, taking a large sip of sweet tea. "That is quite the accomplishment. You can write it down."

"I guess I can."

Boone wanted to change the subject in case this talk about cities led Piper to ask which one he moved from in California. "You agreed to be my accountability partner even after discovering the project."

"True," Piper stated. "I think that counts because at first I definitely had second thoughts, and I am still not quite sure what I have gotten myself into."

"Me neither," Boone laughed.

Piper smirked. "I will write that one down for both of us."

"Starting the class is one for me," Boone shared as Piper wrote.

"I will put that one for each of us as well," she remarked. "Can you think of any others?"

"Not off the top of my head."

The waitress popped in. "Y'all two doing okay?"

"Yes," Piper replied.

Boone shook his head.

"Y'all doing work?" she asked, pointing at the notebook.

"A fun project," Piper called out.

"Ooh that's the best," she remarked. "Do y'all need refills?"

Boone and Piper glanced at Boone's sweet tea at the same time. He drank a little more than he realized. "I guess you can fill mine up."

"You might have to cut him off soon," Piper teased.

Everyone laughed.

"There's unlimited refills."

"Oh my," Piper commented.

Boone smirked.

The server headed for the tea urn and popped back over with a full glass a few moments later.

"The food should be right out."

"Thanks."

Piper and Boone found themselves alone again, staring at the list between them.

"Now, let's list some fears and goals," Piper recommended. "I'll go first since I had some time to think about this last night."

"Alright."

"One of my goals is to buy a house," Piper announced. "I never owned a house, so it's pretty scary."

"I haven't owned a house either." Beth owned the one they lived in for so many years.

"Should I put that on your list?"

An image of the campsite flashed into Boone's mind. "I haven't considered long-term housing plans, whether I want to rent or buy."

"We can always add it."

"That works."

"One of the key points I read about fears is that it is better to face them voluntarily rather than involuntarily."

Boone furrowed his brow. "What do you mean?"

"Like if I choose not to look voluntarily for a house to buy, and then my rental is no longer available at the end of the current term, I would have to look involuntarily for a place," she explained. "Basically it would make things much more difficult because I wouldn't be prepared and there would be a time crunch. With fewer options, I would have to pack up all my belongings quickly and so on. I might even end up homeless for a short time."

Kind of like me. "I understand what you are saying."

"I think it's interesting how voluntarily facing our fears starts an upward spiral," Piper mentioned. "For example, if you hadn't left Oakland, would you have gone to The Roots Beneath Us class?"

"Well no because it wasn't offered in Oakland."

"But if it was?"

Boone's facial expression answered the question. "I wouldn't have," he confirmed.

"If you hadn't shown up for the class and agreed to be my accountability partner, although I guess the latter was somewhere between voluntary and involuntary for both of us, would you have agreed to come with me to lunch?"

"Probably not."

"So once we start overcoming life's obstacles, we build momentum and grow as people."

"Makes sense," Boone noted. "You sound like an expert at this already."

Piper chuckled. "Not at all. I merely read some of the material last night. I think the concept is relatively simple as the opening paragraph mentions. When we start making the best decisions, things begin to fall in place, and challenges become easier to overcome especially when we break them down."

"What do you mean by breaking things down?"

"For example, earlier you alluded to the construction project feeling nearly impossible."

"Yeah it does; I am not sure I can do it."

"You can," Piper encouraged.

"What makes you think that? You don't know anything about my skill set. I could be terrible at construction."

"Even if you were, I think you could do it," she surmised. "But you're not; you have the capability or else your friend wouldn't have entrusted you with this important project." Piper paused for a sip of water through her yellow pasta straw. "Just because we haven't done something doesn't mean we can't do it."

"True." Boone lifted his glass to his lips.

"It probably looks so scary because it is so big," Piper concluded. "What if we break it down into smaller pieces?"

"Like what?"

"Well, you already have the funding, the plans, and the land. That's momentum. What's next?"

Boone considered the question. "Visiting the lot," he decided.

Piper wrote *Building the House Project* under Boone's name. Below that she indented and added *View the Lot*. "That's a pretty simple task. What then?"

"I have to see if it needs to be cleared and surveyed, and if it has water and sewer hookups."

"Have you done all that before?"

"It's never been my responsibility."

"But you have the knowledge," Piper observed. "I wouldn't have known to check on any of that other than whether the land needed to be cleared. That should be pretty obvious," she laughed. "We just keep making the list and check off one task at a time."

"*We*," he examined. "Are you saying you will volunteer your time to help me with this project?" he asked. "Building a house like this will take six to nine months. There will be thousands of little steps."

Piper considered the question and the appropriate answer. She thought about her commitment to volunteer at the dance studio. That was important to her. "I will help as much as possible," she promised, "especially when you need a hand. I realize this might be in the gray area when it comes to the duties of an accountability partner; however, volunteering is one of the things I want to add to my list." She paused for a moment when a thought struck. "Actually I can add that to my list because I have now volunteered for two positions."

"That's honorable."

"I do need to find a paying job as well," she added, snickering.

"You can put that on your list."

"Yeah, sure. Finding a job is a goal, and changing careers is somewhat of a fear, so it covers both."

"What type of work have you done in the past?"

Piper stalled by taking another sip of water. "I worked in physical fitness."

Boone mindlessly studied the visible portion of her body. It added up.

Piper wrote it down but decided to change the subject. "So let's jot down as many of our fears and goals as possible and work on breaking them into smaller parts later," she suggested. "Except for the house project, we can break that down as much as you want right away."

"Sounds good. I will be able to determine more once I see the lot."

"Okay. Can you do that today?"

"I will have to find out how far away it is."

"It's on the island," she reminded him. "I don't remember exactly where the area is but it's not far."

"Far is relative when you are walking."

"You don't have a car?"

"No."

Piper wondered if he didn't have enough money or had a revoked license. He said he hadn't been in any accidents, so she hoped he didn't have DUIs. "How did you get here from California?"

"Train and bus."

"How about your belongings?"

"I only brought a few bags."

Who was she to judge? She only packed what fit in the Jeep. "Shall we add a vehicle to your list?"

Boone snickered. "Probably." *We will also need to include learning how to drive.*

"Oh, and I can drive you to the lot so you can check it out."

"I can't depend on you to drive me everywhere," Boone acknowledged.

"Hey, a car is on the list, so let me *volunteer* to help you until you can check that one off."

Boone snickered at how she emphasized the word volunteer. *It might not be as simple as you think.* "Okay," he agreed.

At the perfect moment the waitress showed up with two plates. "Here's y'all's food," she announced enthusiastically.

While eating, Piper and Boone talked a lot about the house project. He shared some of his past experiences in construction. She told him she knew absolutely nothing about construction, which they laughed about. They wondered aloud who the house might be for; they came up with the names of movie stars, politicians, CEOs, and others but decided it could be for any wealthy person. However, Preston's reaction to the question earlier made them think otherwise.

Piper talked way more than Boone, but she was glad most of his answers were now more than one word.

When they finished eating and the check arrived, Boone reached for the ticket.

"I can pay," Piper offered. "At least for mine."

"I've got it," he said proudly. Yesterday Boone wouldn't have been able to afford this meal. He would have chosen not to come because of money, but now he felt good about how everything worked out.

The lot where the house would sit overlooked the Atlantic Ocean as Piper presumed, but to their surprise, it sat on a narrow stretch of the island. As the plans showed, a deck on top of the home featuring a hot tub and sitting area enclosed by a glass barrier made sense. This new revelation explained the balcony at the front of the house.

When Boone and Piper met at the Jeep's grill, he pointed out that the Currituck Sound across the street would also be visible.

"The views will be gorgeous," Piper imagined.

"For sure," Boone agreed. "This is a valuable piece of land."

"A priceless piece of land. I would live in a tent out here to have this view."

"Me too," Boone replied. He left the tent comment alone for obvious reasons but wondered if setting up camp here while building the house might be an option. "I have good news," Boone shared, pointing at something near the front of the lot. "Water and sewer hookups have already been established, which surprises me, but it's beneficial," he acknowledged. "That's two things out of the way since the lot is cleared."

"Yay," Piper exclaimed with a calm clap.

In unison Boone and Piper stepped toward a clearing perfectly nestled amongst a slew of spidery live oaks that appeared to have been growing for hundreds of years waiting for a house to complement the charming environment.

"This is where the home will sit," Boone projected.

"It's perfect."

Although not touching, Boone's and Piper's bodies slowly turned as if dancing on a dirt floor while taking in their surroundings in awe.

Sand dunes covered with wild sea oats waving at them with the help of a gentle breeze protected the oceanside, and small rolling hills protruding inland created a boundary on either side of the property.

"This is so peaceful," Boone shared.

In the trees birds chirped; squirrels scampered across the ground; and the hum of the ocean's waves filled the air.

"This lot reminds me of the backyard at the house where I am staying but on a grander scale and with an oceanview."

"Must be a nice place."

"It is. I initially rented the home for a week, but now I have it for a month," she shared. "Can you tell if this land has been surveyed?"

Boone glanced in all four directions in which boundaries would generally be set. "I can't see any markers from here," he explained. "However, not far before we turned in, I thought I saw a flag," he mentioned.

"What exactly is a survey?"

"In basic form a survey measures and records the boundaries of a lot. It creates a map of a parcel of land and includes angles, elevation levels, and more details that help with building, irrigation, and other topography needs," Boone explained. "Stakes are usually hammered into the ground at the corners of the property, and if there are any odd angles between one and the next, additional stakes are nailed down. An orange flag is often tied around the top so they'll stand out. These are placed so the land and adjacent owners can know and respect the property lines."

"Oh yeah, I've seen those."

"When we are building the house and creating the yardscape, we will want to make sure the water flows to that ditch," Boone said, pointing to a small drainage ditch mirroring the roadway. "By the way, the fact that there is already a gravel drive across the ditch shaves another step off the early part of the process. That will allow easy access for delivery of materials and supplies."

"That's great news," Piper concluded. "So what comes next?"

"Let's walk the outer edges of the property to see if we can find the stakes."

"Okay."

In less than a minute, Boone found the first flag he saw from the road earlier. From there, they walked toward the ocean.

"All these little hills and climbing trees remind me of a jungle," Piper noted.

"These live oaks would be fun for kids to climb," Boone pointed out.

"Adults too," Piper added before pouncing into one like a leopard.

Boone watched her maneuver from one limb to another as though she climbed trees daily.

"The view is pretty good up here," she announced upon finding a perch. "Are you coming up?"

Boone studied the tree. "I'm not sure; I haven't climbed a tree in a long time."

"Boone, you can climb this tree," Piper argued in a motherly tone. "The branches are like a stepladder."

The low-hanging limbs offered easy access to the tree, and the pattern of the branches made for relatively simple climbing.

Boone stepped on the first branch holding the one above it as he did. He reached for the tree's trunk when his leg stretched to the second branch, and before he knew it he made his way to Piper.

"See, that wasn't so hard," Piper said as their legs dangled about half a dozen feet off the ground.

"The view is pretty nice up here," he stated as they faced the ocean. From their viewpoint, they couldn't see anyone on the beach; there was only sand, water, and sky as far as the eye could see. The waves rolled in steadily, and the sky remained blue with puffy clouds.

Boone hugged the tree trunk with one arm and held the branch beneath him with his other hand. This reminded him of balancing on scaffolding while building a house. He tolerated it and tried not to let the guys know it scared him.

"Hey, look," Piper said, pointing toward the sand dunes. "There is another survey flag."

"Great spot. We now know where the back right corner of the property ends."

"Do you have kids?" Piper asked randomly. Boone furrowed his brow wondering from where the comment originated. Piper noticed. "When you mentioned that these trees would be nice for kids to climb, it made me wonder if you have children."

"Oh, that makes sense. No, I don't have kids. Do you?"

"Nope," she answered. "Do you want kids?"

14

Piper's question about children reminded Boone of his thoughts on the train. "I used to want kids; it just never worked out," he answered.

"I think I would still like to have kids even though I am forty."

"I wondered how old you are," Boone commented. "You don't look forty, but you said something that made me think you were close to my age."

"How old are you?" Piper asked. "Wait, let me guess," she interjected then paused for a moment as the birds danced in the trees around them. "I think you are forty-three."

"Thirty-nine." Boone figured the stress probably added a few years.

Piper covered her mouth with one hand and kept the other balanced on the tree branch. "Oops, I guess that's why everyone says not to guess people's ages," she commented with a snicker.

Boone smirked. "It's okay."

"When do you turn forty?"

"May the eighth."

Piper's cheeks rose with her smile. "Our birthdays are only a week apart," she acknowledged. "Mine was Monday."

"The day you moved here?"

"Yep. I planned it that way."

"That's interesting. What did you do to celebrate?"

As their feet dangled and Boone became a tad more comfortable, Piper told him all about her birthday.

They walked over the sand dunes a few minutes later, and Piper pulled off her shoes.

"This is the first time I have been on the beach since arriving in Duck," Boone reported.

"Take off your shoes," Piper encouraged. "The sand feels so nice between my toes."

Boone reached down and untied one shoelace and then the other. He removed his socks and stuffed them in his shoes, and then they walked to the water's edge where the wind blew flakes of sea-foam like dandelion dust. A pelican soared in the distance, and the sand swirled around their ankles where seashells of all sorts of shapes and colors decorated the beach.

"Can you imagine being able to walk out your back door to this every day?" Piper asked.

"Not really," Boone answered honestly.

They both snickered.

The late afternoon sun felt comforting on Piper's skin. She wondered what she would be doing if she hadn't run into Boone today. Maybe she would have come to the beach or rode her bicycle. She most likely would have worked on the list just like they did.

"So what comes next for the house project?"

"Prepping for the foundation," Boone answered. "I need to order sand for where the house will sit to get that spot precisely level. I also need to start looking for a crew to hire to lay the foundation."

"There's plenty of sand right here," Piper teased, digging her toes in and flicking a few thousand grains onto Boone's feet.

Boone laughed and kicked off the sand. "Are you trying to get me in trouble before I ever start building?"

"Of course not, I'm here to help, remember?"

Boone and Piper walked the rest of the lot and found all the boundary markers. When they climbed back into the Jeep, she pulled the notebook from her bag and checked off the things on the list they discovered.

"It's all falling into place," she acknowledged.

"So far so good."

Piper wrote down the next two steps Boone mentioned. "Do you want to use my phone to order sand?"

"Right now?"

"Why not?"

"I guess I just didn't expect to move so fast." Everything seemed to be happening rapidly, and Boone was still undecided about how that made him feel.

"I say keep the momentum going," Piper reminded him. "And you don't have a phone, so you might want to take advantage of this opportunity."

"True but I have no idea who to call for sand."

Piper pulled her phone from her bag. "I'll search for *sand in Duck*."

Twenty seconds later a few options popped up on the screen. Piper read the list to Boone, and they picked the one with the most interesting sounding name.

Piper handed the phone over, and when it started ringing, Boone couldn't believe this was happening. A lady answered and began to take his order. He estimated the amount of sand the area needed, and she told him they could always bring more later if needed. Piper smiled as Boone talked although she wasn't sure why this brought her so much joy. Maybe knowing what this man went through had something to do with it.

"My phone number?" Boone asked the woman on the other end of the line, his eyes darting at Piper, begging for help.

"Give her mine," Piper whispered.

Boone figured he had no other option. He pulled Piper's phone number from his pocket just like at the bank and read it aloud.

"My billing address?" Boone questioned, his eyes bulging like a cartoon character's.

Boone and Piper stared at each other for a moment.

"I don't have an address where I can get mail," Boone uttered nervously to Piper while holding the phone as far away from his mouth as possible.

"Give her mine," Piper concluded again. She flipped a page in the notebook and quickly wrote down the address. Thankfully she looked it up yesterday for the dance studio application so it remained fresh on her mind.

The lull in the phone conversation made Boone feel awkward especially when the lady asked, "Are you still there?"

Finally, he read off the address, and just like that the sand order became final.

The air in the Jeep remained quiet momentarily, and then Piper burst into laughter.

"That wasn't funny," Boone complained.

"I'm sorry. I felt like we were high schoolers trying to convince our parents of our whereabouts and having to come up with a phone number and address on the fly," she explained. "We did good."

"I guess," Boone remarked. "I think we need to add a phone to my list."

Piper turned back the page. "You are up to three now which puts you one ahead of me. I want a cat," she mentioned randomly, evening out their lists when she put it on paper.

"Okay."

"I better wait until I find a permanent place to live though," she thought out loud.

Boone shook his head in agreement. "Good idea."

"I guess I gave you my address after all," Piper disclosed with a chuckle.

"I probably won't remember it," Boone snickered.

"You might need to if you keep ordering stuff," she mentioned with a grin. She wanted to ask where he lived that didn't have an address where things could be delivered but decided to allow him privacy under the circumstances. He would tell her in time if he wanted, or maybe he would ask her to take him there now. "Speaking of addresses, it's about time for me to head home. I have plans this evening."

"Sounds good."

"Where should I drop you off?"

Boone's face suddenly felt flushed. He hadn't even considered where Piper would take him. Asking her to drive him anywhere other than where he was staying sounded sketchy, especially since she willingly shared her address.

"I need to grab a few things from the general store, so if you can drop me off there, it will save me some steps," he finally figured out. The truth set him free this time.

Boone wandered the aisles of the general store and eventually found a small camping section with a couple of tents, sleeping bags, and various other outdoor conveniences. He stood there for a good while contemplating the options. Adding the money in his pocket to the envelope gave him more than a thousand dollars.

"Sir, can I answer any questions about the camping gear?" an employee asked.

"No thanks," Boone answered. "Just trying to decide what I need."

Boone wished he knew how often he would be paid and how much. He kicked himself for not thinking to ask those questions at the bank, but all the information shared was overwhelming. Adding Piper into the mix with the course expectations and the accountability partner situation made thinking during the meeting even more challenging. He wasn't a businessman; manual labor had always been his thing.

He glanced at his watch and realized the short hand had passed the number five. Returning to the bank today wasn't an option, and the doors wouldn't reopen until Monday morning. He needed to figure out the next three nights before a calculated decision could be made. He didn't want to waste money on a tent if he only needed it for a few nights; however, the campground guy said he must have one tonight.

The options seemed to be renting a place for a few nights, buying the tent, or going back to the campground empty-handed to see if the attendant understood the dilemma and would let him sleep on the ground at the campsite three more nights.

Boone picked up the cheapest tent and sleeping bag putting one under each arm. Almost to the register, Piper's comment about sleeping in a tent on the beach lot came to mind. He stood in the middle of the store motionless for a minute with thought bubbles floating above his head. If the campground owner wouldn't let him stay without a tent, he could always go to the property and camp out under the trees. With no houses in sight, no one would see him there as long as he was careful about coming and going. Building a fire might be risky but he could probably get away with it.

Boone walked back to the camping section and returned the items knowing he needed to save for a cell phone, a vehicle, and many other things. He then left the store with nothing and headed toward the campground.

15

Piper's day turned out much differently than anticipated. Until arriving back at the house, she completely forgot she planned to pick up a novel from the local bookshop and fresh veggies from the Wee Winks Market after the bank. The darkness on the other side of the windows reminded her she wouldn't have a book to read in the bathtub. She considered hopping back in the Jeep and heading to the store but then began to peruse the cabinets, refrigerator, and freezer.

A box of brown rice, a carton of eggs, and a frozen bag of mixed vegetables ended up on the counter.

"Close enough," Piper whispered to herself while thinking it sure would be nice to have the cat to talk to.

It didn't take long to cook fried rice, one of her favorite dishes. She added butter, soy sauce, hoisin sauce, salt, and pepper.

Once again she ate dinner on the back patio overlooking her little jungle. Those last few words came to mind because of her comment to Boone earlier. She admitted to herself she had a lot of fun with the guy today. After a few conversations she was pleasantly surprised by his quality of companionship.

For some reason that thought reminded Piper of her friend Hardy Turner, and she found herself missing their dialogue and excursions.

When Piper felt full, she put away the dishes, poured a glass of wine, and went straight to the master bathroom. A long bath was her big plan for the night. Since she didn't have a book, she grabbed the journey list journal, deciding she might add a few. First, she wanted to read more of the course material for fresh ideas.

❦

Daylight faded by the time Boone reached the squeaky screen door where he knocked, waited for the hippie man to show up, and pleaded his case.

"I'm sorry, my friend; I can't let you stay here without a tent for the rest of the weekend. That's not fair to the other campers."

"I understand," Boone replied. "I will gather my things and leave."

"I know of a shelter on the Outer Banks if you want to stay there," he proposed. "The people who run it are really nice and will feed you three warm meals a day."

"Thank you," Boone responded, "but I have another plan."

"You are welcome to keep the sleeping bag and pillow."

Boone hadn't even thought about that when he put the sleeping bag back on the shelf at the store. He would have been in trouble if the guy made him leave the old one here. Regardless he sure wished he remembered to buy a pillow.

Boone shook his head; he wasn't thinking straight today.

At the campsite he retrieved his suitcases from the bushes where he had left them covered with the sleeping bag. Fortunately no one messed with his stuff.

Several minutes later Boone walked off the property with the bookbag on his back, a suitcase in each hand, and the pillow tucked inside the rolled-up sleeping bag under his arm. On the main road he considered hitchhiking but decided otherwise. Duck was his new home, and being labeled a bum from the onset didn't seem appealing. Thankfully the dark skies should shield his face from anyone driving by.

⁓

Piper undressed and studied her naked body in the tall mirror. Each of the tattoos on her brown skin told a story. The words faith, hope, and love, written in cursive, stretched down the right side of her torso between her armpit and hip. The ink barely had time to dry on this one she got just before leaving Miami. She knew she needed faith and hope to find love again.

Piper felt like she gave up on love around age twenty-five after a bad breakup. Rather than eating ice cream and watching romance movies, she decided to have a sunflower, her favorite, painted around her belly button. It reminded her there would always be brighter days. She often looked at this one when the skies in her life seemed gray. Right now they didn't, but the circular brown center and sprouting yellow pedals were still beautiful.

At age eighteen she nervously asked a tattoo artist to write the words *I hope you dance* on her right foot. The sentence started just below the ankle and ended near her pinky toe. Piper turned her foot to read the saying. Thinking of the dance studio she visited earlier, she smiled from ear to ear.

The red heart on her left breast reminded her of many things. She chose it when a tattoo parlor partnered with blood donors, hosting a fundraiser and giving the full amount of the ink to charity. It also represented her decision to become an organ donor in honor of her friend who died at age twenty-two while waiting on a transplant. Piper's grandmother passed away after battling breast cancer, so the heart always reminded her of their time together. Piper traced the bright image with her pointer finger, remembering the people she loved.

Stepping away from the mirror, she felt proud to know she didn't regret a single tattoo. She chose to place each of them where she could see them without assistance. Glancing over her shoulder at her butt, she could tell the squats every other day still worked after forty. She needed to start running too; she'd slacked off since moving here because so many things required attention. Maybe tomorrow.

Boone should have known that in a small town people liked to help others. On several occasions today Piper brought up the kindness of the locals. Three drivers stopped to ask if he needed a ride as he walked toward the lot. He kept his chin down each time and said, "No thanks," in a muffled voice.

The headlights of another vehicle coming in his direction from up ahead encouraged him to stare at his boots. When the black car slowed as it passed, fear coursed through his body, and without looking back, Boone noticed the swivel of the headlights as the vehicle turned around. When the car made it back to him, the driver rolled down the passenger window and stared in his direction for a few moments as Boone tried not to glance at the person out of the corner of his eye.

"Boone, is that you?" she questioned.

The hot water bounced like popcorn off the bathtub's floor when Piper turned it on, and she let it run while she clicked a lighter. One by one the candles surrounding the tub flickered to life. Lastly, after dimming the lights, she released a bubbly bath bomb.

When Piper sank into paradise, the warmth relaxed her whole body. Her eyelids collapsed, and she breathed in the aromas all around. She loved everything about baths and could stay in one for hours.

Boone had only met a handful of people in Duck. Recognizing a woman's voice immediately ruled out the campground fellow and Preston Bynum. He wished the latter had shown up to answer the questions rattling his mind.

Boone only knew one woman in Duck, and he quickly realized the voice didn't belong to her. He heard Piper talk enough today to pick out her unique sound. Reaching that conclusion, the familiarity of the voice coming from the black vehicle frightened him.

After nearly twenty minutes of stillness, Piper warmed the water. The bubbles floating on top reminded her of snow, but nothing was cold about this experience.

On a nearby table the notebook and a pencil sat on top of a hand towel. Piper flipped open the pages and read over the lists she wrote for her and Boone. Then she reached for her phone and started to read the course material. A couple paragraphs in, she stopped. Reading on without Boone felt wrong, knowing he didn't have a phone to study the information. She decided to put it back.

Boone couldn't believe he got into the car. He should have never lifted his face and let her look him in the eyes. He wished he said, "No, my name isn't Boone," and kept walking. But that would have been a lie.

He thought the hoodie and the darkness would hide his identity, but somehow, she recognized him.

Why hadn't he moved on down the road before she jumped out of the car and hurried to him? Instead he froze and let her take control of the situation. Before they could discuss anything, she grabbed the sleeping bag from beneath his arm, opened the back door, and tossed it in as if he had no other choice.

"Put your bags in there," she instructed.

Where would she take him?

Piper turned her attention to the glass of wine, and as the clock ticked, she sipped slowly until the contents disappeared. The bottle she picked up earlier in the week had enough for one more glass which she poured carefully as the smooth sounds of jazz played through her phone's speaker. She made a mental note to pick up more tomorrow although unsure whether she would get the same pinot noir or try something new.

Boone sat speechless in the passenger seat as the trees on the lonely road flickered by as quickly as his thoughts.

"Where is your girlfriend?" she asked.

Boone glanced sheepishly in her direction. Why did he feel the need to explain as if leaving it alone would get him in trouble? "It's not what you think."

"What do you mean?"

"She's not my girlfriend."

"Oh, then, who is she?"

"We are taking a class together," Boone mentioned.

"The two of you looked pretty friendly earlier."

Boone tensed up even more, wondering what she meant and what she saw. "She is my accountability partner," he confessed.

"It sounds like you two are more than friends," she considered audibly.

"We're not," Boone clarified quickly.

"So she won't be upset I gave you a ride?"

Boone shook his head. "I don't know why she would."

"How long have you known each other?"

"Just a couple of days."

"Oh, y'all didn't move here together?" she inquired. "That's how it seemed."

"No."

Boone cringed. This felt like an interrogation. He hated being questioned, always had. Beth did this to him constantly.

"I know you are a man, and you probably don't think you need help, especially from a woman, but I will take you to my place. You can shower and have a mattress to rest your head on. There's no reason for you to be roaming around."

16

With bubbles floating around her, Piper wondered what Boone was doing. Where had he walked after she left him at the general store? In a way she wished they made plans to get together tomorrow instead of Sunday. Continuing this journey with him excited her. Not only did she want to work on creating the list, but she wanted to start facing fears and checking off accomplishments.

Even though she hadn't read any more of the material or written anything down, she thought of a few things to add to her list. Others came to mind that she didn't feel comfortable sharing with Boone. She didn't want him to know what she did for a living. In fact she never wanted to tell another soul about her career.

Boone realized the black sedan's tires sat in almost the exact spot Piper's Jeep occupied when they viewed the lot earlier. He didn't know why he brought another person here. He intended to keep this place a secret, specifically the part about him staying on the grounds. She threw him off by encouraging him, or more like pushing him, to stay with her.

"I hope offering for you to shower and stay at my place didn't seem like I was trying to seduce you, Daniel Boone," she mentioned. "I just want to help in any way I can, especially since you are new to Duck."

"I appreciate that," Boone replied. Kayla was pretty. A bit ditzy but pretty. He noticed her smile and curly blonde hair when she waited on him and Piper. "So why did you ask me all those questions about Piper?"

"Like I said, I want to help you, but I didn't want to invite another woman's man to my house regardless of the circumstances."

"I see."

"You seem interesting, Daniel Boone," she professed. "I look forward to getting to know more about you."

"Thanks," Boone replied. He didn't know exactly what she meant by that. "I think I need to get settled in first."

A large bird flew across the path of the headlights, startling Boone and Kayla.

"What was that?" Kayla asked, breathing heavily all of a sudden.

"An owl, I think."

"Might have been," she replied, studying the mysterious surroundings. "Do you have a cabin back there in the woods, Daniel Boone?"

Boone really didn't care for people calling him Daniel Boone. A kid in high school, Roger Phelps, always called him by that name, and he hated it. "Something like that," Boone responded.

Kayla wondered why he told her to stop here earlier. She expected to drive up to a house.

"If you drive further your vehicle might get stuck," Boone suggested. "I have to walk the rest of the way to my place."

Honestly he didn't know the location of *his place* yet. However, earlier, he noticed a relatively wooded spot on one of the back corners of the lot and figured it might be the best option to set up camp.

"I'll help you carry your things," Kayla offered.

"There's no need for that," Boone professed.

Kayla wrote her name and number on a random business card she plucked from her cluttered center console. "Call me if you need me," she encouraged.

Boone pulled a flashlight from his backpack but waited until Kayla pulled away to press the button. It didn't take long to find the dense area he remembered, and rolling out the sleeping bag didn't take up much room. He sat his other bags nearby and climbed into the bed.

The ground here felt softer than at the campsite. Probably because no one ever walked through this area. Boone decided against gathering sticks to build a fire. On his first night here, he had already drawn enough attention. He kicked himself for letting Kayla bring him to the lot. As much as she liked to talk, he worried she would tell others, and someone would pry into his business.

Maybe he would only stay here tonight.

Critters rattled in the nearby brush. The owl from earlier hooted. The moonlight snuck through the trees surrounding him. The roar of the ocean rose through the darkness. He loved that sound, and when he couldn't fall asleep, he decided to walk on the beach.

Boone left his shoes near the waterline as a marker, so he would know how to find his way back to the sleeping bag. The sand felt cool and soft beneath his toes although the ocean air was much brisker than when he and Piper walked around midday. The sun really made a difference.

Boone followed the moonlight one lackadaisical step at a time. He had no idea how far he ventured before turning around but liked how the atmosphere calmed his mind and body. He really wished he could sleep out on the beach. The fluffy sand would feel comfortable beneath the sleeping bag, but it wasn't worth the risk. Someone likely patrolled the beach, at least in the morning, and he doubted they would take kindly to a person camping in a random spot near the dunes. The last thing he needed was to be arrested for something so petty.

Boone contemplated everything that happened on his first full day in Duck. Never in a million years would he have expected it to be so full of adventure. He thought about the meeting at the bank, lunch with Piper, making the list, and then being surprised by Kayla. It blew his mind that he could literally be in her house right now. How in the world had he met two attractive women in as many days when he hadn't even tried? In fact he didn't intend to meet anyone. He wanted to lay low, get his life together, and let Beth go one memory at a time while building a new life.

He thought of the two of them lying under the covers together. Sleeping with clothes on this week felt odd because they always slept naked. This was the longest he had gone without sex for as far back as he remembered, and it honestly seemed okay although strange.

In a way Beth's addiction became his addiction. She always wanted him even when she came home smelling like another man's cologne. In fact those nights she seemed to crave him more. He assumed it provided the sexual power she desired.

Thank God she never brought another man home, at least not physically. Boone didn't want to know what went through her mind when they had sex. She called him other men's names occasionally labeling it role play but never had him call her by another name.

Boone figured most men who met Piper and Kayla felt a desire to be intimate with them. He hadn't. He appreciated their beauty, but the idea of touching either of them romantically felt wrong. He wondered if Beth brainwashed him to view all women as sex fiend monsters. There had to be some good ones out there, but he wasn't sure how to tell the difference. Removing the walls Beth built around him would take time.

Boone found himself wanting to add this to his journey list

although he didn't know how to word it. The idea of a healthy relationship seemed so foreign although desirable.

When Boone made it back to his shoes and, ultimately, the sleeping bag, the thoughts he had about Beth, sex, and relationships suddenly caused him to miss having another person's arms wrapped around him. He never knew it would be this hard to be away from Beth or that his body would physically crave her touch. Thinking of that control, his fists slammed into the sand, causing tiny grains to erupt like a volcano and scatter all over the sleeping bag and his face. He spat them from his lips, thinking he could have gone home with Kayla. Maybe she would have had sex with him, consensual sex. That might satisfy his urges and help him forget about Beth, whom he wanted but knew he didn't need.

Piper woke up early on Saturday morning with energy pumping through her veins. Living in a new place always felt refreshing and exciting. She pulled on a pair of dark green leggings and a matching sports bra then ran six miles on the beach.

A handful of other runners waved as they passed, and walkers did the same. It seemed a good portion of the latter group collected freshly unearthed seashells.

As the sun rose a little higher, she finished her morning workout with several sets of squats. She showered at the house, ate breakfast on the front porch, then hopped on her bicycle. Today's ride would be purely for pleasure since she already worked out. The first leg of the journey took her to the bookstore. The owner greeted her with a smile and told her about the history of the bookstore and some local authors.

Piper took her time perusing the shelves. She skipped the bestsellers rack and found the beach reads section. By the time the door jingled on her way out, she read the synopsis of over twenty books. Her final choice, a mystery novel, rested in the bicycle's basket as she pedaled around town, familiarizing herself with new streets and shops.

Scarborough Faire Shops instantly became a favorite. Nestled into a treehouse village atmosphere, two stories of shops including wine, books, coffee, breakfast, clothes, jewelry, and a variety of other unique items provided an unparalleled experience. An open-air area in the center surrounded by the shops, a variety of shade trees, and outdoor staircases made the perfect spot for sipping on a cup of coffee in a natural environment.

Wood plank walkways led to picnic tables, quaint ponds, cornhole boards, and a veranda. Globe lights dangled from tree to tree as if Spiderman hung them while soaring about shooting webs. Random décor like an antique bicycle attached to a staircase, red wooden hearts pinned to tree trunks, and arrow-shaped directional placards added to the place's rustic vibe.

Piper spent time there shopping and relaxing before ending up at Wee Winks Market. She eventually made it home with the ingredients to make a salad for lunch and fresh veggies for dinner. The guy who helped her with the wine selection the last time once again guided her toward another bottle based on her review of the first. She grabbed pinot noir as a backup plan since she enjoyed the taste so much.

Piper spent the rest of her day reading. She bounced around from the patio to the front porch, couch, and beach. Eventually, the grand finale happened in the bathtub. She always wanted to read a whole book in one day, and now she had.

Boone's second night of sleep in Duck proved worse than the first. After climbing into his sleeping bag, he kept worrying someone would catch him even though the chances seemed slim. Could he be charged with trespassing at the worksite? Possibly. Probably.

He guessed it depended on the owner's perspective. Regardless, he didn't want to cause any issues for the project.

He slept a little, stared at the stars through tree limbs, listened to the waves crash, and wondered what Saturday would look like. Buying a pillow definitely became a priority. Sleeping on a stranger's pillow felt gross. He couldn't quit wondering if someone left it behind because of bed bugs, and thinking about that caused him to scratch his head.

In the middle of the night, he randomly contemplated what to do if it rained. He didn't know if the sleeping bag was waterproof and highly doubted his suitcases were. What if all his clothes got soaking wet? He would have to hang them on tree branches to dry. They would probably stink. He never considered all the challenges homeless people dealt with. Even though he didn't think of himself as a bum, reality slapped him in the face. Technically, he was homeless for the first time in his life. Homeless. That word hit hard.

Boone searched his mind to prove that this situation and that word didn't define him. How many homeless people had a job? A thousand dollars in their pocket? Oh no, what if his money got wet, he thought, and then he remembered wet money always dried.

What about the blueprints? The blueprints! Oh no, he left them in Piper's back seat. His face scrunched in frustration. What if he never saw her again? He would or should. They made plans for Sunday. Maybe the blueprints fared better with her. What would he do with them here, nestle them inside his sleeping bag? Probably.

Boone's new priority became finding Piper on Saturday to check on the blueprints. Although they might stay dry with her, he couldn't risk losing them. Those things weren't cheap, and who knew if a master copy existed somewhere on a file or printed. Another question he didn't ask at the bank. The set provided could be the only one. The plan seemed very original.

Boone made a mental note to research the weather forecast and write it down so he could prepare accordingly as long as he lived outside. Piper would probably look it up for him, or he could even ask a stranger if he found the courage to strike up a conversation. He really needed his own phone. What was the first step in that direction? He never bought a phone before. He wasn't a caveman; he knew he needed a plan but didn't know the process. Could he get a phone immediately, or would it take a while? How much would it cost?

Beth handled these things. Boone used her phone some, so he understood the basics of navigating a device, but she insisted it didn't make sense for them to have two phones. He knew what she really meant.

When the sun rose over the horizon, Boone knew he wouldn't sleep another wink. He moved his belongings near a large tree, where thick brush surrounded the trunk, and covered his luggage with the sleeping bag. Then he placed the straps of his bookbag over his shoulders, walked about twenty yards to the closest clearing, and looked back to see if his things were visible. He saw them, but he knew where to look. A random person walking through the lot most likely wouldn't notice them.

Boone moved carefully through the property as if performing a tactical mission. When he neared the road, he stood behind a tree and watched for cars. He appreciated the sappy fragrance of the loblolly pine his shoulder leaned against. The coast became clear, and he hurried to the roadside and began walking toward town.

Today people drove by and waved, but only one person stopped. Since Boone didn't carry suitcases and a sleeping bag, he didn't feel the need to hide his face. He simply told the gentleman he was walking for pleasure. Once he made it into the village area, more people would be walking, and he would blend in although not many tourists would be out this early in the morning.

Boone wanted to go straight to Piper's house but decided she might still be sleeping, and waking her didn't sound like a good idea. He would take care of other tasks first. He needed to check out phones, buy a pillow, and pick up some basic groceries. He wished he could shower. The one yesterday morning at the campground felt so good. He even styled his hair before going to the bank. Today he simply poured water from his bottle onto his hands and formed it as best he could. The curls often posed a challenge and could look like knots after sleeping.

The grocery store would be the only place on the list open this early in the morning. While roaming the aisles, Boone remembered that the absence of refrigeration limited the possibilities for meals and snacks. He first collected items from the fruit section: apples, bananas, and strawberries. Then he grabbed a can of cashews and a six-pack of water. The cart could hold way more, but his backpack would only fit so much. Now he knew why homeless people pushed grocery carts. They were like a giant bookbag or purse that could literally hold the kitchen sink that so many people teased women about.

Boone snickered at that thought, and a man nearby looked at him funny. After he walked out of the Wee Winks Market with a bag in either hand, he sat on the bench outside and transferred everything to his backpack. Then he stuffed the plastic bags into the front section in case he needed them later.

It would be at least another hour before the phone and general stores opened. While waiting, Boone wandered to a boardwalk he caught glimpses of yesterday when riding to the restaurant with Piper. The walkway, literally attached to shops and restaurants, wound through marsh and offered a panoramic view of the Currituck Sound, which Boone calculated as about two miles wide from his vantage point.

He located a bench and pulled out his breakfast—fruits and

nuts. It seemed like a good place to people watch. Others sat on nearby benches; dog owners walked their four-legged friends; amateur photographers snapped pictures; and a few runners scurried by at varying paces.

Boone couldn't remember the last time he jogged or did any exercise other than construction which kept him in relatively decent shape. Usually by the time he arrived home after a long day's work, he felt too physically worn down to consider working out. Beth never asked him to go with her although he would have. She always said gym time meant time with the girls.

A sudden realization hit Boone harder than the bright sun bouncing off his forehead. He needed to get stronger and learn how to defend himself in case Beth showed up or if, God forbid, he found himself in a relationship with someone like her again. This might be a good thing to add to his journey list although telling Piper would make him sound weak.

Boone glanced at his watch which read fifteen minutes after eight. It surprised him how much time passed since checking out at the grocery store. He decided to search for a pillow at the general store before walking to Piper's. He sure hoped he remembered the address because he never wrote it down. That reminded him of a thought from last night; he wanted to ask Mr. Bynum about putting up a mailbox at the lot to receive mail there during the project. He also needed to add secure building permits to the journey list under the Building the House Project before hiring a crew to lay the foundation.

Once he got to Piper's, he would ask her for advice about a cell phone.

The front desk attendant at the general store greeted Boone with a smile. "You were in here last night, weren't you?" he recalled kindly.

"Yes, I couldn't make up my mind about some items," Boone responded. "Do you happen to have pillows?"

The man scrunched his nose. "You know what, that's one item I don't carry," he revealed. "Although I can probably order one for you if you don't mind waiting a few days to a week."

Boone grimaced. "I kind of need it right away."

The guy pointed. "Try Kellogg Supply; they have home furnishings. It's a neat place; they've been around for many years."

Boone decided to buy the sleeping bag he held in his hands last night. After checking out, he followed the sidewalk in the direction the guy explained. There, he found a pillow, and thankfully, the woman who rang him up asked if he needed a pillow case. He grabbed a set of two in case one got dirty.

Thankfully Piper's blue Jeep stood out like a highlighter in the gravel driveway when Boone made it to her road. Otherwise he would have second guessed the street number. With the sleeping bag stuffed in the backpack on his shoulders, he sat the other bags on the porch. A solid white carrying bag housed his pillow, and he had transferred the groceries back into a single plastic bag. With his hands free, Boone knocked on the door.

He waited about thirty seconds and knocked again. When Piper didn't answer, he wandered around the side of the house, thinking she might be sitting on the patio she mentioned. When he didn't find her there, he studied the backyard. It really did look like a smaller version of the vacant lot. Beautiful.

Boone considered knocking on the back door but thought that might seem a bit invasive. He wondered if Piper could be in the bathroom, maybe taking a shower. People often did that in the mornings.

He knocked on the front door again then sat on the steps and took a swig from his water bottle. He waited about fifteen minutes and knocked one last time. When Piper didn't answer, he thought about leaving a note but realized he didn't have a pen or paper. He didn't know what he would write anyway. He guessed he could ask her to stop by the lot. Maybe if he went to the cell phone store first, he would have a number to leave her. Oh well.

Many steps later, Boone ended up in front of a phone display with an overwhelming number of options. The salesperson who helped him seemed pushy. The guy tried to talk him into buying a thousand dollar phone. When Boone told him he barely had that much money, the salesperson said he could split it into payments under one hundred dollars a month for twelve months with a new plan. Eventually he showed Boone the least expensive phone in the store. However, it would still eat nearly a third of his cash even before the monthly payment for service.

Boone decided to wait although he didn't walk out empty-handed. He dropped a complimentary pen and a pad of sticky notes in the zipper pouch with the plastic bag and his flashlight. Now he could write a note.

He ate lunch at Duck Town Park, an eleven-acre public area in the center of the village. Gravel trails led to a playground, an amphitheater, and the boardwalk where he ventured earlier. This time while taking in a unique view of the sound, he enjoyed an apple, a banana, and a few handfuls of cashews.

By late afternoon he ran out of things to do, and his legs grew weary. He went by Piper's house again, but she didn't answer the door. The Jeep still sat idle in the driveway. Boone wondered if she was ignoring him, but that didn't seem like her style although he didn't really know her. He didn't hear any rustling around in the house, see the curtains or blinds move, or anything like that.

Boone pulled out the pen and paper and wrote his earlier thoughts: *Piper, I left the blueprints in your vehicle. If you have a chance will you ride out to the beach lot and see if I am there? I plan to work on some ideas at the property today. -Boone*

Boone spent the rest of the evening at the lot. He wrote down his earlier thoughts about the building permits and mailbox and began making a list of materials to order and additional crews to hire along the way. The project still felt overwhelming, but he appreciated the course and Piper sharing The Roots Beneath Us idea of creating baby steps that led to the primary goal.

When Piper didn't show up by nightfall, Boone doubted he would see her before tomorrow. Hopefully everything worked out. He felt too tired for a beach walk tonight but sat near the edge of the ocean for hours and took in the view and sounds that he didn't know how long he would have. He chose to cherish them while he did.

Boone ate dinner as tiny crabs scampered in the sand, darting in and out of holes as if their lives depended on it. During the day at the busy parts of the beach that might be the case. A couple people walked by with flashlights and said hello. Boone played it cool. He watched a raccoon run from the sand dunes to the water and back up a few minutes later. Birds chattered in the air and on the beach. For a while his eyes followed their little footprints.

The only negative about being near the ocean was the salt air that caked on his glasses. He wiped the lenses several times throughout the evening with his shirt.

Climbing into his new sleeping bag and resting his head on the fresh pillow comforted Boone. He thought of Beth but didn't physically crave her as he did last night. He remembered contemplating consensual relations with Kayla and shook his head in disgust.

Boone wanted to know the intimacy of making love to a woman rather than having sex with one.

17

On Sunday morning, Boone sat atop the sleeping bag and pulled on a pair of shorts. Shirtless and shoeless, he followed the winding path through the dunes and looked in either direction at the end as though a stop sign existed. All clear. Rather than walk at a normal pace toward the water and tiptoe his way in, he ran across the beach into the ocean until almost waist deep and then dove through the first big wave.

The cold water immediately penetrated his skin, sending his whole body into a temporary state of shock. Beneath the surface, he desired to emerge, get out quickly, and find warmth. However, Boone forced himself to stay under and swim until nearly out of breath.

When Boone's head popped up, he turned and faced the shore, probably forty yards away. He didn't intend to stay in long; he only wanted to rinse the sweat and stench from his body. After walking so much the past couple days and being engrossed by a sleeping bag, his body held an odor and an icky sensation until now. With only his head above water, he wished he brought a bar of soap.

Boone dove under again and swam around until his body advised him to get out. Feeling refreshed yet cold, he scampered through the sand toward the dunes. He didn't have a towel, so drying off with a shirt would have to suffice.

When Boone crossed over the hill on the narrow path leading back to the property, he felt panic when he saw someone approaching. Suddenly it was just the two of them surrounded by low-lying brush.

"Boone, what are you doing?"

Boone stopped in his tracks, his body shivering and wet feet covered in sand. "Swimming," he answered, his teeth chattering.

"Isn't the water cold?"

"Yes," he answered, insecurely wrapping his arms around himself.

"Where is your towel?" Piper asked, glancing at his body and empty hands.

"I didn't bring one."

"Gracious," she exclaimed. "You are going to freeze to death." How did the man plan to dry off, leaves? "I have one in the Jeep," Piper reported then turned and jogged to her vehicle. Since day two in Duck, she kept a beach bag with her for spontaneous beach trips although she hadn't been brave enough to jump in the ocean yet.

Boone moved in her direction trying to keep his blood flowing. "Thanks," he offered when she handed over the towel.

When Boone reached out, Piper noticed how skinny he looked, probably a little too scrawny. She could see his ribs. "You're welcome. The air is probably as cold as the water," she predicted.

"Possibly. The water felt refreshing," Boone explained. "But I am colder out than in."

"I imagine. Do you have something warm to change into?" she asked, looking at his dripping red shorts. After checking the weather this morning, she decided on a pair of ripped jeans, a burgundy lightweight knit sweater, and tan boots.

"My bag is hidden in some brush over there," Boone shared, looking in the direction where he set up camp. He was thankful nothing appeared visible from this vantage point.

"Okay. I found your note this morning," Piper reported. "When did you leave it?"

Boone realized he didn't include a date or time. "Yesterday."

"I figured. I went in and out of the back door most of the day, so I didn't see it until I walked out on the porch this morning to eat breakfast," she explained. "I didn't expect to find you here, but now I am glad I stopped by. Do you want to change and ride with me to the park?"

They planned to meet at Duck Town Park at ten thirty—about an hour from now—to work on their lists.

"Yeah, that will save me some steps."

"Great. I will give you some privacy so you can change."

"Thanks."

"Would you like to change in the Jeep? It might be warmer, and you can even turn on the heater," Piper offered, holding out the keys. "I will walk down to the beach, and you can come down when you are ready."

Boone considered the idea. Not only would it be warmer in the vehicle, but it would put less attention on the campsite. He didn't know if Piper would be able to see him through the trees in the thicket. From the beach he knew she couldn't, but if she came back up the trail and he stood stark naked, she probably wouldn't miss him.

"Sure, that would be nice if you don't mind," Boone accepted, letting her drop the keys in his hand.

"Not at all."

Piper meandered through the dunes while Boone gathered his clothes.

Being naked in Piper's vehicle felt a bit awkward especially when Boone thought about how nervous he felt yesterday simply riding in the Jeep. He didn't take the time to turn on the heater; he just hopped in the back seat for concealment purposes yet still peered through the tinted windows every few seconds looking out for cars or in case Piper returned prematurely.

When Boone finished changing into jeans and a black long-sleeved t-shirt, she hadn't emerged. He left his backpack and the towel in the Jeep and hung the wet shorts on a low-hanging limb at the campsite. He crossed the dunes and found Piper sitting on the sand staring at the ocean as if it were a painting.

"Thanks again for the towel," Boone reiterated, bending down to sit a few feet from his accountability partner.

"Of course," she obliged.

"I need to tell you something," Boone proclaimed. He wasn't sure if his body still shook from the cold water that seemed to permeate his bones or because he decided lies of omission were as harmful as any other lies.

"Sure," Piper accepted.

Boone traced the sand between his outstretched legs with his finger. "I spent the last two nights out here," he disclosed.

"Like camped out?" Piper inquired.

"Yeah kind of." He dug his heels into the soft granules below.

Piper glanced at Boone but didn't keep her attention on him. She could sense his nervousness. "That sounds fun."

"I don't have a place to stay yet, like a house or an apartment."

"I thought you might not," Piper revealed. "Where did you stay the first night?"

"At a campground."

"Why did you leave there?"

Boone told her the story as the waves rolled one over the other and sea-foam bubbled at the shoreline.

"I appreciate you sharing that with me. I understand not wanting to buy a tent if you don't know how long you need it."

"Thanks. I was afraid if I told you I am basically homeless that you wouldn't want to be my accountability partner."

As the wind blew Piper's long black hair in Boone's direction, she turned and looked into his green eyes. "I know there are a lot of things you don't know about me yet, but I am not shallow," she told him. "I have friends who are millionaires, others who live on the streets, and plenty somewhere in between."

"That's good to know," Boone responded, his gaze locked on her caramel brown eyes. He previously noticed how big and beautiful they were, but this marked the first time a connection traveled much deeper than his mind. In fact he never recalled feeling this way when looking at another human being, and it felt good yet frightened him at the same time. "I don't have enough money right now to waste any."

"Let me guess, your ex controlled all the money, so you left with basically nothing besides the clothes on your back?" She'd known more than enough women in his shoes.

Boone pursed his lips. "And a couple of suitcases."

"How long has it been since you left her?" Piper asked, assuming somewhat recently.

"I left on Monday."

Piper did the math. "You hopped on a train and came straight here?"

Boone shook his head as seagulls soared above searching for food.

"Did you tell her you were leaving?"

Boone closed his eyes and his lips curled inward, tightening more. His jaw muscles shook as he tried to hold back the tears. "No," he uttered through a small opening his mouth formed.

"Boone, it's okay to cry," she encouraged him. "In fact, you probably need to."

As if her permission was all he needed, Boone dropped his head between his legs, and the floodgates opened beneath the rim of his glasses. He never cried in front of anyone about Beth, not even Claude, so this openness with Piper surprised him.

Piper stretched her arm toward Boone's shoulder and closed

the gap between them. She held him firm with her hand.

"I know it's hard, friend, but you are in a better place," Piper promised. "Never be afraid to cry in front of me or anyone else. Sharing your emotions with another human being is one of the bravest things a person can do, and right now, I am beyond proud to be your accountability partner."

Tears streamed down Boone's face, and the sand absorbed each drop one at a time, just like the many raindrops that pounded this beach for years on top of years.

Piper rubbed Boone's right shoulder. "Don't ever be afraid to ask for help," she reassured.

When Boone eventually stopped crying, he gasped for air. He didn't even realize he'd been holding his breath.

"You okay?" Piper asked.

Boone shook his head from north to south.

"Where are you showering?" she inquired.

Boone lifted his head and gazed at the ocean. "The outdoor shower at the campground the first day and out there this morning."

"Ah, now the cold plunge makes more sense."

Boone snickered and sniffled at the same time.

"You are welcome to shower at my place anytime," Piper offered.

"Thanks," Boone replied. He was much more comfortable with Piper's offer than Kayla's although confident both came from the heart.

Boone and Piper sat quietly in the sand, taking in the wind, the waves, and the spectacular view. Piper asked, "Do you feel like going to the park, or would you rather stay here?"

"I definitely want to work on the program and list-"

"We can do that either place," Piper interjected with a smile. "Actually I think we have already started and accomplished much more than you realize."

"Let's go to the park," Boone decided. "It would be nice to be somewhere different."

"I love the sound of that."

❦

Sitting on a bench that faced the sound, Piper read from The Roots Beneath Us website. The material asked them to think about their pasts, specifically people who hurt them or times they hurt others. It encouraged forgiving and asking forgiveness from anyone they wronged.

"This is going to be hard," Piper admitted.

"Yeah," Boone agreed. "Who do you need to forgive?"

"My parents," Piper answered simply.

Boone immediately thought of his parents and couldn't imagine forgiving them. "What for?"

"Judging me and my decisions," Piper shared. "I'm not sure I can."

"I understand. The lesson mentioned writing it down was the first step in the right direction even if we felt like forgiveness was out of reach." Boone almost wished he didn't remind himself of that; he was preaching to the choir.

"That's true."

Piper added it to her list. "Who do you need to forgive?"

Boone snickered. "My parents, but they don't deserve forgiveness," he concluded. "They deserve—" Boone stopped and gritted his teeth.

Piper remembered what he said at the bank about being abused his whole life. "Want me to write them down and we can return to the parents topic later?"

"Fair enough."

"I need someone's forgiveness, too, but I've never really thought about it that way until now." Piper's mind flashed back to a high school dance. "I hurt my best friend, and I haven't talked to her since I moved away from home after graduating."

Boone shook his head and listened. Piper wrote down her friend's name.

"I need to reach out to her," Piper mentioned, remembering the guilt from all those years ago which she struggled with for quite some time although she rarely thought about it these days. However, writing down the request for forgiveness felt intrinsically rewarding.

"I can't physically forgive all the people my parents let hurt me," Boone unveiled.

Piper wondered what Boone meant by the people his parents *let* hurt him. "The lesson mentioned following your heart on the forgiveness path—looking some people in the eye, talking on the phone to others, and even writing letters, some to mail and some to burn. Maybe the latter is an option to put your feelings on paper. Have you ever tried that?"

"No."

"Would you consider it?"

"Probably."

Piper began to think about all the people who mistreated her over the years. Although she put herself in vulnerable situations, their words and actions still hurt. "You know, I might need to write and burn some letters myself." She remembered forgiving Hardy. Early on he said and did things she didn't appreciate. She recalled how much better she felt when he verbally asked for forgiveness when they visited the Eiffel tower. Their friendship really blossomed afterward.

"Sounds like we can plan a bonfire."

Piper chuckled. "Yeah let's do that."

"We can roast paper instead of s'mores."

Piper laughed all over herself. "Both might be nice," she acknowledged. "Let's trade in bad memories for good chocolate."

The park was relatively busy for a Sunday morning. A couple of moms pushed strollers. Several people chatted in a nearby gazebo.

A group appeared to be having a Bible study on the grassy lawn. The squirrels and birds seemed active.

"Do you remember that church we passed on the way here?" Piper asked.

"The one where you said, 'Wow, there are a lot of people at that church?'"

"Yes, that one," she verified and paused momentarily. "What do you believe?"

"I agree, the nearby lots appeared at capacity, and cars were parked all over the place."

Piper snickered. "I mean, do you believe in God?"

Boone contemplated the question as the water lapped against a tree. "I guess. Do you?"

"Yeah, but I haven't been to a church since I moved out of my parents' house."

"Why not?"

"My parents were those overbearing religious people. I had to attend church every Sunday morning and night, on Wednesday evenings, and almost anytime the doors opened."

"My parents were the polar opposite. They didn't believe in God. Drugs were their God. They hated religion and rules. They were *anything goes* type people." Boone paused for a moment. "I wish they believed in God; then maybe they would have had consciences."

"Why do you believe in God if they didn't?"

"I said *I guess* I believe in God," Boone reminded Piper. "I've never been to church or studied the Bible although I have read verses here and there. A lot of them seem to make sense. Plus I figure something or someone created us, and there has to be a purpose."

"You are almost forty and have never attended a church service?"

"That's right. My dad wouldn't step foot in a church even for a wedding or funeral," Boone shared. "I remember him saying he didn't believe in good and evil."

Piper turned up her nose. "Really?"

"Yes. I recall coming to the realization that anyone who doesn't believe in evil is either involved in it or okay with it."

Piper took a moment to absorb the comment. "That makes a lot of sense," she agreed. "My friend Hardy used to say God wants people to believe He exists, and the devil attempts to convince people that neither he nor God exists."

"That sounds about right."

"That reminds me, have you ever realized that the word devil is evil with a d in front?"

Boone thought about that for several seconds. "I can't say I have."

"Spiritual health was one of the things the journey mentioned early on. I am trying to figure out what that looks like for me now. I have kind of just avoided it altogether in my adulthood."

"My friend Claude once said, 'Believing in God doesn't make Him real. God is either real or He isn't regardless of what anyone believes.'"

"True. I think we often forget that truth is truth no matter how we wish things to be," Piper declared. "Maybe we should put *Figure out who God is* on our lists."

"How do we do that?"

"I guess it starts with a conversation like the one we are having."

"With questions?" Boone asked.

"Sure. We can't find answers if we don't ask questions."

"Maybe we can break it down into steps like the other big things on the list."

"Makes sense because I doubt we will figure it out today," Piper articulated. "On that note, what is a fear or goal we can work on today?"

"I need a phone."

"We can get you one."

Boone told Piper about his experience at the phone store.

"You can get a phone for under two hundred dollars and buy data as you go."

"The salesman told me the cheapest phone is a flip phone that only allows calls and texts."

"Yeah, but I think you need a smartphone for research because of the building project."

"You are probably right. It's just that I only have a thousand dollars to my name."

"Even if you have to wait a little while to get a phone, I think it will be worth it. Plus like I mentioned previously, you are welcome to use mine."

"I know, and I really appreciate that. I should know more about my income once I talk to Preston at the bank tomorrow."

"Why don't you wait until tomorrow to decide about the phone?"

"I can; I just feel like I am waiting on everything: my housing situation, the sand, the phone, and the vehicle."

"What if we break *Getting a vehicle* down into smaller pieces so we can make progress on that today?"

"What do you mean?"

"A vehicle can be a lot of things. What if we got you a bicycle today?"

Boone's eyebrows rose. "That would save me from walking so much."

"Duck is the perfect place to ride a bike. I have been riding mine everywhere: to the grocery store, shops, and restaurants."

"A new bike isn't cheap either, though."

"A used bike would serve you just as well, and I noticed a shop on the island that sells them. Want to go check out the options?"

"Sure," Boone decided.

"Okay. I am writing it down so you can check it off today," Piper noted with a smile.

It only took a few minutes to drive to the shop where a row of previously owned bicycles lined the sidewalk. Boone and Piper walked from one to the next checking the price tags hanging from the handlebars.

"These are pricier than I expected," Piper concluded.

"Welcome, guys," a man with a surfer voice called out as he stepped out of the shop's front door.

Boone and Piper said hello.

"You all in the market for some wheels today?"

"Yeah," Boone replied but the more he studied the price tags the less feasible the idea became.

"These are all used, and I also have brand new bikes inside."

"We are in the market for a used one," Boone confirmed.

"Sure thing. These are all in good condition. When the bicycles come in, I fix any issues with the brakes, steering, chains, and so forth."

"Oh, that's cool," Piper acknowledged, touching the handlebars of one with fat tires.

"If anything goes wrong with the bicycle after purchase, just bring it back, and I'll take care of it. Owner's guarantee."

"Are you the owner?" Piper asked.

The man shook his head yes.

"That's nice," Boone responded. A blue vintage bicycle on the end of the row drew his attention. The style and white-walled tires reminded him of an era when bikes were more special.

"She's a beauty, isn't she," the shop's owner pointed out.

"Yeah," Boone smiled then looked at the hefty price tag. "It's a bit out of my budget."

"Is that the one you want?" the man asked.

"Yeah, but like I said, I can't afford it," Boone reiterated.

Piper almost chimed in because she could see Boone getting nervous, but the owner spoke again.

"If you want it, it's yours," the guy replied, combing his long blond hair back with his fingers.

"What do you mean?"

"The preacher man from the little white church up the road brought it in this morning on his way to service. He asked me to give it to the first person who showed interest."

"As in free?" Piper checked.

"No strings attached," he promised. "Well except the string looped onto the price tag, but that was just for show, and I'll cut it off."

"Are you serious?" Boone checked. "You are just giving it away?"

"That's what the preacher man wanted."

Boone nearly broke down in tears. "Thanks," he murmured.

"That's awesome," Piper added.

Thankfully Piper kept the rack on the Jeep, and after the shop owner walked back inside with a smile, Piper taught Boone how to strap on his new ride.

"Hey, what do you think about heading to my house to grab my bike and going for a ride to celebrate your new wheels?"

"Sure, sounds fun."

"By the way, I love the one you picked out," Piper remarked. "When you see my bicycle, you will understand why."

At Piper's house, she let Boone pull his bike off the rack as she walked around back to get hers. When she wheeled it around the corner, Boone's eyes lit up.

"Our bicycles might as well be twins," Piper announced.

Boone studied the frames. "Other than the colors and the basket, they look identical."

"We need to get you a basket."

Boone chuckled. "I don't know about that."

"You might change your mind after a few trips into the village."

"For now I will use my backpack." He grabbed it from the back seat. "Oh, and here is your towel. It's still a little wet. Would you like me to hang it somewhere?"

"We can hang it on the patio railing."

"I love your backyard," Boone pointed out when they draped the towel to dry.

"Thanks. Doesn't it remind you of yours; I mean, the lot for the house?"

"It does."

"I am going to run inside and put on something more comfortable; it's gotten a bit warm out," Piper mentioned. "Do you need anything or want to change clothes?"

"Nah, I am good."

About ten minutes later atop their matching cruisers, Boone and Piper rode through her neighborhood for him to test out and learn his new bicycle. He double-checked the back and front brakes, made sure the chain grasped the sprocket firmly, and watched the wheel alignment. As a kid riding his bicycle offered an escape from reality, but he hadn't ridden much in adulthood. He and Beth owned bikes but only hopped on them a couple times a summer. The two of them spent more time indoors binge-watching television shows.

"Ready to head to NC 12?"

"Sure."

"I am sure you noticed the sidewalk and bike path on the main road throughout Duck."

"I have walked on it quite a bit."

"That makes sense," she acknowledged. "I am getting hungry; do you want to grab lunch while we are out?"

"I could eat."

"Do you want to go back to Roadside for more syrupy-tasting sweet tea?" Piper asked giggling.

18

Trying to think, ride, and talk simultaneously caused Boone to wiggle his handlebars a bit much as he and Piper turned out of the neighborhood onto the bike path. Thankfully he kept his balance and was behind Piper, so she missed his near fall.

When Boone steadied the bicycle, he thought about Kayla. "Can we try something different than Roadside?" he asked, wanting to avoid that situation.

"Of course. Seafood?"

"Sure."

"The place I have in mind, The Village Table and Tavern, is about a mile outside of the village. Are you okay with that?"

"Sounds good to me."

On some parts of the trail, Boone and Piper rode side by side, and at other points he fell in behind and let her lead. The lane wasn't crowded, especially once they ventured beyond the close-knit village area, but other cyclists, walkers, and joggers passed by occasionally. They dodged a couple tree limbs and a bump here and there, but the asphalt rode smoothly overall.

At the restaurant Piper and Boone parked their bicycles and climbed a rather tall staircase that led from the gravel parking lot to the front door. One of the first things they noticed once inside was the wall of windows providing a spectacular view of the Currituck. Piper and Boone requested the outdoor patio to be even closer to the water and to soak in the pleasant weather.

"Good choice," Boone acknowledged taking in the scenery. Behind the restaurant a grassy area sloped toward the sound where bulkhead framing held the water at bay.

"Even if the food happens to be average, this view will be worth the cost of lunch," Piper pointed out. The sun holding steady over the water warmed up the day, and Piper was glad she changed into a comfortable blue t-shirt and a pair of yellow shorts highlighting her dark legs. "By the way, I am paying today."

"I have enough money to buy lunch," Boone disclosed.

"You paid Friday. It's my turn."

Piper and Boone ordered cornmeal crusted local white fish, French fries, and goat cheese hushpuppies. Boone opted for sweet tea again and discovered this recipe to be even sweeter than the one before.

"Wow, that's delicious," he claimed, and Piper laughed at him.

They talked about their bicycles, the places in Duck they wanted to visit, and basked in the stellar view. The atmosphere seemed a bit more formal than their previous meal yet still relaxed especially on the balcony. The server wore fancy attire and presented things elegantly while engaging in casual conversation.

"Do you want me to join you at the bank in the morning?" Piper asked after their meal arrived.

"If you can make it, that might be helpful. There are so many questions to ask, and I am sure you will think of some that I won't."

"The only thing I have scheduled specifically is volunteering at the dance studio at three thirty. Other than that, I usually check on potential jobs and look at houses."

"And ride your bike," Boone pointed out and then took a bite of a fry.

"I think that is the one thing I have done every day."

Boone clued Piper in on a few questions for the banker as they savored the taste of their food, especially the uniqueness of the hushpuppies.

"Don't forget to grab the plans when we return to my place," Piper reminded him.

"Oh yeah, maybe one of us will remember this time."

"Are you sure it is safe to keep them outdoors?" Piper asked. "I can store them in the house if you like."

"Maybe I will leave them with you tonight, and we can find out tomorrow if there is another set."

"If not, can we have a copy made?"

"I am sure we can, but I haven't done it before, so I will have to figure out where. Blueprints can't be copied on a normal machine like what the bank probably has for typical business documents."

"I think most office supply stores can copy large plans," she suggested. "I imagine there is one on the island."

"I think so. My boss's assistant always took care of those things."

"Makes sense."

After settling up at the restaurant, Piper and Boone explored the streets of Duck. She showed him the dance studio, and he took her on a ride by the unofficial campground and pointed out where he spent the night. They discovered that the picturesque and popular boardwalk stretched one-mile, the northern end starting at The Waterfront Shops and the southern end rounding out at Aqua Restaurant & Spa. It pretty much paralleled the village which took roughly five to ten minutes of leisurely biking from one end to the other.

Town rules required walking bicycles on the boardwalk for safety purposes which also allowed Piper and Boone more time to watch the sunset paint beautiful pink and blue hues in the sky that the Currituck reflected like a perfectly placed mirror. They wandered onto a couple docks, rested once at a bench, watched boats cruise by, and pointed out interesting objects the tide brought to the marsh. Large pieces of driftwood sat on the shore along with random items like a beach ball and an Adirondack chair.

Piper and Boone pedaled back to Piper's house at dusk and parked their bikes near the patio.

"Would you like to shower?" Piper asked Boone.

He sweated quite a bit today and would prefer to be as presentable as possible at the bank tomorrow given the circumstances. "Yes, please, if you are sure you don't mind."

"Of course I don't. While you shower I can cut up fruit and make us fruit bowls for dinner."

It was hard to believe they rode bicycles long enough for it to be dinnertime already. "Okay, thanks."

Piper showed Boone to the bathroom, the only one in the house. An access door entered from her bedroom and another from the kitchen of all places. She walked him through the latter in case she left delicate items lying around the bedroom.

"Here is a towel and a washcloth," she offered from the closet.

Bookbag over one shoulder, Boone collected the items.

"I think everything else is self-explanatory," Piper added. "Both doors lock from the inside, but it's just me here, so I think you will be safe."

Not sure how to respond, Boone smirked.

Once alone, he pulled out a fresh set of clothes and undressed. It felt odd being naked, knowing a woman other than Beth occupied the adjacent room, and only an unlocked door stood between them. Boone stepped in that direction, quietly twisting one lock and then taking care of the other.

When the showerhead came to life, the warm water felt amazing on his skin. He definitely took showering for granted all these years. If not at Piper's, he would probably stay in twice as long and maybe even bathe. He liked baths although Beth hated them. She vowed that sitting in dirty, stagnant water was disgusting, and she didn't want him bathing.

When Boone toweled off, he dressed in front of the same mirror Piper stood at every day.

The door handle felt moist when he opened it carrying his dirty clothes in his other hand.

"Do you want me to wash those?" Piper asked through a quaint laugh because he caught her with a piece of fruit in her mouth.

"I can't ask you to wash my clothes."

Piper swallowed then pursed her lips, moved her mouth side to side, and made a face at him. "I am pretty sure I did the asking," she reminded Boone. "Just say yes," she laughed.

"Yes, ma'am."

"Not yes, ma'am, that makes me feel old."

"Well, you are older than me," he teased.

Piper punched Boone in the arm. "Maybe I will rescind my offer." Boone winced and then snickered, and Piper realized what she just did. "I'm sorry. Did it bother you that I just hit you?"

Boone hesitated for a moment. "No," he concluded. "That was playful; there is a big difference," he pointed out realizing the inference. Maybe even flirty. Maybe.

"Just let me know if I ever cross the line."

"Will do."

Boone spotted two large bowls on the kitchen counter filled to the brim with assorted fruit, the colors beautifully arranged. "Wow, you have been busy."

Piper put away the cutting board and tossed the waste in the trash can. "It didn't take long," she acknowledged. "You are welcome to munch on the fruit in your bowl while I shower."

"I will wait."

While Piper showered, Boone sat on the couch beneath a perfectly hung antique decorative door featuring two hand-painted sea turtles that appeared to be kissing. He thought about how the look fit the island, and he began to notice the theme throughout the house.

When Piper emerged, she sat on the couch cushion next to the one beneath Boone, her dangling wet hair leaving a water ring on her fresh t-shirt. They chatted loosely about the art pieces before grabbing the fruit bowls.

"Do you want to eat here, on the patio, or on the front porch?" Piper asked.

Boone appreciated how she asked what he wanted although he tried his best to get a feel for what she preferred because he was accustomed to pleasing Beth. "All of them sound nice."

"The front porch offers an open view, and a few cars drive by, and people walk, jog, or ride bicycles on the road occasionally; the patio provides the little jungle experience with a serene atmosphere; and the couch features the antique island art gallery."

Piper's contagious smile prompted Boone to follow suit. "Where would you prefer to eat?" Boone asked.

"I enjoy spending the evenings on the patio."

A few minutes later they sat at the outdoor table, and Piper told Boone about her idea to drape lights in the trees. Once again the music from a neighboring yard wafted through the darkness.

"What is your favorite type of music?" Piper inquired.

"Anything soft," Boone announced. "My parents always played loud music which I grew to hate."

"You know, I have been around way more loud music than I cared to as well, so I am with you. I am learning to appreciate jazz and classical music."

One piece of fruit at a time, Boone and Piper eased their way to the bottom of the bowls while enjoying a peaceful evening, fresh conversations, and each other's company.

"Would you like me to drive you home?" Piper asked when she realized the time.

"That might be a good idea because we rode so much today,

especially since I haven't ridden in a while."

Throughout the evening Boone's legs tightened, and this time when he got up to walk, they felt like mush.

After helping load Boone's bike, Piper asked if he wanted to drive the Jeep. "How long has it been since you drove a vehicle?" Piper teased, playing off the length of time since he pedaled a bicycle. "Honestly, I don't see as well in the dark as I used to, and I have been putting off going to the eye doctor for years."

"Sounds like a fear to add to the list."

"Thanks for calling me out," Piper announced.

"If it makes you feel any better, I will call myself out too," Boone offered. "I don't have a license," he admitted.

Piper remembered wondering if his license had been revoked. She cocked her head. "And why not?"

Surprisingly Boone comfortably shared the truth with Piper this time. "I have never had a license."

"What? You are full of surprises, Mr. Winters," Piper remarked. "So you just drive illegally?"

Boone smirked. "I have never driven illegally because I have never driven a vehicle."

Piper's face glared with astonishment. "Really?"

"I have lived a sheltered life."

Piper knew what that meant. "I thought you said you wanted a car."

"I do. It's a major fear and a huge goal."

"I guess we each have some of those," Piper reported. "We will break them down together and reach them."

"I have to learn how to drive," Boone said aloud for the first time in—maybe ever.

"You can do it."

Boone appreciated Piper's optimism.

"I can teach you how to drive," Piper added.

"You are that brave?"

"Sure. Baby steps, remember?"

Piper hopped behind the wheel, and when they made it to the beach property, she switched off the headlights. Boone grabbed his new bicycle, and then Piper followed him and his flashlight's beam to the small campsite area he claimed in the thicket. On the way over she told him she would teach him to drive during the daytime, and she offered to wash the dirty clothes stashed in grocery bags in one of his suitcases.

Boone pulled out a few tied grocery bags filled with clothes. It felt kind of odd knowing Piper would handle his underwear, but what other option did he have? A laundromat, he realized, but he already left the outfit from today, including a pair of boxers, at Piper's house. So at this point what difference did several more make?

"This place is so neat," Piper remarked.

"Yeah, especially at nighttime," Boone mentioned. "I can roll out my sleeping bag if you want to sit down?"

"Sure, I will hang out for a bit."

Piper and Boone sat with their legs crisscrossed, the flashlight between them pointing up at the sky through an array of tree limbs.

"Do you see how the light illuminates the branches?" Piper asked.

"Yeah."

"I love that," she remarked.

"That's how the branches at your place would look with lights strung in the trees."

"Exactly."

The waves crashed on the other side of the dunes. The owls hooted back and forth. Other rodents scampered in the distance.

"Do you worry about the critters out here at night?" Piper inquired.

"Not really."

Piper studied the trees as best she could. She and Boone had been searching for the owls since the first let out a hoot.

"Now that my eyes adjusted to the dark, I can see the stars through the trees."

"You should see what it looks like lying here with the flashlight off."

Piper reached for the button, and the air around them went dark a moment later. She could still see Boone's silhouette but couldn't completely make out his features or gauge his reaction. She stretched her neck back as far as possible and took in the sky.

"I can open the bag all the way if you want the full effect," Boone offered.

"Let's do it."

Boone flipped the flashlight on, and they stood temporarily while he unzipped the bag. Piper helped him lay it flat like a blanket on the beach. She relaxed on her back, and Boone clicked off the light and joined her. When he settled in, his arm wedged against hers, and his hand touched her fingers. He didn't intend to make contact, but the instant it happened, waves of electricity flooded his body in the dark of night.

19

It surprised Piper when Boone's skin touched hers. She wondered if he meant to be so close. Part of her liked it. Lying here with him felt comfortable even though she hadn't been romantically attracted. Something about Boone seemed different than any other man she met. She felt safe in his presence.

For a moment, Boone froze. He knew he should probably move his arm before it became awkward, but all he could do was stare through the trees at the stars even though he wanted to turn and look at Piper.

Piper considered scooting over an inch to create space, but then as the moonlight filtered and the stars twinkled through the silhouette of hundreds of tree branches, she decided she was okay with Boone's arm being pressed against hers. A couple of his fingers settled on hers delicately like a fallen leaf on the summer grass.

"Boone, this is lovely," she admitted.

Boone began to breathe again although he didn't know what to say. "It is," he finally uttered.

"You were right about this view. I think I could lie here all night."

Neither of them spoke a word for the longest time. They simply basked in the ambiance surrounding their lives at the present moment.

Eventually Piper broke the silence. "Sometimes I try to count the stars."

Boone smiled in the dark. "That sounds fun."

"You're fun, Boone," Piper stated, wrapping her pinky around one of his fingers. She turned and looked at him. "You deserve this freedom."

Boone didn't know precisely what freedom she meant, but he felt as free as the owls in the trees. The way her pinky wrapped around his finger made him more alive than he ever remembered. "Thanks," he responded, slowly turning his head to meet Piper's gaze. The clarity of her charming brown eyes surprised him, and once again he experienced that previous connection.

Piper studied Boone's green eyes. "No matter what happens, you never ever have to go back to her."

"I know," Boone replied, trying his hardest to believe it. Suddenly he wanted to kiss Piper's lips but couldn't. He could write that on his journey list a thousand times but doubted he ever would, and right now he couldn't muster up the courage. *Baby steps*, he heard someone on his shoulder say.

Piper considered rolling onto Boone and kissing him gently. She doubted he would make the first move. Almost any other guy would have already jumped on top of her but not Boone Winters. He was scared and scarred but also a gentleman. This man had been taken advantage of so many times he understood the danger in crossing boundaries. She understood his delicacy and wanted to treat him with the respect he deserved, realizing most of the women he encountered probably jumped on top of him.

Piper and Boone didn't say much more the rest of the waking night. They just let things be. Mostly they stared at the stars. Their bodies didn't move, not even their fingers, slightly intertwined like many of the branches above.

It shocked Piper when Boone dozed off to sleep, but it made her glad to know he felt comfortable. She knew she needed to leave but hated to wake him, so she kept gazing at the stars and listening to the ocean, imagining he would wake up soon.

As Piper listened to the steady rhythm of the rise and fall of Boone's breath, the owls hooted, the sky glowed, and before she realized it, her eyelids collapsed, and sleep captured her body.

The moon moved across the North Carolina sky. The branches slowly danced to the breeze blowing off the Atlantic Ocean. The critters went on about their night. Everything seemed completely peaceful, and then something unexpected happened.

20

Without notice, the rain came fast and furiously. Both Boone and Piper immediately woke as it pelted their exposed bodies. Instinctively, they each tugged at the edge of the sleeping bag on their respective side and pulled it over top of them. Boone quickly found the zipper, and as the rain pounded, they became cocooned together inside a bed made for one.

A small breathing hole remained at the top of the bag, and on the inside, the air warmed quickly as Boone and Piper shared body heat in the cramped space.

Piper laughed, and Boone chimed in.

"Eventually the rain is going to soak through the sleeping bag," Piper predicted with a whisper.

"Actually, it shouldn't. When I decided not to get a tent, I sprung for the waterproof bag for this reason."

Boone had never nestled inside a sleeping bag with another person but quickly found the way their bodies naturally formed around each other to be the only comfortable way—legs intertwined, arms wrapped, and faces mere inches apart.

"So you picked out the bag for *this* reason?" Piper teased smiling widely inside the dark of the bag just in time for a flash of lightning to illuminate her facial features. A strong clap of thunder followed, and she shuddered in Boone's arms.

Piper heard the quick and steady breaths erupting from Boone's lips. She was glad she asked if he wanted to brush his teeth before they left her house, and even more relieved she brushed her own although she never imagined their mouths being this close together.

"Well—"

The rain fell so hard through the tree limbs that Piper and Boone could feel it punching the outside of the sleeping bag like pellets shot from the sky.

"You could have warned me that we were going to accidentally fall asleep beneath the stars only to be awakened by a torrential downpour."

Boone laughed as Piper's eyes mesmerized him. "Would you have still come?" he surprised himself by asking.

"Absolutely," Piper answered.

Sparks flew through Boone's and Piper's veins as their bodies woke up and recognized each other's embrace.

Whether fate or happenstance brought them to this moment in the middle of their lives, they were here—together. Slowly and carefully, the short distance between their lips narrowed, and they met in the middle.

Boone's eyes closed, and Piper's followed. The taste of salty air and rain present on Boone's lower lip traced Piper's lips. Tenderly their mouths danced with one another as the thunderstorm played a melody seemingly created for this moment. Lightning lit up the sky, and thunder rolled across the ocean, but Boone's and Piper's lips remained connected as if the world around them became a part of them.

Boone felt the tip of Piper's tongue touch his, and he reciprocated as their entire bodies moved in unison with their first kiss.

Similar to counting stars, the kiss lasted longer than either dared to count. It never sped up or seemed wrong, only meant to be.

Boone somehow forgot about all the moments that brought him to this place. He released every forced kiss that ever trespassed his lips. At almost forty years old, this kiss became the first he ever experienced consensually, and it shattered expectations. Piper's lips and her body felt so amazing, so tempting that he could barely handle himself.

Piper had kissed her fair share of men, but not one compared to this experience. She couldn't explain it and didn't need to; she just etched the memory into her mind. The night was perfect. The setting was perfect. She was so glad she hadn't kissed Boone earlier, so thankful this moment hadn't been planned, expected, or even desired. It just happened, and she knew she would never be able to explain it to a friend. It was an understanding that only she and Boone would know and share for the rest of their lives, regardless of where they went from here.

21

While the rain pounded the ground around them, Piper and Boone talked in whispers inside the sleeping bag. The kiss they shared seemed natural, leaving Piper feeling like she had kissed Boone a thousand times.

Eventually the thunderstorm subsided, and the two emerged from their cocoon to a muddy mess. Piper recommended going back to her place, where they took showers in the middle of the night. She tossed their clothes in the washing machine but decided to start the cycle in the morning. Before leaving the campsite, they had grabbed all of Boone's belongings, including the soaked suitcases and sleeping bag, and threw everything in the back of the Jeep.

Boone slept in the guest room, and each lay in their respective beds wide awake thinking about the intimate moments they shared.

Piper never saw that coming. Although Boone's personality quickly grew on her and she found him cute in his own way, a physical attraction hadn't previously presented itself.

Boone labeled Piper attractive the moment he first saw her in the parking lot but never imagined kissing her. He had other priorities, and honestly, Beth still had a hold on him. But not anymore. He was on his own now and kissed the most beautiful woman he ever met, which seemed unreal. He considered Piper out of his league from the beginning and still did. He previously figured she showed him kindness because she felt bad for him.

Piper woke first and started the laundry. When Boone heard her moving around, he joined her in the kitchen. Thankfully it didn't feel awkward for either of them to wake up in the same house and meet in the common area even though Boone wore a baggy pair of yellow and white striped lounge pants Piper let him borrow.

"Looking good," Piper complimented, studying him from head to toe for a round of laughter.

Boone took the bait, glanced down, and a smirk became a chuckle. "Good morning, silly," he replied, somehow emerging as a new man.

Boone figured he should be grateful Piper hadn't handed him the beige mélange cotton blend ribbed pajama set that caught his eye the moment he stepped into the room. The short shorts with overlocked edges at the hems looked much better featuring her form and long tanned legs than they would on him. The long-sleeved, V-neck matching top with a window to something way more attractive than his chest hair reminded him of the surrealness of waking up in this beautiful woman's house.

Piper responded with the same. She then initiated a hug and kissed Boone tenderly for a couple of seconds to let him know she didn't regret what happened last night in the sleeping bag. She asked how he slept and said she didn't sleep great either.

They ate bagels on the front porch and dressed for the bank trip. Thankfully, along with the boxers and t-shirt Boone wore to bed, he unearthed a pair of jeans and another shirt that somehow stayed dry in one of the suitcases during the thunderstorm.

Piper appeared from her bedroom wearing gray pants and a dressy beige lace-trimmed camisole top. She noticed a little more joy in Boone's face this morning, and she imagined it came because he faced one of the greatest fears possible. He kissed her. Not specifically her but someone other than the woman who controlled him all these years. She figured that loosened some chains, and she was happy for him.

❧

"Good morning, Mr. Winters and Ms. Luck," Preston announced when he greeted them in the bank lobby.

They followed him into his office and sat in the same chairs as last time.

"What can I help you two with this morning?"

"I have a lot of questions since Friday," Boone announced.

"I figured you might. There was and is so much to cover. That's why I took the liberty to read Claude's detailed notes on Friday after you all left. So, fire away," he requested.

"How often will I be paid?"

"Your pay schedule will be the same as in California, weekly on Monday."

Boone recalled Claude telling him that construction workers should be paid once a week on Monday because when paid on Friday most spent every dollar before the weekend ended.

"Okay." The day of the week didn't really matter to him although he understood Claude's reasoning and hoped that his workers would spend the money on their family's needs rather than hedonistic wants. "What is the pay?"

"The same amount you made there, along with bonuses when certain stages of the project are completed."

"That sounds good." Boone figured he could make it on his usual salary, and the bonuses would help get him on his feet. In the past, Claude surprised the guys with a bonus every now and then, and he became more generous in the later years of his life.

"We can open a personal account for you here at the bank if

you like and set up direct deposit for your pay."

"Alright."

"Would you like to take care of that now?"

"Yes, please."

"I only need your social security number and driver's license."

Boone and Piper turned to each other with question marks in their eyes.

"I don't have a license."

"Alright. I know you just moved here, so I doubt you have a North Carolina ID, but do you have one from California?" he asked. "If I have that and proof of a local address, I can work around things."

"I do have a California ID." Boone decided he better not reveal his current living situation. "I don't have an address here yet. I've only stayed places temporarily."

"You can use my address," Piper offered hoping Preston wouldn't dig into where Boone stayed.

"Thanks," Boone accepted graciously. "Will that work?" he asked Preston.

"Under the circumstances I might be able to allow it."

"That reminds me, can I set up a mailbox at the building lot to receive construction-related mail?"

Preston's brow furrowed. "Normally I would say no. However, I think it will be fine because of how Mr. James set things up."

It surprised Piper that Preston agreed without talking to the owner. Mail seemed to be a funny thing. She forwarded mail from so many places who knew where some of it ended up. Thankfully she managed to stay out of debt.

"We can even use the beach lot address for the banking account if you like," Preston suggested. "Piper, I recall you mentioning your address might be short-term, so that would keep Boone from having to change it if you move."

Piper shook her head in agreement.

"Sounds perfect," Boone acknowledged.

Once they nailed down the details, opening the account didn't take long. Boone handed Mr. Bynum cash for the initial deposit.

Boone told Preston about the sand, and Preston reminded him to simply bring in the invoice, which he would pay from the construction account.

"Is there an extra set of blueprints?" Piper asked on Boone's behalf.

Boone was relieved because he forgot to ask. He was also glad he agreed to leave the plans at Piper's house; otherwise, they might be drenched along with the rest of his belongings, currently airing out at Piper's.

"The set I gave you is the only printed set I know of, but we have the master on file, and we can share it electronically for printing if needed."

"Not at this time, but I wanted to know just in case."

"It's always nice to have a backup plan," Preston assured.

"Do you think it would be okay if I set up a temporary place at the construction site so I can be there anytime rather than going back and forth?"

"Something like an office trailer?" Preston inquired with a raised eyebrow.

Boone hadn't thought of that angle. They sometimes set these up at commercial project sites and even some residential although no one ever lived there. However, he knew guys who stayed overnight occasionally, usually without permission.

"Yeah something like that. I don't have a car yet, so I have been walking everywhere, but I just got a bicycle. So having a spot on-site would be beneficial." Maybe a trailer, perhaps a tent.

Preston pondered the idea. "There are no major building restrictions or an HOA for that lot, but with this being beachfront property, I think you will need to be careful; otherwise you might end up at a town hall meeting because of complaints. That said, it might be easier to ask forgiveness than permission."

This all sounded like music to Boone's ears. He expected to hear different answers. If he didn't have to pay rent and other housing expenses, he could reach the other goals quicker.

"Perfect. I will make sure to be respectful of the neighbors," he promised. He would rather no one know his whereabouts anyway. "When does the building project need to be completed?"

Preston glanced at the notes on his computer. "Mr. James said the project should take six months to a year, depending on weather and the availability of crews and materials."

Grateful for the generous window of time, Boone envisioned all the floor-to-ceiling windows planned for the home's oceanside. The view would be spectacular.

When the bank meeting ended, Boone and Piper returned to her house to finish laundry. Piper pulled clothes from the dryer and immediately filled it with the second load from the washer.

"I thought the meeting with Preston went really well this morning," Piper mentioned. "Did you get all your questions answered adequately?" she asked while dumping the clean laundry from the basket onto the couch.

"I agree, and I think so."

The two of them sat on either side of the pile to pluck out and fold their respective clothes.

"So are you planning to live on the beach lot while building the house?"

"Yeah, I think so," Boone acknowledged. Folding his boxers in front of Piper seemed a bit awkward, but imagining her folding them on her own might be even more so.

"Do you think you will buy or rent a trailer like Preston mentioned?"

"Probably not. I want to save up as much as possible for the car, phone, a future place to live, and other living expenses."

"So you plan to live in the sleeping bag?" she asked, folding her underwear but not nearly as self-consciously as Boone.

"I think I will get the nicest tent the general store has," he replied, stacking a shirt on top of a pair of jeans. "The weather this time of year is perfect for camping."

"I think that's really cool," Piper announced.

"You do?" Boone surprisingly asked.

"Yes, especially after last night. Being out there underneath the stars and listening to the waves felt magical," she revealed. "I never camped at the beach before."

"I really liked it too." Staying at the beach lot alone was fine, but having Piper there made it an unbelievable adventure.

"Did the meeting this morning make you think of anything else you want to add to your journey list?"

"It reminded me that I need to apply for the building permits and find a crew to install footings and pour the foundation," he reported. "I also need to keep dissecting the steps so the project doesn't look so big. Having six months to a year to build sounds like a long time, but I know it can go by quickly, and there is so much to fit into the schedule."

"How many crews will you need to hire throughout the process?"

"Probably over twenty."

Piper's eyes bulged. "Holy cow."

Boone began naming some. "Framer, roofer, electrician, plumber, floorer, window installer, cabinets installer, landscaper . . . the list goes on."

"I guess it does take a lot of specialists to build a house. Do you know the order in which you have to hire them?"

"Yep, it's pretty much the same for every house."

"That's valuable knowledge, Boone. I would have no idea."

"The challenge is I don't know anyone here. I have no clue who does quality work, and this is certainly a project where I need the best subcontractors available."

"I am sure we can figure it out."

Boone appreciated the way his accountability partner always said *we*. "Thanks for saying that," he acknowledged. "You have already been such a huge help."

"My privilege," Piper responded, grabbing their journey list journal as well as another notebook from her bag. "I have an idea," she mentioned.

"What is it?"

"I think we should use a separate notebook solely for the building project since there are so many steps and intricate details. What do you think?"

"Sure, that is a good idea."

Piper flipped open to the page in the journal where she wrote down their goals and fears and began copying the building project list into the new notebook. "So applying for the building permits is next, right?" she double checked.

"Yes."

"Where is that handled?"

"The local municipal office."

Piper jotted that down. "Do you want to go there today?" she asked, glancing at the clock. "If it doesn't take long, I think we have time to eat lunch and do that before I have to be at the dance studio."

Piper and Boone made turkey and cheese sandwiches and ate on the back porch while she read another lesson from The Roots Beneath Us. It discussed physical health goals and fears and focused on being proactive rather than reactive. A few pages encouraged healthcare over sick care.

"What is something you would like to add to your list?" Boone asked. "I feel like we have been so focused on mine."

"Well, I mentioned yesterday that I need to see the eye doctor which I put on the list. I think I need to make an appointment."

"You should do that now," Boone encouraged.

"Do you want me to make you an appointment as well?"

"I went regularly at home," Boone answered, pointing to his glasses. "But I might as well establish a provider here."

Piper searched for eye doctors and quickly found several in the area. She called the highest rated one and made an appointment for her and Boone within minutes.

"Wow, that was so easy," she noted. "This will be my first eye care appointment since moving out of my parents' house."

Boone smiled. "The ball is rolling in the right direction."

"Definitely. Now that I am not required to stay physically fit for my job, I want to ensure I continue exercising regularly, which I have already mentally added to my list." Piper officially wrote it down along with some specific workout ideas. "How about you, Boone; have you been avoiding any doctors?" she checked. "Do you have physical fitness goals?"

Boone found himself wanting to avoid the latter question. "I have a lot of pains from years in construction. I fell off ladders, took hammers to the head, and endured all kinds of other crazy accidents."

"Have you gone to the doctor for any of it?"

"Only to get stitches a couple of times."

"How about for the chronic pain?" Piper asked. "It seems that is what you are describing."

"I am used to hurting," Boone acknowledged. "Plus my insurance is through Beth, so I can't use that, and I don't want to pay out of my pocket for expensive exams. I can handle an eye appointment but not X-rays and MRIs."

Piper's shoulders dropped. "That's unfortunate. Maybe in time you can get your own insurance."

"Hopefully."

"Do you run, lift weights, or do other workouts?"

"Not really."

"Does that stuff not interest you?"

Boone thought about his desire to learn self-defense. "As a kid

I always wanted to take karate classes, but my parents wouldn't let me because of time and money."

"You should do it now."

"I don't know, I have the physical issues we discussed, and I am getting old. I turn forty tomorrow."

"That's right. We have to celebrate our birthdays," Piper exclaimed. "What do you want to do?" she inquired with a smile. "But we are coming back to the physical fitness topic." Piper knew exercise would do a person in Boone's shoes wonders.

Boone snickered. "Maybe lunch or dinner."

"Since it's our fortieth birthdays, how about we go all out and celebrate all day?"

"Okay. Doing what?"

"Breakfast, lunch, and dinner out, and some other fun stuff in between. Have you ever done that?"

"I doubt it. Have you?"

"I always wanted to."

"I guess tomorrow is the day then," Boone accepted. "Although this idea won't help us with physical fitness," he laughed.

"True, but maybe we can exercise some too."

"Okay," Boone agreed hesitantly, knowing he couldn't keep up with her. She already wore him out on the bicycles.

"Perfect. How about you pick a restaurant, I will choose one, and we will select the third together?"

"Sounds fun."

"Can I have breakfast?" Piper inquired giddily. "There is a breakfast place I want to try."

"Sure."

"Do you want to pick lunch or dinner?"

"Lunch."

"Okay, we can choose the dinner restaurant together. Where do you want to eat lunch?"

"I have no idea," Boone revealed. "I will have to check out the options."

"Alright. What else?"

"Ride bikes, maybe."

"Yes, definitely. We will have lots of calories to burn." Piper paused when a memory slid into her mind. "While running the other day, I saw people riding horses on the beach, and it looked like a blast." Boone looked unsure. "Would you do it?"

"I don't know; I have never ridden a horse, and to be honest, I have always been intimidated when I stand near one. Horses are huge."

"I don't know, Boone, this kind of sounds like a fear you should face," she teased.

"What if I get thrown off?"

"At least we will be on sand."

"True, but it would still hurt."

"We can ride at a slow pace. I will teach you the ropes," she offered. "Pun intended."

"You know how to ride?"

"A good friend of mine owned horses, and we rode a lot." That reminded her that she needed to call Leslie and apologize.

"So you are going to teach me how to ride a horse and drive a car?"

"Yes," Piper exclaimed, "and on the same day. We can have our first lessons tomorrow."

"Okay to driving, and maybe to horseback riding."

"You have the rest of the day to think about it," she said, then thought better. "Actually they may not have availability this late, so we should try to book ASAP."

Boone smirked. "Hopefully they're booked."

"How about if I call and they have an opening, we go, and if they don't, we don't have to go."

Boone laughed. "Wait, that's not fair. If they don't have tomorrow open, we can't go anyway."

Piper giggled. "I was hoping you wouldn't think about it that way. How about if tomorrow isn't open, you never have to go."

"Let me think about it." Boone shook his head. He enjoyed her little games, and she was good at convincing him without being pushy.

"Deal. We better go check on the building permits."

Piper put away the dishes while Boone grabbed the plans and paperwork Preston gave him.

At the planning office, Boone filled out various forms providing the details Claude eloquently laid out. He feared he would struggle to deal with these folks, but he didn't. The man walking him through the process proved to be quite helpful especially when Boone told him this was his first time applying for permits and that he was building the house on behalf of Claude James. The guy knew of Claude and his work and was somewhat in awe of the project.

It would take time to process the paperwork, but when Boone and Piper walked out of the office, he felt good about the permits. However, the application process took longer than expected, and Piper barely had time to drop off Boone at the beach lot before heading to dance class.

Kelly introduced Piper to the instructor she would work with today, and then she met all the parents and kids as they arrived. The six and seven-year-olds looked adorable in their dance outfits.

They started class by forming a circle in the middle of the dance floor and stretching together. Each child then told Piper their favorite style of dance and favorite song.

Piper told them she liked ballet best and her favorite song was "Hero" by Mariah Carey. She danced to that song a thousand times.

As the class proceeded, Piper thought more like a student than a teacher while she learned their routines. She understood everything they practiced and helped with one-on-one instruction for kids who needed an extra hand. Piper didn't dance much, but she showed the kids that she worked with a few maneuvers to overcome the obstacles they faced.

By the end of the lesson, she thought she might explode from the amount of joy in her heart. The instructor thanked her for volunteering and said she hoped to see her next week. On the way out Kelly hugged Piper like a long-lost friend and told her how impressed she was with her ability to fit in so quickly.

On the ride home, Piper's face beamed. She wanted to tell someone about the experience, and Boone came to mind first.

Since she couldn't call him, Piper searched for the group that provided horseback riding and called them, although she opted not to blurt out how much she loved dance class. When the woman said they had one opening tomorrow afternoon, it surprised her almost as much as when Boone agreed to let her check when she dropped him off before dance.

Piper thought about stopping by the lot since no other option for talking to Boone existed. However, they spent quite a bit of time together the last couple of days and would be with each other all day tomorrow. She decided some alone time might benefit both of them, and her body reminded her she needed sleep.

Piper made two stops on the way home, poured a glass of wine, grabbed her book, ran a bubble bath, and stayed there the rest of the night.

The highlight of Boone's afternoon came when a dump truck pulled in and dropped off the first load of sand. Another followed, and the cycle continued until the abundance of sand looked like a new beach might be formed on this side of the dunes.

Once the last load slid out of the truck, Boone biked to the general store but didn't get the tent because the one he wanted was gone. He picked up a couple other items instead, and when checking out, the man at the counter told him he would order the same tent to replace the sold one.

Boone fell asleep early in a clean sleeping bag thanks to Piper. Although he wished she were there to share the accomplishment, he discerned the project officially started today.

22

Piper arrived at Boone's campsite at eight o'clock, kissed him softly, and greeted him, "Happy birthday, handsome."

Boone grinned and replied, "Happy birthday celebration day, beautiful."

He thought every outfit looked good on Piper and couldn't help but notice the curves she wore so well in a pair of black leggings and a partially tucked-in tan top. She resembled a model on a magazine cover at the grocery store checkout.

They loaded Boone's bicycle on the rack behind Piper's, and Boone tossed his bookbag in the backseat. Piper watched him climb into the Jeep, and she appreciated the rugged look he pulled off in a pair of dark jeans and a gray shirt that fit just right. While helping with his laundry yesterday, she confirmed what she already assumed—his ex knew good taste in men's clothes.

Piper and Boone ate breakfast at Treehouse Café & Coffee where she poured out her heart about her first dance lesson with the kids. Having someone to share life's excitements with was gratifying, so she carried on about her bubble bath and told him how she dozed off several times while reading before forcing herself to towel off and climb into bed.

Boone talked about the sand he proudly showed Piper when she picked him up earlier, and then they took off their shoes for an impromptu beach walk. It seemed like the Atlantic Ocean and Currituck Sound were within walking distance of nearly every place on this island. With Duck's charming features packed into a cozy 3.7 square miles—2.4 of land and 1.3 of water—the ease of accessibility made sense to Piper, and sharing these simple island luxuries both thrilled and calmed her heart.

As the sea oat framed dunes gave way to a landscape of white sand, Boone and Piper tiptoed through shell piles swept in lines by the ebbing tide. More than once, Piper grabbed Boone's arm to steady her bare feet over broken oyster and clam shells until they reached the soft sand beyond. The surfaces of these broken and polished treasures rested in the sun, sparkling with gem-colored interiors now laid open and bare.

A fellow beachcomber, who happened to be a retired marine paleontologist, ended up at the same pile where Boone and Piper knelt. As she scooped handfuls of shells through her fingers, sorting the spiral coned auger shells from smooth, round shark eyes, she gave an informal lesson on the formations of modern and fossilized remains lining the beach bringing the three of them warm smiles while appreciating the awe-inspiring landscape set out before them.

The ocean created a paint brushed drawing with swaths of pastel lines over a milky background. Varying shapes of swirls and layered colors illuminated from the surfaces. In some places haphazardly scattered shells grouped together away from the isolated ones. Still other shells rocked in the wash of the shoreline waiting for the next adventure of a new inhabitant or final resting place at the top of the tide.

Piper adored the coquinas who played in the waves, popping up with each rise and quickly burying themselves when the water abated. Their distinctive butterfly shape was a favorite of hers, and she gleamed each time she found one fully intact in the shell beds.

Together they discovered a variety of whole shells including whelk, oyster, cockle, scallop, moon snail, clam, and slipper. Boone found the elongated halves of Atlantic jackknife clams and teased Piper by placing them on top of his fingernails to look like manicured tips.

Piper laughed jubilantly at the sight of this grown man acting so young as they played in the sand. She couldn't help snapping a photo in this moment when he let down a wall, showcasing his playful side.

Boone and Piper wandered along the length of the beach, dodging the rising water and feeling the harder, wet sand firm beneath their steps giving a rest from the more difficult treks through the sugary, dry sand. They stopped here and there for more shell collecting and to inspect the beach washed flotsam. A seagull picked up a small piece of driftwood and dropped it in their path, and Piper enthusiastically picked up the gift from above. It was something so small and insignificant—a bit of random wood, pock marked with bored holes and encrusted with barnacles; however, Piper knew this rustic memento would fit in perfectly with the décor in her house.

The footprints of others led the way to more discoveries like the fossilized shark tooth Boone found as the sun shimmered on the last group of shells they combed through. As the walk came to an end, their hands, pockets, and hearts overflowed with treasures.

"I am good at this kind of exercise," Boone revealed.

"Start," Piper reminded him. "We have to start somewhere."

"So I hear," Boone replied with a smile.

"Speaking of which, are you ready to start driving?"

"As ready as I will ever be."

Finding a remote spot in Duck for Boone's first driving lesson almost proved impossible. Only one road led in and out of the village, with no side streets on the sound side, just shops and restaurants between NC 12 and the boardwalk that ran along the

Currituck. Large abandoned parking lots didn't exist, nor did old dirt roads in the middle of nowhere. The island was far too quaint for the latter. Eventually they chose a back road on the ocean side that seemed relatively quiet.

Piper and Boone jumped out of the Jeep and ran around the vehicle as if playing the stoplight game.

"I nearly got arrested for that in my twenties," Piper told Boone, grinning at the memory.

"Thanks for telling me now," he responded, settling into the driver's seat.

They laughed, and Boone's first driving lesson began on his fortieth birthday.

"You are probably going to laugh at me, but I have to ask the obvious questions to ensure we stay alive," Piper announced. "Do you know which pedal is the gas and which is the brake?"

Boone glanced at the floorboard. "Yes, the brake is the wider pedal on the left, and the gas is the longer pedal on the right."

Piper smirked. "Moving right along. If at any point you panic, press the brake and hold it down until we figure out what to do next, okay?"

"Got it."

"The mirrors are your friends," Piper pointed out, then encouraged Boone to adjust each one to his liking. "Only glance at them for a second each time you want to check your surroundings; otherwise, you will find yourself running off the road or veering into the other lane."

"Okay," Boone responded. He adjusted each one to match his height.

"Do you know how to start the vehicle?" Piper asked even though the engine continued to purr.

"Yes, I do." Beth had him do that on cold mornings, and he considered taking off more than once.

"So you know you have to press the brake while you turn the key in the ignition?"

"Yes."

"Just checking," she confirmed, sliding a strand of hair behind her ear. "You must also hold the brake down to put the vehicle in gear." Piper explained the letters on the dashboard although she figured he probably knew what each stood for. She then went over the rest of the gauges. "So, go ahead and grab the gearshift and move it into drive."

Boone followed her instructions although the gearshift didn't seem to move as fluidly as when he watched others, and he feared he might have broken something when he heard the grinding sound. "Did I do that right?" he asked with the drive symbol highlighted.

"Yes, it will go more smoothly as you get a better feel for it," she noted. "Now ease off the brake and let the Jeep start to roll."

The Jeep moved slowly, and Piper couldn't tell if Boone's face revealed excitement or fear, but most likely, a mixture created the look.

"Give it a little gas and keep the steering wheel steady."

Suddenly, Boone's and Piper's bodies lunged backward as if on a roller coaster. Boone pressed the gas harder than she expected and more than he meant. An instant later their torsos whipped forward when his foot slammed on the brake pedal.

"Whoa, cowboy," Piper remarked. "You have a lead foot."

Boone's heart raced. "Sorry about that," he said, checking their surroundings.

"Nothing to be sorry about; it's your first time. Now that you understand the capabilities of the gas and the brake pedal, try again."

Boone pressed the gas slower this time; however, keeping his foot steady presented a challenge as he worked the steering wheel simultaneously. The vehicle jerked back and forth although not as violently as in the beginning, and when he pressed the brake several times, it did the same.

Piper let him drive straight ahead for a reasonable distance before letting him attempt turning around. Boone did that cautiously, and it surprised him how much effort twisting the steering wheel required to make a U-turn.

Talking Boone through every step reminded Piper of her dad teaching her to drive as a teenager. She remembered being eager but nervous.

"This isn't too hard," Boone commented.

"You are getting the hang of it pretty fast." On the one hand it made sense that a mature adult who rode in the passenger seat all those years picked up on many of the intricate details of driving. However, the fear probably increased because of the missed opportunities and the possibility of failing.

Boone began to get a feel for the gas pedal and the brake as they headed back in the direction from which they came. He kept his eyes peeled on the road and hoped no other vehicles would appear. When the first one did, he held the steering wheel with a death grip and slowed as they passed within feet of one another. For some reason staying between the white and yellow lines seemed much more challenging with other vehicles on the road. Only a few passed as he drove up and down the street over and over like a teenager falling in love with driving for the first time. As he gained confidence behind the wheel, he didn't want to stop.

"This is so much fun," Boone shared.

Piper's smile stretched from ear to ear. She relished the excitement on Boone's face and in his voice. He reminded her of a giddy kid, and it was one of the cutest things she ever saw.

Boone drove for nearly an hour. She taught him how to make a three-point turn, pull onto the side of the road, merge on, back out of driveways, and slam on brakes. However, he pretty much did that involuntarily at the onset.

After the driving lesson, Boone chose a Mexican restaurant, Coastal Cantina, for lunch where he and Piper dunked too many chips in salsa and cheese dip. They felt so full by the time their meals arrived, each only ate a few bites. Piper dropped off the leftovers at her house so they wouldn't spoil, and then they headed to the beach for horseback riding.

When Boone climbed onto the horse saddled for him to ride, he thought he might have a panic attack. He sat way higher than expected, almost as if sitting atop an elephant. Holding on tightly, he listened to the owner's instructions given from her saddle. She already asked them a bunch of questions on the ground and found out he never rode before.

"I will spend about thirty minutes with you all making sure you understand the animals, and if we are all confident with you going out on your own, you may. Otherwise, I will continue to ride with you for your comfort."

Boone glanced at Piper. Sitting on a light brown beauty with a healthy mane, she looked more like an extension of the horse than a rider. Everything about her posture appeared at ease, and he noticed the trainer didn't even pay attention to her. He certainly wasn't offended; in fact, he prayed the woman wouldn't leave him alone with this animal for one second.

"This is so scary," Boone admitted, imagining the horse taking off and throwing him into the ocean where he would hit his head and drown.

"Think of the first time you rode a bicycle or learned how to drive a car," the trainer compared. Boone couldn't muster up a chuckle, but Piper had no trouble silently laughing all over herself while the woman went on. "At first it was frightening, but then suddenly you got the hang of it. Riding a horse is similar; however, the animal can sense your fear."

With their horses step for step, she walked Boone around and taught him how to use the reins to guide his horse. When he understood the basics, she asked if he wanted to try it on his own for a little bit. At first it went okay, but then he experienced another gas pedal moment when he pulled the reins too hard. The horse took off as if shooting out of a gate at the derby, and all of a sudden sand flew from beneath the animal's hooves while Boone held on for dear life.

Thankfully about fifty yards down the beach, he remembered how to ask the horse to slow down, and it seemed to have already figured out he didn't know what he was doing.

On their respective horses, Piper and the trainer caught up quickly, and Boone envisioned being lassoed like a steer at a bull riding event.

"How did that feel?" the trainer asked Boone, coming in close enough to massage the horse. "Good girl," she commended.

"I thought I was going to die," Boone stammered, breathing heavily through his words.

"You didn't," Piper reminded him and then reached over and rubbed his shoulder.

"This horse is about as calm as they come. She won't throw you off as long as you hold on."

"That's good to know, but I'm not crazy about this," Boone stated bluntly as his heart continued to pound.

Piper could see the fear in his face, and something made her think of Beth telling him to shut up and ride. "Would you like to ride with me instead of being on a horse by yourself?" she asked.

"Yes," Boone answered without hesitation.

"Is that okay?" Piper asked the trainer.

"Of course. I want everyone to be comfortable."

Boone felt relief the moment he climbed off the horse even though she appeared to be a gentle giant. He walked through the sand for a bit to calm his nerves then climbed aboard Piper's horse and nestled in on the saddle behind her. Wrapping his arms tightly around Piper's waist, he felt much more confident with her in control of the animal.

They rode down the beach with the trainer for a couple minutes as she led the other horse back to the starting point. There, the woman asked Piper and Boone to meet her at this same spot in two hours.

Once on their own, Piper guided the horse to walk for a couple hundred yards until she felt Boone's heartbeat calm, and then she let him know they would increase to a trot. Boone was so glad Piper offered for him to hop in the saddle with her, and as he settled in, he enjoyed the ride and the views. It also felt nice to hold Piper. Occasionally she let one of her hands fall onto his as they followed the shoreline toward the sun.

After about thirty minutes of riding, Piper stopped the horse, turned her torso, and leaned into Boone. She slid her arm around him while his arms still circled her waist, and their lips met as the waves crashed and the sand glistened beneath them.

Boone closed his eyes and kissed Piper as passionately as the first time in the sleeping bag. It seemed memorable kisses might be their thing as their mouths once again moved in unison. Her lips felt soft and sweet, and for a few moments, he forgot they were on a horse. He connected with her and the animal, and even though he didn't have the reins, it was like riding a bicycle or driving a car—lovely.

When Piper's and Boone's lips parted, their eyes met.

"Thank you for riding with me," Piper said.

Boone smirked. "Thank you for letting me," he replied. "I never imagined riding a horse could be this much fun."

"Me neither," Piper agreed. "Riding is always fun, but this was much better than I've ever experienced."

"I'm so glad you talked me into it."

"Me too," Piper reported. "Are you ready to ride again?"

Boone smiled and shook his head, and then their bodies twisted back into place. Piper led the horse from a walk to a trot to a canter and eventually into a gallop. At each gait speed she checked to make sure Boone was still comfortable. Like driving the Jeep he just needed to get used to it.

As the sun sank on the horizon, they rode for the next hour and a half, stopping every once in a while to absorb the views. They spotted a pod of dolphins, watched pelicans catch fish, talked about the large ships in the distant haze, and cantered through the surf letting the saltwater splash around them.

This was one of the most romantic things either ever did, and they couldn't wait to see what came next.

23

Walking felt different after Boone climbed off the horse. He imagined his movements looked funny to others at the beach as he appeared to straddle thin air. "I guess riding really opens up the hips," Boone commented.

Piper grimaced. "Yeah I forgot to warn you about that."

He noticed her walk looked a little different but not as obvious.

"I might not be able to ride bikes after dinner," he predicted.

Piper laughed. "You will be back to normal soon," she promised. "Where do you want to eat?"

"What have we not had yet?"

"Pizza."

They returned to Piper's house to freshen up and then ventured to Duck Pizza Company where the parking lot was tucked beneath several buildings of shops and restaurants built on stilts to survive hurricane flooding. Over a veggie pizza, Boone and Piper talked about all the fun things they did today.

"I wish you could have seen your face when you decided you wanted off that horse," Piper laughed.

Boone tried not to laugh. "I guess I failed miserably at horse riding."

"Not at all," Piper reasoned. "You tried it. Even though you didn't like it, you faced the fear. If that had been on your journey list, I would say you deserved to check it off."

"You are probably right."

"On top of that, you jumped right back on a horse with me."

"True," Boone acknowledged. "I guess that counts for something."

"Facing our fears doesn't mean we are not afraid anymore; it means we had the guts to do it," Piper articulated. "Tomorrow I plan on starting my letters to the people who have hurt me," Piper shared. "I might also call Leslie, my high school best friend, to apologize."

"That's great."

"Have you started your letters?"

"I haven't had time, but last night, I thought about what I might say."

Piper fiddled with her fork. "If this is none of my business, you can tell me—when we started talking about letters the other day, I wondered if you left one for Beth?"

Boone's eyes dropped to the plate in front of him, and he stared at the random dollops of sauce, unintentionally biting his lower lip. "Yeah," he eventually answered.

"That was thoughtful of you."

"Why do you say that?"

"If you hadn't left a note, she might have worried that you were in danger or, by now, dead or something tragic like that."

"That was the main reason I left a letter. I didn't want her to suffer from the unknown or call the police and have everyone looking for me. I decided if she did the latter, she would be more likely to find clues that might lead her to me."

"Leaving a note was honorable, and I think the best thing for both of you and everyone else involved. You are a sweet man, Boone Winters," Piper disclosed reaching across the table for his hand.

"Thanks," he replied shyly, and he looked up at her when he

felt her fingers begin to work their way between his fingers.

"I know this is hard for you," Piper mentioned. "Starting over after any relationship is a challenge."

"It's been harder than I thought it would be," Boone shared thinking about the sluggish days between when he left and when Piper became his accountability partner. In his mind, his relationship with Beth had been over for a long time, and he figured in a way that made it easier to move forward. "But I'm glad God brought you into my life at just the right time."

Piper grinned. "You think God did that?"

Boone shrugged his shoulders. "Can you think of a better explanation?"

Piper considered the question and the possibilities. "I guess it could be happenstance or fate."

"Possibly, or maybe God orchestrates happenstance and fate."

Those words might have been the most intelligent she ever heard from the mouth of a construction worker. "Maybe."

Piper and Boone sat silently for a moment as the busy restaurant carried on around them. People drank wine, ate pizza, conversed, and laughed. Servers danced between the tables. Italian music serenaded the dimly lit atmosphere.

"I am not sure how I would have made it through my birthday without you." For the first time all day, Boone thought about how Beth might feel on his birthday without him there. They celebrated so many birthdays together. He realized this thought would have popped into his mind much sooner, probably first thing this morning if he hadn't been with Piper all day. However, hopes, goals, and dreams propelled him away from thoughts of Beth.

Piper smiled from ear to ear and squeezed his hand. "It's been an honor to spend this special day with you," she announced proudly. "But it's not over yet," she reminded him. "There is still more celebrating ahead."

By the time the check arrived, Piper and Boone devised a plan for paying. "I paid for breakfast, you paid for lunch, and I think we should split dinner," Piper recommended.

"Sounds fair," Boone agreed. "Much fairer than your horseback riding deal."

Piper chuckled. "You can't blame a girl for trying."

When they walked out of the restaurant and into the darkness holding hands, Piper told Boone she had a surprise for him at her house. He tried to guess what it might be as she drove the short distance down NC 12 and pulled into her neighborhood.

Once they arrived, she made him sit at the outdoor patio table while she went inside. "You must keep your eyes closed until you hear my voice," she instructed.

As Boone waited, the brisk air crawling across his skin comforted him. He figured having his eyes closed heightened his senses. The rustle of the leaves in the trees seemed more present, and he smelled the Atlantic Ocean.

When the back door opened, a new and lovely sound introduced itself—Piper's harmonious voice singing, "Happy birthday to you, happy birthday to you, happy birthday dear Boone, happy birthday to you."

He turned as the first few notes floated into his ears and discovered Piper waltzing in his direction, wearing a smile and carrying two oversized pieces of cake. A candle flickered atop the one in her right hand as she lowered it onto the table in front of him.

"Make a wish," Piper encouraged.

Boone dropped his eyelids and wished his new life would always be this wonderful, then he opened his eyes and blew out the candle through the tiny circle formed between his lips.

"This is amazing," Boone proclaimed, "and the cake looks delicious."

Piper sat down beside Boone and kissed him on the cheek. "Let's find out."

"Wait," Boone requested, holding up a finger. "Where is the lighter?"

"Inside on the counter."

"I'll be right back," Boone announced.

A minute later, he emerged, plucked the candle from his cake, stuck it in Piper's piece, and lit it again.

The second he asked about the lighter, Piper realized his intentions. Still when he finished the process, she couldn't help but smile as widely as if he completely surprised her.

The shock came when he sang Happy Birthday. Shy, quiet Boone Winters sang a solo for her. Grinning from ear to ear, she blew out the candle and wished this new beginning would never end.

"Thank you, sweet man," she whispered.

"You're welcome, birthday girl."

"It's exciting that our birthdays are only a week apart, and we can celebrate like this."

"I know."

Piper picked up her fork and pointed to the cake. "So the piece in front of you is a caramel layer cake, and this one is lemon meringue angel. Do you want to share, or is there one you prefer?"

"Sharing sounds good; they both look yummy."

"I had a piece of red velvet cake on my birthday from the same place these came from, Tullio's Bakery, and it was to die for."

"When did you have time to get these without me noticing?"

"Yesterday on the way home from dance class."

Piper's comment sparked a memory. "Last night I thought of something else I want to add to my journey list," Boone stated.

Piper's eyes lit up. "What?"

"I want to learn how to dance."

"Really? Are you serious? Because that is not something you joke about with someone who loves to dance."

Boone chuckled. "Really," he confirmed. "I never got to go to any of the dances in high school and never danced anywhere else."

"Not even at a wedding?"

"I don't have friends," he reminded her.

Piper pushed her chair back with urgency, grabbed Boone by the hand, and led him to the darkness beneath the trees in her backyard.

"Let's dance," she insisted.

Boone instantly glanced down at their feet but could barely see them. "Don't I need to be able to see what to do?"

"I brought you into the dark for a reason," she announced, wrapping her arms loosely around his neck. "All you need is to feel. Feel your body," she explained moving closer until their bodies became flush. "Feel mine," she added, and Boone wrapped his arms around her waist. "Do you see how that came naturally," she pointed out.

"Yeah," he replied with his hands holding her lower back.

"Feel the connection of our bodies and let their movement become one," she encouraged, pausing as their bodies began swaying in the same directions. "There are no mistakes on this dance floor; there is only what we do. Don't think, just move. Dance like we did in the sleeping bag two nights ago—this is the same thing, just the standing up version."

As Piper whispered, Boone's body loosened and electricity streamed through his bones. He recognized Piper's body firmly against him—her thighs, her stomach, her breasts. Then he stepped on her foot, tensed up, and jerked backward.

Before Boone could speak, Piper swiftly pulled him back into her. "Our bodies become one dancing unit when they're connected," she revealed. "Stepping on each other's toes is part of the dance," she noted, "until we become so in tune with each other that we realize where the other will step without seeing our feet, without planning our movements."

Piper and Boone slow danced for nearly half an hour as the

cake waited at the table. Their feet found each other a handful of times as did their lips. They laughed, talked, and kissed slowly as their bodies moved in unison. Eventually, Piper rested her head on Boone's chest and listened to the music of his heartbeat.

"You are a natural, Boone Winters."

"Thanks. You are a good dance instructor, Piper Luck."

What he liked most about Piper was how nothing with her felt forced. Things just happened, and one adventure always led to another.

"Do you think we should get back to our birthday cake?"

"Yes," Piper responded. Enjoying their first dance, she nearly forgot about the cake. "Would you like milk?" she asked as they walked hand in hand toward the patio.

"Sure."

Piper fetched two glasses of milk and then sat next to Boone. They each took a bite of the piece of cake in front of them, and then Piper fed Boone a forkful of hers.

"Which do you like best?" she asked.

"They are both good, but I think the caramel is the winner."

"Yay, I picked the right one to put your candle in."

Boone forked a piece of the caramel cake and fed Piper. Some topping dripped off and oozed down her chin, and she laughed and scooped it with her finger.

When both plates held only crumbs, they took them in and rinsed them off along with the milk glasses.

Piper excused herself to her bedroom and returned with a large box wrapped in yellow Happy Birthday paper.

"What is this?" Boone asked.

Piper stated the obvious. "A gift for you."

"Oh my goodness," Boone replied when he tore the paper and saw the image of the tent on the box.

"I bought you a house," Piper giggled, clasping her hands and smiling as her tiptoes lifted her body.

"You sure did." Boone's mind wandered back to yesterday. "I rode to the general store last night to get this, but it was gone. I had no idea—"

Piper smiled even wider. "I was one step ahead of you, Mr. Winters."

Boone smirked and shook his head in appreciation. "I have a gift for you too," he revealed. Boone debated whether or when to give it to her especially after their time on the dark dance floor, but now it seemed fitting. "You have to stay inside for about ten minutes while I do something, and promise not to peek out the windows."

Piper's face showcased her curiosity.

Boone hurried out the back door and grabbed his backpack from the Jeep. He reached to the bottom underneath the clothes, where the gift took up most of the bag, then headed for the trees.

Eager to know Boone's plan, Piper washed dishes to keep the excitement at bay.

"You have to close your eyes," Boone instructed when he walked back inside.

"You are returning the closed eyes favor, huh?"

Outside when Boone asked Piper to open her eyes, she gasped as she followed the string of globe lights dangling from the low-hanging tree limbs surrounding their dance floor.

"I absolutely love it," Piper exclaimed with her hands covering her mouth. "This is perfect." She leaped into Boone's arms and kissed him. "Now we have to dance again."

"I thought I wasn't supposed to be able to see us dancing."

"You can close your eyes."

Piper played background music on the phone this time, and she and Boone enjoyed their second dance beneath the magical ambiance she envisioned when she first stepped foot in this backyard.

Before the night grew too late, they ventured to the beach lot and put together Boone's tent beneath the moonlight with help from the light on Piper's phone and Boone's flashlight.

Piper read the instructions one step at a time, but as the process progressed, she realized how Boone's mechanical mind worked. It became apparent that he could probably build anything. Once all the flexible poles were connected, the stakes installed, and all the other intricate details put together, they moved in Boone's belongings just like at a new house.

Boone spread out his sleeping bag in the center of the tent, and Piper found places to neatly arrange his clean clothes. Once finished, they nestled together to enjoy the fruits of their labor.

The large gray tent featured a cushioned floor, several windows with screens, and Piper's favorite, a screened moonroof at the top. Through it they could see the tree branches swaying in the wind, the stars twinkling in the night sky, and, of course, the glow of the bright Carolina moon.

The sounds of the ocean played the background music to a well-lived day. Piper and Boone snuggled closely, and it didn't take long for Boone to roll on top of Piper. They kissed and danced intimately on the soft floor as the creatures outside chirped, hummed, and buzzed.

Boone never enjoyed a birthday as much as this one and possibly never enjoyed a day so much, at least not as an adult. Spending time with Piper somehow reignited the hope of childhood, and life's possibilities once again seemed limitless.

24

iper and Boone continued spending time together, and one adventure led to the next. Most days flew by; the sun rose and set as fast as a time lapse video. Boone loved his new tent. It kept out the rain which was nice now that he and Piper didn't need a thunderstorm to fold them into a cocoon. They spent equal time at her place, the beach lot campsite, and wandering the island by bicycle, Jeep, and foot.

Nearly every day they read a lesson from The Roots Beneath Us journey guide. They checked fears and goals off their lists and added new ones. The week after the birthday celebration, Boone and Piper wrote letters independently to the people who hurt them. One thought chased another as Boone relived the sexual abuse of his teenage years that carried over into the long-term relationship with Beth. He cried a lot. He screamed at God. Piper did some of the same. Although she had never been sexually abused, some tried, and to those she wrote forgiveness letters. She prayed they changed in the way her friend Hardy Turner did. He never put his hands on her but said some very inappropriate comments before he turned his life around.

The hardest part for Piper seemed to be forgiving herself for the vulnerable situations she chose. She missed the action from her old life, as well as the friends and coworkers, but she didn't miss the danger. She wished Boone had known how to defend himself like she did. She hit people, kicked them, maced faces, and even choked some out.

When Boone and Piper finished the letters, they built a campfire at Boone's and talked about the parts they were willing to relive with their accountability partner. Then they tossed the letters into the flames one by one and watched them burn. As their pasts began to drift away with the smoke in the night, they held each other tightly.

Piper called Leslie that same week and apologized for stealing her boyfriend in high school marking the first time they talked since graduating. She figured her friend would hang up on her, but Leslie didn't. She listened to Piper's sincere apology, and the two spoke for nearly an hour. She told Piper she ended up marrying that same guy. They went to college together, became doctors, and had two kids. Recently, they moved back to their hometown for new positions at the hospital. Before the call ended, Leslie invited Piper to check in occasionally and reach out if she returned home for a visit.

Letting go of Beth officially made its way onto Boone's journey list, and the indented column beneath that goal grew rapidly. He started attending professional counseling. The sessions proved hard especially at first, but as the weeks passed, he noticed growth as he became his own person. He wrote Beth a goodbye letter and threw it in a campfire while alone one evening.

Kayla randomly showed up that night. She said she drove by, thought she saw a fire, and decided to check on Boone. The two of them sat within reaching distance of the hot flames and talked about life on the island. Kayla mentioned wondering what happened to him since she hadn't seen him at the restaurant or heard from him. Keeping his promise to be transparent with everyone, Boone told her that he and Piper had been spending a lot of time together and were now a thing.

If this news bothered Kayla, she didn't reveal it. She rambled about all sorts of things and asked many questions about Piper, what they had been up to, and how they were settling in here in Duck. Before leaving, Kayla told Boone she hoped he and Piper would stop by to see her sometime. He concluded she must not have been interested in him the night she offered to let him shower at her place; maybe Southern hospitality ran in her blood.

The next time Boone built a fire, the purpose was to warm his and Piper's toes after a late night dip in the ocean. During their chat about the journey list, Boone briefly retreated to the tent and returned with a picture of Beth.

"What is that?" Piper asked, noticing Boone holding a thin square as if germs contaminated every inch.

"Will you throw this photo of Beth in the fire for me?" Boone asked.

Piper cringed and shook her head. "No."

Boone studied his accountability partner's brown eyes as the glow of the fire flickered in the mirrors of her pupils. A few barely noticeable tears slid down his cheek, following the wrinkles built by age and stress. He looked at the picture, then at the fire, and back at Piper.

"When you are ready, you will throw it in," Piper concluded.

Boone stood above the flames and held the picture over the top as if about to drop a golf ball after accidentally losing one in a water hazard. His mind flashed back to the first night at the campsite when he held the photo near the crackling fire. This time, he released his pinched fingers, and the image of Beth floated slowly, spinning like a wing-shaped maple seed liberated by a tree that no longer needed the attachment.

The picture fell onto a cluster of dry sticks Boone gathered during the daylight hours, but now they crackled with heat. The edges of the photo paper quickly crumpled like arthritic fingers, and Boone watched Beth's face fade away.

There were days when Piper realized Boone needed more space than others. Moving forward meant hurting and healing.

"The healing rarely comes without the hurting," she read from one of the lessons.

Once the building permits gained approval, the beach lot project moved quickly. Boone and Piper met with Preston, who shared news that was a perfect fit for both Boone and Piper.

"Claude put money in the budget for you to hire an assistant," Preston announced to Boone. "I think you might already have one in your accountability partner over here," he added nodding toward Piper with a big grin.

"Now I can pay her," Boone exclaimed, turning his attention from Preston to Piper and touching her arm gently. "If you want the position, that is," he concluded.

Piper smiled widely. "Of course I will take the job," Piper agreed jubilantly. Her job search on the island hit one wall after another, and she recently mentioned considering a waitressing job.

As the ball started rolling, Piper loved managing the project with Boone. Although he acquired his own phone and could now research subcontractors, make calls, and handle most things associated with building the house, she still tackled many of the administrative tasks while he attempted to balance planning and physical labor. Plus she often teased that she spent more time teaching him how to use his phone than working.

They rented a backhoe and bulldozer, and watching Boone operate the machinery to clear debris, dig the holes and trenches for the foundation, and perform other site preparation work fascinated Piper. She liked it when he took his shirt off because she found the sight of sweat running down his chest and back while he worked very attractive. Time in the sun added layers of tan to his pale skin, and muscles started forming from the physical labor and workouts they performed together.

Piper appreciated that Boone let her climb aboard the heavy equipment. He patiently showed her how to drive and operate all the gears, knobs, and pedals. However, initially, it intimidated her almost as much as the horse frightened Boone.

"No wonder you caught on to driving a vehicle so easily," Piper exclaimed one day. "You already knew how to drive; you just needed to adjust to the speed and share the roadway."

When Boone finished that fundamental piece of the project, a crew came in to pour concrete and install rebar to establish the footings, then they formed and poured the foundation walls. Once the concrete cured, waterproofing and initial plumbing happened. Afterward came the first inspection; the inspector checked that installations met county codes.

Thankfully Boone knew a lot about inspections from prior experience. Still, he studied the North Carolina building codes which helped him avoid a few mistakes. He spent many daytime hours on-site, often analyzing the plans and progress to catch snags early. Piper visited the lot almost daily. Sometimes she brought lunch, and they would proudly watch the construction progress or sit by the beach to enjoy the scenery and the sunshine. They celebrated with a day off when the work passed inspection on the first visit.

Tourist season seemed to kick off on Memorial Day in late May. People from all over the world showed up in Duck. The streets filled with vehicles, the shops and restaurants buzzed with patrons, and beachgoers packed the vacation rentals. The absence of public beach access kept the local strand from overcrowding, but some of the adjacent Outer Banks towns offered areas for those not within walking distance of the ocean and others visiting for the day. Amongst all the hustle and bustle, Boone and Piper became even fonder of their mostly private beach oasis at the oceanfront lot.

Piper continued to look for houses but couldn't find the right fit. She fell deeper in love with the rental and compared every home to the one she came to cherish but forged on because one of her top journey list goals was to buy. She rented her whole adult life and desired to experience the joys and challenges of home ownership. One day fate, or happenstance, or God intervened. The owners set a meeting with her and the real estate agent. After a thirty minute conversation in the living room, they asked if Piper wanted to buy their house.

The day after the closing, Boone handed Piper a box that meowed. She pulled out the most beautiful kitten she ever saw, a brown spotted Savannah cat with the cutest pointy ears. Piper gently rubbed the soft, warm brown fur dotted with dark brown spots. The kitten resembled a leopard and snuggled on the couch with her for about an hour, and she instantly fell in love.

"Bailey, you are the most adorable kitten in the world," Piper announced in a tone of voice reserved for animals and babies as she held up the kitty, letting its long, skinny legs dangle. She already picked the name when she and Boone recently perused cat photos online. Piper was so grateful he remembered precisely which breed caught her eye. "Boone, you are the most amazing boyfriend in the world," she added with a long smile.

Within twenty-four hours, Boone built a cat door leading to the patio. He strung more globe lights in the trees and started on other projects around the house to help make it Piper's. Dance lessons continued, and Boone rarely stepped on Piper's feet although Bailey often attempted to trip them when not climbing the trees, frequently getting stuck, and calling for a rescue.

After volunteering at the dance studio for quite some time, Piper shared with Boone during a walk along the boardwalk that she would love to open her own one day. They leisurely added this idea to her journey list although she didn't know if there would be room for another dance school in Duck. However, the dream still existed. The opportunity to work with Boone allowed her to continue volunteering and save money for her own studio or another venture if that didn't work out.

As they explored dreams, Piper asked Boone what he wanted to do once he finished the building project, and his mind began churning. During June the frame went up, and as all the pieces came together, the project started to look like a house. When Piper mentioned that the process reminded her of building with Legos, but at actual size, Boone shared how much he loved creating houses, towns, and all kinds of other things with Legos as a kid.

"I thought about going to college," Boone mentioned one day while walking at the lot, appreciating the progress with Piper. She liked picking up the loosely discarded nails so no one would step on them although each time Boone guaranteed there would be more tomorrow. "But I don't think that's what I want. I love construction. I want to get my contractor's license."

Piper supported Boone one hundred percent. She watched the man build things with his bare hands that seemed impossible. Even though he hired crews for nearly every step of the process, he did so many projects himself especially to create the critical details Claude requested. Piper believed there were no limits to what Boone could accomplish regarding construction. Together, they made a great team, and she could see herself working with him long term.

On the flip side of the coin, she didn't envision talking him into joining the dance instructor team as an option, but maybe one day he would build her studio. Hopefully they would create and live their dreams together. He did continue to dance with her in the backyard under the trees, on the beach while the wind blew their hair, and in other random places when the mood struck.

One of the lessons they read in The Roots Beneath Us guide talked about the need for a group of friends, especially a couple close ones. Piper developed that with Kelly, who recently announced she was pregnant, and other instructors at the studio. They went out for dinner occasionally, spent a day at the beach together here and there, and talked like they knew each other forever. Of course she had Bailey too.

Piper knew it would take Boone longer to find his tribe although he too fell in love with Bailey, who followed him around the house more than Piper.

Boone's and Piper's journey to figure out God eventually led them to the church they passed on the way to the park the day Boone got the bicycle. At the second service they attended, Boone thanked the pastor for the bike and told him he didn't have a driver's license or car at that time. Since then Boone took the necessary steps to obtain a license, but instead of purchasing a vehicle, he bought a golf cart which he and Piper quickly learned was the preferred transportation method for locals on the island during the busy season.

When not driving the golf cart, Boone often rode his bicycle with Piper and began cycling with a few other friends. It turned out that the shop owner where Boone got the bike started going to the same church, and he and Boone ended up in a men's group together where Boone made several friends.

Through the church, Boone and Piper found additional reputable subcontractors who helped tremendously. Being able to depend on them made the house project move even smoother during the dog days of summer. After applying sheathing to the exterior walls, some friends helped Boone install the windows and exterior doors. A crew put in the HVAC system; the plumber returned for the rough plumbing; and an electrician installed wires and panels. The progress made in July brought out the inspector a couple of times, resulting in approval stamps to continue.

When August rolled around, Piper and Boone found it hard

to believe they had been living in Duck for three months, and both realized they fit in well. Along with getting to know many of the locals and building friendships, they learned about hidden gems in the area as well as how to avoid traffic, busy restaurants, and other touristy places. They both liked their new eye doctor, whom they saw a couple of months ago when Piper joined Boone's glasses club. Thankfully she only needed them for reading. She convinced Boone to read a couple of books with her, and she even joined a book club. Once he decided to obtain his contractor's license, however, he began spending his time reading material related to that goal. Regardless of what they read, Bailey, who seemed to grow taller each day, liked to climb on them like a jungle gym and snuggle.

Boone and Piper explored the Outer Banks with day trips and random weekend excursions. They drove from the most northern point in Corolla where the pavement of NC 12 literally turned into sand for beach access to four-wheel drive vehicles only all the way to Ocracoke, a quaint community only accessible by ferry. Of course they couldn't pass up the opportunity to drive the Jeep on the beach which proved to be even more exhilarating than expected as did sitting still in the Jeep as it sat atop the ferry. They climbed Jockey's Ridge, walked the runway where the Wright Brothers took their first flight, and visited the Ocracoke, Hatteras, Bodie Island, and Currituck Lighthouses that guarded the Graveyard of the Atlantic.

People all over the island became interested in the house Boone was building. Most didn't know about the hidden campsite in the trees, but some found out, and a few complained. One evening Boone came home after being at Piper's to find a crab in his tent. He didn't think much of it but a few nights later discovered a tent full of crabs. Odd things like that continued to happen. Boone didn't know if the teenagers who previously left trash at the unfinished beach house were the culprits—he ran them off a few times—or adults fully aware of their intentions. The NO TRESPASSING signs didn't seem to detour the issue. The latest thing that happened was a sign taped on his tent that read: Go home or else!

Boone hoped he wouldn't have to defend himself or the property but felt more confident after spending part of his summer taking private self-defense classes with a retired military hand-to-hand combat instructor. He almost signed up for karate, but Piper convinced him to meet with a parent she met at the dance studio. The man promised he could have Boone prepared to defend himself against almost any attacker within weeks or months, depending on the pace rather than the years it would take with a traditional self-defense course.

After a few lessons, Boone believed him. The instructor explained that he didn't teach people only how to fight but, more importantly, how to end a fight. He pointed out that street fights weren't fair like fights in a ring and were often life and death situations. This hit home with Boone because no fight with Beth had ever been fair; she used all kinds of things against him; and there had never been a referee to stop her.

Boone quickly learned protection modes, pressure points, submission techniques, and disabling skills. Eating well along with Piper, he put on weight and muscle as they worked out together, sometimes jogging on the beach, lifting weights at a local gym they joined, or doing yoga at her house and on the beach.

They began meditating regularly to relax their minds and draw closer to God. They prayed together, worked on breathing exercises, and fasted. It amazed both of them how their minds and bodies began to transform. They had more energy, thought clearer, worked harder, and enjoyed more adventures.

All of a sudden unexplainable things began to happen more frequently.

25

"Boone, did you bring the mail in today?" Piper asked after returning from a run.

"No, you always check the mail," he reminded her.

"Are you sure? Because the mail was sitting on the table when I came in, but I didn't bring it in," she reported pointing to a small stack of envelopes. "I know I didn't because I checked the box before I walked inside, and it was empty."

"That's odd."

"Do you remember how yesterday the air temperature was five degrees higher than we normally keep it?"

"Yes."

"Are you sure you didn't touch the thermostat?" Piper verified.

"No, I didn't; I promise," Boone claimed. "Are you sure you didn't leave the freezer door wide open this past weekend?"

"Boone, I already told you three times I didn't."

"I know."

"Either one or both of us is going crazy, or someone is coming into this house."

"Do you think it is the same people messing around at the beach lot?"

More odd things occurred there too. Sea shells surrounded Boone's tent one morning; his pillow disappeared; and the creepiest was when he came home from Piper's one night to find a dead bird hanging from a tree branch.

"I am not sure, but I imagine there is a connection," Piper postulated.

"Do you think we should call the police?"

Piper contemplated the question which she previously considered. She kept a detailed list of the things that happened at both her place and Boone's, including the dates, times, and other specifics that could prove significant.

"Why don't we set up cameras instead to see if we can figure out who is doing these things," Piper recommended.

"That is a good idea."

"But for now, I need to shower so we are not late for your appointment with the neurosurgeon."

Once Boone obtained medical insurance, Piper convinced him to see an orthopedist about his chronic pain. When she and Boone initially spoke about his condition, he vaguely complained about body aches. However, through discussing the issue in more depth and her closely watching the movements that bothered him, they pinpointed his left shoulder as the troublesome area. The orthopedist tried an injection, prescribed physical therapy, and a few other remedies. None of that seemed to help, so he referred Boone to a nearby specialist.

This morning, they traveled for a second visit with the neurosurgeon to review the results of an MRI and myelogram.

"Mr. Winters, I want to be frank with you," the neurosurgeon started, looking confidently over the tip of the glasses perched on his nose. He glanced between the notes in his hands and the faces of Boone and Piper. "You need surgery on your neck."

When they met previously, the neurosurgeon explained how the pain Boone felt in the shoulder quite possibly stemmed from an issue with the cervical spine even though that area didn't bother Boone.

Speechless, Boone stared at the man, probably twenty years his elder, who wore mint green scrubs.

"What caused this?" Piper investigated.

"Most likely a traumatic injury which over time has worsened and presented itself in the form of pain in the left shoulder." He explained how the nerves, tissue, bones, and other body parts in that area connect and affect one another.

Boone finally spoke up. "Do you think this happened during my hand-to-hand combat training?" His instructor slammed him on the mat plenty of times. Boone would kick himself if he severely injured his neck while trying to learn how to defend himself from Beth or someone else intending to inflict pain on him.

"Absolutely not," the neurosurgeon confirmed, pulling a pen from his shirt pocket. He flipped a switch beneath a light box that highlighted the test images and began to point at the bones in Boone's neck.

"This is the root issue," he claimed. "Right here in the C4 and C5 area. There are markers here that indicate this injury happened many years ago." He explained those in more detail, but the dialogue mostly drifted over Boone's head or at least in one ear and out the other.

Boone's mind played a reel of old injuries: falling out of a swing as a child, his father pushing him down a set of stairs, falling off ladders at work, and Beth constantly shoving him, often resulting in forceful impacts.

"How come it only started bothering me more now, especially in my shoulder?"

"Time reveals many things. Wear and tear over the years probably began to irritate it especially with you working in construction. It also may be that you did something in your physical training regimen that bothered your neck, but you can rest assured this issue has been around for a while."

Piper felt and appeared dejected. Neck surgery was a big deal. She recognized most of the medical terminology this man used because her dad specialized in this area of medicine and surgery. She suddenly wished he were here so she could ask him a thousand questions.

"How serious is this injury?" Piper asked. "I mean, are you saying Boone needs surgery right away, or is this something we have time to think about?" She could hear her dad now: *Always get a second opinion.*

"Ms. Luck, I will shoot straight with you all because I believe my patients deserve the truth. This surgery is needed sooner rather than later. In fact, Boone, I strongly advise you to relinquish all physical contact activity that could possibly cause damage to your spine." He pointed to the screen again to emphasize his point. "These two discs are pushing against the spine, and a significant blow could cause further damage. Let's say, for example, you got into a car accident; you would be at high risk for paralysis due to the whiplash."

"I could become paralyzed?" Boone screeched. Of course anyone could become paralyzed, but this news scared him tremendously.

"I am not saying paralysis would occur, but it could. The only reason I mention this is to explain the surgery's urgency and encourage caution in all activities."

Boone walked out of the office drained. He kept his eyes on his feet as he walked to the Jeep. He drove here but now handed the keys to Piper.

"You have way more driving experience," he uttered, unwilling to make eye contact.

Piper accepted the keys knowing precisely what he meant.

"I have told you my dad is a surgeon," she mentioned after cranking the vehicle.

"Yeah," Boone replied.

"What I haven't told you is that he is the best," she proclaimed, maneuvering through the parking lot toward the exit. "Probably the best in the country, possibly in the world. Daddy is a neurosurgeon who receives cases most others don't want to touch."

"Really?" Boone responded as Piper pulled into traffic making sure to leave plenty of space.

"I am going to call him."

"But you haven't talked to your dad since we met."

"Boone, forgiving my parents has been at the top of my journey list since we made it," she reminded him. "I think this might be God's way of saying now is the time."

"What do you mean?"

"You are more important than me holding a grudge."

Boone felt like he might cry. "That means a lot to me," he whimpered. "I am really scared."

"I know, and I am here for you," she reminded him, reaching over with her right hand to caress his arm.

"You should probably keep both hands on the wheel at ten and two like you taught me," he advised.

Piper quickly found the position.

"I am going to call my dad."

"You probably don't need to hold a phone either," Boone mentioned.

"We will put him on speaker."

"What? I have never talked to your dad; that might be awkward for me and him."

"Boone, the sooner the better," she reminded him.

"Okay."

The phone rang loudly through the speakers. Once. Twice. Three times. On the fourth ring, someone picked up.

"Hello, Piper," the voice sounded jubilantly.

"Hi, Daddy."

"How are you, darling?"

"Overall, I am well. How are you and Mom?"

"We are blessed, and we miss you. We have called you but haven't received a response."

"I apologize for not answering or calling back," Piper responded. "How much time do you have?" She knew to ask that question during daytime hours; her dad only answered calls between surgeries or appointments.

"Several minutes; my team is prepping for surgery as we speak."

"Dad, my boyfriend Boone is in the car with me, and I have you on speaker phone."

"Hello, Boone," her dad greeted without missing a beat.

"Hey, sir," Boone replied sheepishly, his heart beating as fast as in the surgeon's office, if not faster.

"Daddy, since you are pressed for time, we need to skip the small talk," Piper announced. "Boone and I need your help."

"You know I will do anything I can, sweetheart," he replied, his voice lined with concern.

She explained the results from the appointment with the neurosurgeon as precisely as possible.

"Boone, I am sorry you are dealing with this trauma," Piper's dad offered sincerely. "I want you two to have all the images and radiologist's notes sent to my office right away. I am being paged into the operating room now but will forward you to my assistant, and she will provide the transmission information. I promise to look over everything at my earliest convenience."

"Thank you, Daddy."

"Thanks, Dr. Luck."

Piper's dad's assistant shared the information, then Piper and Boone called to have the records forwarded to her dad.

The rest of the ride home was interesting. Boone remained quiet for the most part, only answering questions. Piper tried to keep things upbeat, but she could tell the surgery frightened Boone greatly.

"Would you like to cancel our dinner plans?" Piper asked at some point on the drive home.

"No, that's not necessary."

That evening Piper and Boone served dinner on the patio to a group of friends, including people from the dance studio and the church, as well as spouses and children who came along. They grilled fish, played cornhole on boards Boone made, and danced under the globe lights to the music floating from the speakers they installed in the trees several weeks back. Boone barely conversed with anyone. He didn't participate in the games nor touch the dance floor. Mostly, he sat in a chair with Bailey on his lap. When Piper asked why, Boone referenced the fear of injuring his neck worse.

When the last car pulled out of the driveway, Boone and Piper walked to the backyard to begin the cleanup. Then to their surprise a person stumbled up the driveway causing fear to instantly flood Piper's body. Her hands trembled while her mind connected this individual to everything odd that happened lately.

"Hey guys," the person shouted, raising a cup, obviously drunk.

"What are you doing here?" Piper asked firmly.

Boone looked at the person and then at Piper.

"I saw you all were having a party, and I wanted to join."

"The party is over," Piper announced. "And you weren't invited anyway."

"That's no way to treat an ex."

Boone's shoulders tightened, and he didn't know whether to speak up or let Piper handle the situation.

"Leave," Piper demanded. "Or we will call the police."

"Call the police?" the drunkard slurred. "Can't you and your boyfriend defend yourselves?"

"Just leave."

"Aren't you going to introduce me to him?" the individual

clamored, pointing the cup at Boone while drawing closer.

"No, he doesn't want to know you, Derek."

"Does he know you?" Derek chuckled.

"Yes, he knows me very well."

"Then we're all friends."

"Derek, we are not friends anymore."

Derek stumbled around them and headed toward the dance floor beneath the trees. "I saw you all dancing tonight," he claimed eerily.

Piper wished she told Boone about Derek, but never in a million years did she expect him to show up here. She hadn't seen him in years. How had he known where to find her?

"Where's the pole?" Derek asked, scratching his thick beard when he reached the dance floor.

Derek was the bad breakup in Piper's mid twenties, the reason behind the sunflower tattoo Boone loved to trace when they lie in bed together. It reminded Piper there would always be brighter days, but she suddenly didn't like this one.

"What is he talking about?" Boone whispered to Piper. "Who is he?"

"I am Derek," the man proclaimed loudly, spinning around as the music played, almost falling but catching himself with his free hand while his cup poured out what little alcohol remained.

Boone realized his words came out louder than intended.

"Derek, I am calling the police," Piper threatened looking for her phone.

"First, come dance with me, baby," he insisted, "or *for* me," he added with a hideous laugh. "For us, you'd probably like it too," he declared to Boone. "Do you know who Piper is?"

"Yes," Boone replied aggressively, surprising himself.

"She's a stripper," Derek announced, leaving his mouth wide open after the last word.

The sun in Piper's sky had been shining brightly these past few months in Duck, but everything suddenly seemed gray as she scurried toward the dance floor with purpose.

"How did you know where to find me?" Piper demanded.

Out of fear of what the man might attempt once Piper reached him, Boone followed quickly although this guy's muscles made his arms look puny. All Boone could think about was the word the neurosurgeon used—paralysis.

"Felecia," Derek laughed. "When she gets drunk and I put enough cash in her G-string, she will tell me anything."

Piper knew she shouldn't have told a soul about the move. She didn't tell Felecia but a mutual friend must have spilled the beans. Hardy even warned her that when she finally walked away not to tell anyone who didn't have to know.

It shocked Boone when the man grabbed Piper's arm, but the tables turned rapidly. Piper swatted the cup from Derek's hand, and before the last drop of beer landed, she performed a sweep kick taking his legs from under him, and he hit the dirt hard.

Boone stopped in mid-stride. What he witnessed reminded him of the professional videos his hand to hand combat instructor shared.

Piper lunged toward Derek's body, his back lying flat on the ground, and dropped her knee in his mid-section with force. He immediately gasped for air. Two seconds later she somehow spun the large man over and shoved her knee into his back and cupped his throat with her arm.

Boone stepped in their direction, not sure what to do. Piper obviously didn't need his help, but did he need to intervene?

"Piper," Boone uttered cautiously.

Eventually Piper released the hold, and the man's body collapsed onto the ground like a rag doll tossed aside by a little girl.

"Is he—dead?" Boone asked, fright lining his shaky voice.

"No, I choked him out," Piper answered assuredly, checking his pulse.

She calmly explained what she did and then tied Derek's hands behind his back with a piece of rope Boone recently used for an outdoor project.

Piper called the police, and by the time the first squad car arrived, Derek had begun moving. Boone breathed a sigh of relief because he literally thought the man to be dead even after Piper claimed otherwise.

Everything happened so quickly that Boone and Piper barely had a chance to talk until after the police asked a plethora of questions before eventually leaving with Derek handcuffed in the back seat of one of the patrol cars.

"Who is that man?" Boone asked once he and Piper were alone.

"My ex," Piper answered, then explained the story.

"Were you a stripper?" Boone quizzed furrowing his brow.

Piper's eyelids collapsed. "Yes," she admitted, although she put that life behind her.

"When? How long?"

"My whole adult life," she confessed. "I have done things I regret and never wanted to discuss again. I moved here to leave that life behind."

"Me too," Boone barked in an elevated tone. "Like being abused by my parents' friends and Beth. But I told you about those things because you were my accountability partner, friend, and eventually girlfriend. I thought we told each other everything."

"There are some things we don't want others to know, ever."

"Yeah like that I got beat up by a woman *my whole adult life*," Boone clamored. "Do you know how embarrassing that is?"

With tears streaming down her dusty face, Piper's lips pursed together.

"I don't want to love a stripper?" Boone clamored.

Piper sniffled. "You love me?" she inquired.

"No, I don't *want* to love a stripper," he said again.

"I am not a stripper."

"You were," he argued. "You just admitted you have been your whole adult life."

"That's true, but there is much more to the story."

"I don't want to hear the story; not at this point. Don't you remember all the lessons we read? We are supposed to confront our fears voluntarily to avoid facing them involuntarily. You should have told me you were a stripper."

"I am sorry, Boone. I didn't want you to judge me like everyone else always has."

"I don't want to hear it. You are a stripper and a liar, and I am done with you and with us."

Boone stomped into Piper's house and gathered everything he could find that belonged to him. He stuffed as much as possible into his bookbag and then picked up Bailey. Even though he wanted to rush out of the house, he took the time to hug the kitten tightly and tell her how much he loved her before eventually setting her down cautiously. Lastly, he walked out the front door, slamming it behind him.

Piper sat on the patio with her head in the palms of her hands for what seemed like hours. She wanted to leave all this behind. She wanted a real relationship. She never wanted anyone to look at her as a stripper again, but apparently, she failed. The life she left in the rearview mirror caught up with her. She thought she found love, real love, but Boone just walked away like every other good man, reminding her that the only men who wanted a stripper were the ones she didn't want or need, men like Derek.

26

Thankfully Boone's golf cart sat in Piper's driveway when he walked out of the house, so that this time leaving a woman who wronged him didn't require hitching a ride. He tossed his backpack on the empty seat beside him and placed several plastic grocery bags filled with his things in the wire basket on the back. He held the original rolled-up house plans with his non-steering hand, although he had a working copy at the beach lot that endured the elements.

The gravel crunched beneath the tires as Boone drove off, planning never to return. He faced this fear once which helped him gain the courage to do it again. The wind on his face reduced the summer heat present even at nighttime as he drove along NC 12. Thinking straight seemed challenging, so he mostly mumbled under his breath and groaned as the wheels rolled toward his destination. After all he shared with Piper, how could she not tell him about being a stripper?

He couldn't believe the woman he fell in love with took her clothes off in front of others and danced provocatively for money. Boone was so glad he never told Piper he loved her.

"What kind of luck do I have?" Boone shouted into the open air to God.

After escaping a long-term abusive relationship, what were the chances of ending up with a stripper? He tried not to imagine Piper twirling around a silver dance pole, but since Derek asked why one wasn't on *their* dance floor, he couldn't remove the image from his mind. How many people saw his girlfriend—scratch that, ex-girlfriend—basically naked?

At the campsite Boone scrambled in the dark for loose sticks to build a fire. When he accumulated a few handfuls, he lit a match and tossed it in the bottom where a birds-like nest fueled the flames.

As the blaze grew along with Boone's frustration, he plucked a notebook from inside the tent and began writing his thoughts, the ones from the drive home and others that popped up. He wrote a paragraph, yanked the paper off the wired ring, and threw it into the fire. He then did the same thing over and over. He wished he could throw in a picture of Piper, but he stored those on his phone rather than carrying printed ones. They snapped so many over the summer; if his phone held less value, he would toss in the device and watch it burn.

He remembered how long it took to let go of Beth and didn't want to drag this out with Piper. He considered his options. For some reason, running home to Beth came to mind. He could return to a familiar life in a comfortable home and forget that this whole trip across the country ever happened. He wondered if Beth would even take him back and how badly she would beat him once the truth surfaced. However, he could defend himself now. Maybe once he showed her that, the physical abuse would cease. But how about his neck? One blow to the face might paralyze him for life.

Thinking of Beth, Boone stared through his glasses into the fire, listening to the crackle, and feeling the heat on his pale skin.

No. No way would he ever go back to Beth. No matter who hurt him or how many other women broke his heart, he wouldn't do it.

Suddenly Kayla popped into his mind. He still had her number somewhere. He could call or visit her at the restaurant. She would talk to him. Maybe having someone to share his feelings with would help calm his anger. He wanted to hit something or someone. He wanted to deck that guy Derek like Piper did. Even though he felt he owed the jerk a thank you for exposing Piper, the man still deserved what she gave him.

That thought brought Boone's mind back to the skirmish. How, when, and where did Piper learn to fight like that? She took down a guy who probably outweighed her by a hundred pounds in a few seconds. Sure, he was inebriated but still. Her swiftness, accuracy, and force reminded him of his hand-to-hand combat instructor.

Boone shook his curly hair viciously. None of this mattered. Piper lied to him. If she lied about her past, what else did she neglect to share? He tried to come up with other reasons he shouldn't like her as he did with Beth. He wrote down page after page about Beth but couldn't think of a single negative thing to write about Piper other than what he learned tonight.

Piper was kind and thoughtful and adventurous and hospitable and sweet and beautiful . . . and a stripper. That word was where any thought about Piper ended. Even if Boone tried to make things work with her, he imagined his mind would always go back there.

Kayla. Boone's mind wandered back to Kayla. She was pretty and sweet and funny and blonde and ditsy and . . . no. No, he didn't need to run to another woman. Was that what he did with Piper? Ran from Beth to her? Everything happened so quickly that he never had time to think about it, to heal on his own. However, it seemed like Piper helped him heal. She was his accountability partner, for goodness sake. They walked through his pain, and their pains, together. She always talked about starting a new life too, and now he knew exactly what she meant.

❦

Piper thought about chasing after Boone. She wanted to tell him so many things but doubted he would listen. She wanted this new life so people would see her differently. She wanted others to see her for her true self, not for what she had done in the past. She knew if she told Boone about stripping, he would judge her just like everyone else who ever found out. Even the people who pretended not to judge her judged her, and she understood why.

Strip clubs were sad places. The dancers devalued their bodies by showing them off to anyone and everyone who paid to walk through the doors. Creeps, perverts, and all kinds of other people with disgusting problems who pay to watch others take off their clothes filled the audience. Many of the men showed aggression. Many of the women allowed it. They allowed the guys to take advantage of them, and in return, the strippers took advantage of the men, especially the ones with money.

Piper tried to help as many women stuck in the crooked world of strip clubs as possible—women who suffered physical, mental, and emotional abuse like Boone. She wanted to tell him why she became a stripper. Now, since that part of her past revealed itself, maybe she should unveil more. Perhaps not all secrets were meant to be kept. But would he listen? More importantly, would he understand?

Boone climbed into the tent and stuffed his face into his pillow while the fire dwindled. Angry tears soaked the soft casing that smelled like Beth each time he sniffed. Odd, he thought. At other times these past few months, he thought he smelled her especially early on, but this time, her scent seemed stronger. It was interesting how attachments became etched in the mind even after being gone for so long.

Suddenly, a thought hit him like a baseball bat over the head—his pillow *was* gone.

Piper's phone rang. She had been sitting on the patio crying because she didn't know what to do besides cuddle with Bailey. The thought of calling Boone crossed her mind every few minutes, but she didn't. She wanted to let him calm down. Maybe then the two of them could talk clearly. Right now, a conversation would probably only worsen things.

"Dad," Piper answered, attempting to hide her sniffles.

"Sweetheart, are you okay?"

The dark sky seemed to collapse on her as the emotional toll of not being able to talk to her daddy about her life caught up with her. "No, I am not. This has been a horrible day," she divulged.

"I can only imagine," Piper's dad sympathized. "I have bad news and good news," he shared.

She didn't need any more bad news today. "What is the good news?"

"I want to perform Boone's surgery."

"You do?" she asked, rubbing Bailey's soft fur. "So he does, in fact, need the surgery?"

"Yes, immediately. The other part of the good news is that my team is handling every step of the process to get the two of you here tomorrow."

"Wait, what?" Piper questioned. Had she heard him right? "Tomorrow?" she chirped. "What do you mean?"

"I reviewed Boone's images and the notes with my top radiologist. The surgery is very intensive and more time sensitive than the other neurosurgeon suspected. There is no room for error, and I cannot allow another surgeon to perform surgery on the man you love."

"Daddy, are you sure?" she asked as the pace of her hand petting Bailey sped up unnoticed. "And I didn't say I loved him."

"You didn't have to, sweetie. It was obvious," he concluded. "I want the two of you on the first flight to Rochester in the morning. My assistant will call you and will handle everything. The flight will be paid for, a car will pick you up from the airport, and I have reserved the operating room after my last procedure tomorrow."

"What if we can't make it tomorrow?"

"I can assure you there is not a more pressing matter in Boone's life right now."

Boone heard footsteps outside the tent when suddenly two hands appeared on either side of the entrance's opened zipper. He swallowed the lump in his throat and crawled backward on his elbows as if retreating to the corner could help him escape. The tent's entrance opened wide, and he saw a face that did and didn't surprise him.

"What are you doing here?" Boone barked.

"I am the one who gets to ask that question," Beth proclaimed with fire in her eyes.

"I live here," Boone stated, attempting to sound proud to be on his own.

"You live in a tent?" she laughed. "That is sad."

"What do you want?"

"What do I want?" she asked, moving closer.

"Yes."

"I want what is mine," she demanded while standing over him.

"I am not yours anymore," Boone declared.

"I bought you from parents who loved you so much they sold you," she reminded him sarcastically. "I saved you from them and from so many others. I took care of you. You are mine. You always have been and always will be."

The image of Piper sweep kicking Derek flashed into Boone's mind, and he considered trying the move on Beth. However, it didn't seem worth the risk. They would surely end up in a scuffle, and he knew from experience that she didn't have any qualms about punching him in the face or slamming his shoulders into the ground.

"I have missed you, Boone," Beth divulged, bending down and straddling his midsection. She forced herself against him and placed her hands on his shoulders with authority. "I want you."

Boone remembered something his hand-to-hand combat instructor taught him: "Children fight with their fists on the playground because they don't know any better way to handle conflict. Wise adults fight with words. Words are always the best offense and defense; only use physical force when there is no other option."

"Let's talk," Boone suggested.

"Talk is cheap, Boone," Beth replied, grinding against him in a pair of black shorts that showcased her quadriceps. "Actions speak louder."

"I want things to change," Boone said, realizing that pretending to go along with what Beth wanted might be the best option to avoid a physical altercation.

"You made that pretty obvious when you left me," she stated, her voice revealing the built-up anger.

"I don't want to fight with you anymore."

"You never put up much of a fight, darling," Beth reminded him, lowering her face to his and kissing his lower lip then biting it hard enough to draw blood.

Boone sucked his lip and tasted the blood. "Let's go somewhere and talk."

"I will let you talk while you give me what I want," Beth offered. "I missed your magic," she said, pushing against him and gnawing on his ear. "Didn't you miss me?" she asked, placing one of his hands atop her black tank top forcing him to cup one of her breasts.

Boone wanted to squirm. He wanted to shove Beth off him and distance himself from her as quickly as possible. "Yeah," he answered. "I missed you."

Beth reached down, unbuckled his belt, and yanked it through the loops of his khaki shorts.

Boone hated that he felt aroused physically. He didn't want her, didn't want to have anything to do with her. This already felt like cheating on Piper.

Beth pushed herself on him and kissed him again while digging her fingernails into his chest. "Where did these muscles come from?" she inquired with passion in her eyes.

"I have been working out," he acknowledged.

"For that other woman?" she quizzed.

Boone didn't realize his heart could race any faster. "What other woman?"

"Do you want her to be here with us?" Beth asked. "Is that why you left? I didn't satisfy you?"

"No, that's not it."

"You want a threesome?"

"No." Boone just wanted Piper. Well, before tonight, at least.

"I might be willing," Beth offered seductively.

"What are you talking about?"

"Is Piper good in bed?"

Hearing Beth speak Piper's name sent chills down his spine.

"Is she better than me?" Beth asked.

"I don't want to talk about this."

"Call her?" Beth dared. "Invite her to join us."

"No thanks," Boone replied.

"That wasn't a question, Boone. Call her and ask her to join us," Beth demanded placing her hands around Boone's throat.

"No," he replied firmly, even though gagging. *May the cards fall where they will*, Boone decided. He wasn't Beth's toy anymore, and he made a pact with himself to be transparent with everyone, including her. "I love Piper, and I will never have sex with you again. Not now, not ever."

As the words rolled off Boone's tongue, he knew what he had to do. He practiced this very move in case anyone ever placed their hands around his throat.

Grabbing the pressure points on Beth's wrists immediately loosened her grip. When her body fell on top of his, Boone lifted his knee into her midsection and threw her toward the zipper door.

Beth was one tough cookie, and he knew she would retaliate quickly, so he pounced to his feet to prepare for her revenge. An instant later, like a flash of lightning, a third person entered the tent.

Piper slid baseball-player-style between Beth's legs as Beth stood glaring at Boone with fury in her green eyes. Somehow, Piper quickly contorted her body and grabbed Beth's torso with her legs, capturing her in a scissor grip like a Venus fly trap.

Wide-eyed, Boone held a defensive stance.

Beth's arms flailed at Piper's face, but Piper blocked every punch with her elbows. A few seconds into the brawl, Piper pinned Beth on the ground in a tightly locked submission hold.

"There won't be any threesomes tonight," Piper declared.

Beth snickered. "I like your aggressiveness," Beth stated, biting her own lip.

"I don't like anything about you," Piper sneered. "Especially what you were trying to do to Boone just now."

"Boone and I were about to have consensual sex," Beth cried. "He doesn't want you anymore, stripper." Hiding in the bushes, Beth heard what the drunk man said, and when Boone left Piper's house, Beth decided that was the moment she'd been waiting for to win him back.

"That's not true," Boone shouted. "Neither part of it," he clarified.

"You don't have to defend yourself, Boone," Piper noted. "I trust you."

"Never trust a man," Beth snickered. "They will always leave you."

Piper thought about how Boone had just left her, but that

wasn't the most important thing right now. "I heard every word both of you said since the moment you snuck into Boone's tent," Piper revealed. "I was behind you on the road, and when you rounded that corner and cut off your headlights, I did the same, and then I watched you pull in here."

"What are you, like a secret agent or something?" Beth asked, trying to wiggle her way out of the hold but with no luck.

"Something like that," Piper answered.

"Boone's weak. He needs a woman to protect him."

"Boone's the strongest man I know," Piper declared.

"So why did you have to come to his rescue?" Beth questioned with a mischievous grin while also grimacing.

"Why do you think I stood outside the tent and listened to everything when I already knew Boone didn't want you here?" Piper asked rhetorically. "I waited for Boone to show you that you are not his boss anymore. He didn't need my help, but I am his accountability partner, and we work together in and through everything, unlike you."

"It sounds like the only work you know how to do is be a stripper," Beth jabbed.

Piper released one of her hands long enough to backhand Beth across the cheek. "That's for calling me a stripper." Just as quickly, Piper regained the position, relinquished her hold on the opposite arm, and smacked Beth's other cheek. "That's for messing with my man."

For the second time tonight, Piper hogtied another human being. When the police arrived, they conducted an extra long interrogation with Boone and Piper since this was their second time visiting them tonight in as many locations.

When the authorities finished their business, Piper wrapped her arms around Boone. "I love you, Boone Winters." Speechless, Boone studied her caramel brown eyes. "You don't have to respond to that, but I have to tell you about the phone call I just had with my dad, and regardless of whether you love me or never want to see my face again, I beg you to go with me to Rochester tomorrow," she reasoned. "Or go without me, it doesn't matter. I just want you in my dad's hands."

"What?" Boone asked, his brow furrowed tightly.

Through tears from all the mixed emotions of the night, Piper shared the conversation she had with her dad that brought her here tonight. "The timing was fate, happenstance, or God," she declared.

Boone wrapped his arms around Piper and kissed her lips slowly and passionately. When he pulled back, he uttered, "God. It was God."

27

Neither Boone nor Piper slept a wink that night even though the two people responsible for the shenanigans interrupting their lives ended up behind bars in the same jail. Each of their minds chased thoughts from one of the wildest nights imaginable. Boone faced his greatest fear—telling Beth to her face that he didn't want to be with her and physically standing up to her bullying. He wondered what would have happened if Piper hadn't shown up; nonetheless, he thanked God she did. He could be paralyzed now if the fight between him and Beth continued.

Something Beth spewed out in their final conversation turned Boone's wheels. After Piper restrained her, Boone asked Beth how she found him.

"Boone, men aren't just pigs; they are sheep," she blabbered. "It didn't take long for me to find one of your coworkers who would follow me anywhere I wanted him to go. That led me to people who know things, and one of them followed me too."

Boone knew precisely what Beth meant—she seduced them.

"There are always trails," Beth continued. "My new friend told me about all the company projects and researched the property owned by Claude and the company, and then intuition helped narrow down the possibilities. It took some time, but I found you, and I will always be able to find you," she reminded him with a sly grin on her dirty face.

"Sure you will," Boone agreed, astonishing Beth. "I don't have to run from you anymore. I will be right here in Duck, North Carolina."

He would file a restraining order soon so that if at any time Beth harassed him, she would go to jail.

"You might want to return to California," Beth eventually responded.

"There is nothing there for me anymore."

"Your mom died, and your dad was looking for you," Beth said nonchalantly.

Boone's heart raced like a horse sprinting around a track. "What?" he asked. Had this happened since he left? "When?"

"A few years ago. Your dad contacted me several times, but I told him to go away."

"Why didn't you tell me?" Boone pleaded.

"They are no good for you."

"Maybe not but they are my parents."

"You said you never wanted to see them again."

"I know I said that, but I would have gone to my mother's funeral."

"Maybe you can go to your dad's," Beth stated vindictively. "But don't come to mine."

Boone spent the night processing this revelation along with the newfound fact about his girlfriend being a stripper with a set of skills that would make Liam Neeson jealous.

Not long after sunrise, Piper drove to the closest airport with Boone in the passenger seat.

"I have never flown," Boone disclosed nervously as they carried their bags toward the terminal.

"It is a piece of cake."

"Says the woman who has flown all over the country and beyond."

"You will do fine," Piper promised. "You have an experienced flier with you," she assured with a smile.

Piper guided Boone through the check in and boarding processes, and when the pilot announced, "Please buckle your seatbelts for takeoff," she spotted fear in Boone's eyes.

"What if I get whiplash when the airplane takes off and I become paralyzed?"

"Oh, I should have already told you that my dad mentioned this part specifically and said you will be okay. He said to just relax your head against the headrest."

The back of Boone's head didn't feel relaxed, but it definitely appeared glued to the headrest when the wheels began to roll at a much faster speed than any he ever experienced. The force pushed his whole body against the seat, and even though Piper promised he would be okay, he couldn't help but wonder. He felt the same way last night while trying to sleep. He kept imagining waking up paralyzed on the morning of surgery.

When the plane reached cruising altitude and the pilot turned off the seatbelt light, Boone's body relaxed slightly, especially when passengers began moving around. Some went to the restroom; others grabbed personal belongings from the overhead compartments; and the flight attendants walked the aisles checking on everyone.

"What did you mean last night when Beth asked if you were a secret agent or something, and you said, 'Something like that'?" Boone whispered close to Piper's ear.

Piper held eye contact with Boone and then studied her surroundings as a force of habit. "Remember after you asked if I was a stripper, and I said there was more to the story," she responded privately.

Boone licked his lips. "Kind of, but I honestly don't remember hearing much of anything you said after you confessed to being a stripper."

"Well, there is more to the story," Piper stated. "I graduated from Harvard Law School with a Juris Doctorate degree in Criminal Law."

Boone's eyes inflated like a balloon at a child's birthday party. He recognized Piper's intellect all along, but a law degree from Harvard, wow.

"My parents wanted me to practice law, but I chose to become a secret agent for a classified agency. They found the latter intriguing but risky and encouraged me to reconsider. When I told them my undergraduate minor, dance, made me the perfect candidate for an assignment posing as a stripper, they begged me to choose a different option."

Boone felt mixed emotions as the flight attendant wheeled a cart to their seats. She stopped to hand them a beverage and snack. One of the thoughts that circled Boone's mind last night after learning Piper stripped was that she seemed smarter than what he imagined from a person who took her clothes off for other people's pleasure for a living. The degrees and secret agent position confirmed her intelligence; however, it didn't change the fact that she stripped.

"I understand your parents' perspective," Boone agreed, surprising himself with the blunt response after the flight attendant moved to the next row. "Stripping for a good cause is still stripping."

Piper swallowed the lump in her throat as she processed Boone's response. "That's pretty much what my parents said, and I hear the point loud and clear, always have, and even agree."

"Then why did you do it?"

"First, I want to say that I can't take back the decision now," she reminded him. "Secondly, if you think my choice will cause you to look at me differently long term, I can't change that either."

"All I know is how I feel now, Piper."

"Yeah you have made that pretty clear."

"Why did you choose the assignment?" he asked again, looking around to ensure no one was listening. "More importantly, why did you continue stripping until age forty?"

"It all started in college," she explained. "Believe it or not, many law students strip for various reasons. Some are rebelling against their parents, others need financial assistance with tuition, and most enjoy the spending money. That's why a lot of strippers never move on to anything else; it's a lucrative position; and they realize they might earn more than with their college degree. Some choose to graduate college, and others drop out."

"Did you strip in college?" Boone asked, finding it hard to keep this conversation at a whisper.

"Yes, briefly."

"Briefly?" Feeling uncomfortable, Boone squirmed in the high-back chair.

"Some of my roommates were strippers, and early on, they convinced me to try it. So I did it for the rebellious reason I mentioned before, but I didn't like it. I didn't care for the way the men treated me or my friends, and I didn't like how exposing my body to anyone and everyone who wanted to see it felt. Guys from the college would come to watch—some invited and others who made me nauseous with their gestures and comments."

Boone wanted to ask: *If you didn't like it, why did you choose it as a career?* However, he held his tongue thinking Piper might explain.

"I recognized the mistreatment of the women and watched many fall into abusive relationships, and I felt a strong desire to help them. The same desire I detected with you. I wanted to be an advocate for them, an accountability partner for the ones who would allow it."

Boone sighed as he looked across Piper's tanned face and out the window, where he could see puffy white clouds beyond the airplane's wing.

Piper continued to explain. "While in college, I was able to help some, but once no longer part of the inner circle after I quit stripping, many claimed I didn't understand. They said the treatment came with the job," she shared. "So when I had the opportunity to accept the assignment through the agency, I realized I put myself in a vulnerable position, but I did it for two reasons. One was business, the other personal. My goal for the agency included gaining intel on people who visited the strip clubs to recruit prostitutes and, even worse, human trafficking victims. My personal goal was to help abused women, and the agency allowed me to use the money I made at the club to fund that endeavor. Over the years, I witnessed women's lives change. Many got out of abusive relationships, and others got out of the industry."

Boone placed his hand on Piper's leg. Other than their kiss last night, this marked the first time he touched her romantically since discovering her past.

"It sounds like your heart was in it for the right reasons," Boone acknowledged. However, he still didn't know if he could move forward in a relationship with someone who stripped and, more importantly, who led him through a lie of omission for months. "I wish you had told me."

"Boone, the secrets are one of the reasons I retired as an agent. The lifestyle is challenging. There are things I can never tell anyone. We learn that keeping secrets is often the difference between life and death, so we master the art," she explained. "In this case, there is a difference between a secret and a lie, but I don't expect you to understand or accept that."

"I get your point, but either way, you are still hiding details that are important to a relationship."

"I thought I could move to Duck and put my past behind me. That's what I planned and what I still hope to do. I longed for a real relationship where the person looking into my eyes every night wouldn't think of me as a stripper or a secret agent but as the person they loved."

Eventually the pilot turned on the seatbelt lights again and engaged the landing gear. Boone's and Piper's conversation drifted through their thoughts as they prepared for a short layover before the final flight.

Once on the ground in Rochester, a car picked them up at the airport as promised and took them to the hospital, where a patient ambassador ushered them to a small office on the third floor of a large building lined with glass windows. There, Boone filled out paperwork with a trembling hand.

Sensing his discomfort, Piper sat close, placed her hands on Boone's back, and helped him through the forms as much as possible. A moment later a knock came at the door, then it opened.

"Dad," Piper exhaled when her father entered the small room. She rose quickly from the padded chair and hugged him. Even though they didn't see eye to eye, she still loved and missed her father.

"Hey, sweetie," he greeted, kissing the top of her head during the lengthy embrace.

Boone noticed how Dr. Luck's eyes closed as he hugged his daughter. He thought he saw a tear run down the man's cheek and disappear beneath his chin, but he wasn't certain. Nervous Boone set down the pen, and when Piper's dad opened his eyes, he smiled warmly in Boone's direction.

"You must be Boone," he considered. "I am Warren Luck."

Boone shook his head and then the hand of the man who would perform surgery on him in less than an hour. "Yes, sir."

"It is a pleasure to meet you," Warren greeted and then returned his attention to Piper. "I have a surprise for you," he announced.

Piper waited, and then the door, still partially open, moved.

"Mom," Piper exclaimed, and another round of hugs began.

Boone was surprised at how tightly Piper's mom held him, but he appreciated the compassion. "Son, you are in good hands," she guaranteed, placing her palm on his chest while speaking.

Boone endured the stress of meeting Piper's parents and the anxiety of the looming surgery all at once, and he also sensed the comfort of being welcomed along with their daughter. If he didn't know better, he would never guess any animosity existed. They seemed sincere and loving.

"Mom, you never come to the hospital," Piper proclaimed.

"I wanted to be here for you and Boone," she explained. "If it's okay, I will sit with you in the waiting room, or we can get dinner in the cafeteria, whatever you want."

"Thank you so much, Mom." Piper appreciated her parents welcoming Boone so kindly, and some of the tears she released fell because she didn't know if she and Boone would be together after this trip. She felt close to him in some ways, but there also seemed to be a vast distance between them.

Things began to move fast. Once Boone signed the last document, Dr. Luck, although he had yet to claim the distinguished title, led them to an examining room. Upon entering, Boone immediately noticed images of his neck on the wall-mounted screens. Everyone sat, and Dr. Luck explained the issue in layman's terms, pointing out each area of concern and explaining how he planned to resolve the issue.

"I will make a small incision at the front of your neck in the throat area, probably right here where this crease is so that it won't even be noticeable once healed. We will have to move some things around in your throat to access your neck. You will have a breathing tube inserted during the procedure which will leave your throat scratchy when you wake up. So, do not let that alarm you."

Dr. Luck explained the delicate nature of the surgery and briefly mentioned the risks although he encouraged Boone not to focus on anything associated with a small percentage. "You have the best team in the United States handling this surgery," he mentioned proudly.

"Daddy, how long is recovery?"

Dr. Luck walked through the recovery steps pointing out that Boone would be in the hospital for several days, leave wearing a neck brace, and should be back to most normal activities in three to six months.

"Do you have any questions, Boone?" Dr. Luck asked.

"Are there long-term side effects?"

"The only noticeable change will be a limitation in range of motion, but I expect it to be minimal in your case. The pain should subside, and you will soon be able to walk, jog, drive, and do most of the things typical human beings your age do," he projected.

When the medical talk concluded, Mrs. Luck spoke for the first time since entering the exam room. "Boone, may I pray for you?" she inquired.

"Of course," Boone allowed.

The woman he met today spoke a short, powerful prayer while holding a hand on his back. All the while Piper's fingers were intertwined with Boone's.

Dr. Luck headed to prepare for the surgery, and a care team member took Boone to preop, which would have ordinarily been done in advance. However, the tight window and Piper's father's status changed things. Thankfully Piper got to be by Boone's side pretty much all the way to the operating room. She even stood next to him as the anesthesiologist administered anesthesia that would keep Boone asleep during the surgery and block his brain from responding to reflexes or pain signals.

Piper held his hand tightly as the medicine passed through the

IV. "Boone, I will be here when you wake up," she promised, trying to keep herself together, but she could feel her face contorting the way it did when she was about to cry.

"I love you, Piper Luck," Boone announced.

Piper smiled widely as tears fell from her eyes. She wanted to hear those three words—needed to hear them. She prayed they came before the laughing gas took effect, but it didn't matter because she knew Boone loved her.

"I love you too, Boone Winters."

Soon after, the best part of the surgery process happened when Boone began to say silly stuff.

"Will I be naked during surgery?"

"Don't worry," the anesthesiologist answered. "We will all be naked; it's a naked party."

Boone's eyes bulged. "I've never been to one of those."

Piper laughed. "You won't even know you are there."

"Most people at naked parties probably don't know they are there," Boone claimed.

The anesthesiologist snickered. "Very true. Don't worry, we will keep you covered, and I don't want to see any of the people I work with naked."

"I want to see Piper naked," Boone said smiling.

Piper giggled.

"Maybe you will," the anesthesiologist responded.

"I don't want to see you naked," Boone declared.

"I don't blame you, my friend."

"Will there be any frogs in there?" Boone asked.

"We usually don't allow animals in the operating room."

Piper appreciated the anesthesiologist's humor and wished she had videoed this conversation for Boone to watch after surgery.

"One time I flew on a dragon," Boone claimed, staring into Piper's eyes with amazement.

"I bet that was a fun adventure," she responded.

"It's better than sex," he declared.

Boone's improv comedy routine ended when his eyes grew heavy and eventually shut for the last time before being wheeled into the operation room.

28

Piper's mom sat with her in the surgery waiting area as the clock on the wall ticked slowly. Everyone in the room seemed nervous while holding out for an update about loved ones. Even though Piper knew going to the cafeteria or out for dinner at a nearby restaurant—her dad said there would be time for either—would seemingly make the clock hands circle faster, she chose to stay in the closest spot to Boone available. She would be in the operating room if her dad allowed it. Nonetheless, she wanted to be within sight of the door her dad would walk through once he finished the procedure, or heaven forbid, if anything went wrong.

"Tell me about Boone," Piper's mom requested once they settled in.

Piper told her about the man she met and grew to love in Duck, North Carolina. She shared how he was initially shy and still quiet, but he eventually came out of his shell. She talked about his sweet personality, quirks, hard-working nature, and construction skills. Although she told her mom that he grew up in California and lived there until recently, she left out the part about him being abused. She didn't think Boone would want her to share that with her parents, at least not this soon. He opened up to his therapist and the church men's group. It shocked her when Boone came to her house after one of their meetings and told her he shared his past with his new friends.

"Mom, Boone knows about my past," she revealed, quietly telling her how he found out.

"This all occurred yesterday?" her mom whispered.

Piper nodded her head up and down. "Yes. I am not sure if he will forgive me."

"Why wouldn't he?"

"The same reason you and Dad haven't forgiven me," she proclaimed. "But I hope you will now that I left that lifestyle behind me," she requested.

"Honey, we love you for who you are. We didn't support your decision, but that didn't mean we held it against you. Have you been pulling away from us all this time because you wanted us to forgive you?"

Tears streamed down Piper's cheeks. "Yes."

"I'm so sorry," she uttered, stretching her arms around her daughter. "We never verbalized forgiveness because we never held your choice against you regardless of whether or not we liked it. There was nothing for us to forgive."

"I thought you saw me as a sinner in need of forgiveness, and I felt like I had to quit to get that from you."

"That's between you and God," Piper's mom declared. "It's not my position to say whether your actions were wrong. There is a lot of gray area, but we understood the greater good you aspired to accomplish."

"You did?"

"We tried to tell you that."

Piper played a reel in her mind of all the conversations, especially from the early years, ultimately leading to avoiding the topic altogether and long spans without seeing each other. "I guess all I heard was that you didn't want your daughter to be a stripper."

"I can't imagine any parent in their right mind wanting their child to be a stripper. We feared what you would go through mentally, emotionally, physically, and beyond. We knew it would be difficult for you to create a steady relationship with a true gentleman, get married, and have children. You used to talk about how much you wanted that, and it pained us when you told us the way men treated you and that you couldn't keep a relationship with a man of solid character. Even though you didn't always come out and say why they didn't stick around, we knew. We simply wanted the best for you and still do."

"Thank you, Mom."

The door that led from surgery opened, and out of the corner of Piper's eye, she spotted a man in a lab coat. When she turned to look at him, she realized it wasn't her dad.

"I am proud of the woman you have become," Piper's mom commented.

"You are?"

"Of course. For example, look at what you have done for Boone. By calling your dad on Boone's behalf, you put this forgiveness quest aside for his well-being. You even came here with him, not knowing if your relationship will continue after this surgery. Those are examples of outstanding character in the face of a storm."

"I hope he forgives me," Piper cried.

"I pray so too, sweet girl," she reasoned. "I sure forgive you if you feel like you need it although I still don't," she reminded Piper. "I love you, and your dad feels the same way."

"Are you certain?"

"He will be delighted to know we talked about this and broke down the wall that stood between us for so many years."

"You have no idea how much relief that brings me."

"Your dad brags on you all the time."

"He does?"

"Yes. He doesn't tell his friends about your specific assignments, but he talks about you defending women and helping reduce human trafficking. His favorites are the stories about you jumping out of helicopters, off trains, and all the moments that scare a mother half to death."

Piper smiled. "I am glad to know that."

"I think they scared him too, but talking about it seems to be his therapy," Piper's mom laughed.

The surgery door opened and closed a few more times, but on each occasion, a person Piper didn't recognize emerged to talk to people in the waiting area whose faces became familiar. She should have known that she and her mother would be the last two people in this room. The only way her dad fit the surgery in so soon was because he scheduled it after his final regularly scheduled procedure.

Although Piper's stomach growled she knew she couldn't eat until she heard the outcome of Boone's surgery. Her mother snacked on a granola bar and peanuts from her purse but, otherwise, waited to eat dinner.

When the door opened this time, the empty waiting area reminded Piper who would walk out. She studied her father's face and mannerisms as he stepped toward them. However, he did this so often that his look remained neutral. She wanted to stand and meet him halfway but couldn't muster the energy to move. When he reached her chair, he knelt on one knee, took both of her hands in his, and looked into the caramel brown eyes he fell in love with the day of her birth.

29

"Boone's surgery went as well as could be expected," Piper's dad revealed. "He is on the way to recovery now, and you will be able to see him shortly."

Piper hugged her dad, and then her mom hugged her.

"So there were no surprises or complications?" Piper questioned. "Future concerns?" she added.

"Absolutely nothing. When I got in there, everything looked exactly as anticipated, and I followed procedure."

"So we can remove the word 'paralyzed' from our vocabulary?" Piper asked. Although she neglected to speak her thoughts while in the waiting room, she feared something would go wrong leaving Boone confined to a wheelchair for the remainder of his life.

Noticing the concern written on his daughter's face, Piper's dad smiled cautiously. "Yes, you may. Boone now has hardware— a plate and screws—holding everything together nicely," he reported. "He will need ample time to recover from the invasiveness of the surgery itself. The entire area needs to heal. While he is at the hospital, we will watch for infection and ensure he receives plenty of fluids and proper nutrition."

"Thank you so much, Daddy," Piper replied, hugging her dad's neck again.

"It was my pleasure, darling," he offered. "Once Boone is discharged, if you two are staying with us, I will check on him daily, before and after my appointments and procedures."

"Having you keep an eye on him will be a major relief."

Piper's mom touched Piper's arm. "I will be there to help with anything you all need."

"Thank you, Mom."

"Have you two eaten dinner?" Piper's dad asked.

"Not yet, I didn't have an appetite," Piper confessed.

"Why don't you visit the cafeteria and grab something, and by the time you get back, Boone should be in a room and ready for visitors."

"What do you think?" Piper's mom asked.

"I believe I can eat now."

The hallways seemed relatively calm as Piper and her mother followed signs to the cafeteria. A man with a mop and bucket cleaned the floor methodically. Members of the hospital staff walked with a purpose in various directions. A woman and a young child stared out the large glass window lining one side of the hallway looking into a courtyard filled with grass, trees, picnic tables, and walkways.

"Would you and Boone like separate rooms at the house or do you prefer to be with him?" Piper's mom asked. "I washed the bedding in your old room and the guest bedroom in case you each want your own space."

Piper imagined that her mom would want them in separate rooms under normal circumstances since they weren't married. Prepping two rooms might hint at that direction, or she may have simply planned for either option.

"I would like to be with him, please, if he is okay with that." Two days ago she would have known the answer.

"That is fine. Are you planning to come home tonight?"

"I think I will stay here with Boone if he will let me."

"Do you need me to bring you all anything from home—a pillow, fresh clothes?" she asked. "Where is your luggage?"

"I think we have everything we need. The patient ambassador took our luggage and said it would be stored in a secure place until Boone received a room assignment. It will be brought there."

"I hope that person follows through."

"He seemed to be on top of things."

In the cafeteria Piper and her mom perused the options.

"I think I will have a salad," Piper's mom decided.

"I might have the same," Piper replied after meandering through the area longer than necessary. Nothing beneath the glass cases looked appetizing at the moment, especially greasy food. "Do you think I should get Boone something, like applesauce or pudding?"

"Your dad may start him on a liquid diet. Either way the nurses will let you all know, and he can order what is available under his nutrition plan from the room."

"That makes sense."

After picking out a salad, Piper wandered to the beverage center. "I probably need one of those energy drinks," she teased.

"Those things are terrible for your health."

"I know, I don't drink them." She grabbed a juice and her mother reached for a bottled water.

"I will take care of our meals," Piper's mom offered at the register. "When did you move to Duck?" she asked as they walked out with full hands.

Piper felt terrible for not previously informing her parents about the move. However, she wanted to prove to herself she could leave her old life behind before telling them she retired.

"On my birthday."

"We talked on your birthday," her mom exclaimed.

"I know, I was driving up I-95."

"You should have told me."

Piper shared her earlier thoughts and added, "You and Dad should visit sometime."

"Do you mean that or are you just being nice?"

Piper couldn't remember the last time her parents visited. "I am serious. I want to spend more time with you and Dad."

"Maybe I can get your father to take some vacation time. He probably has months-worth saved."

"I will convince him," Piper offered with a grin.

Piper's mom's eyes lit up. "That may work better."

"My new house could fit inside yours a few times," Piper joked.

"I bet it's perfect."

"I love it," Piper professed. "You should see the house Boone is building on the ocean."

"I would like to," she replied. "A beachfront home, huh? He must have a lucrative career."

"Oh, the house isn't for him, he is the contractor."

"That is a reputable profession."

Piper didn't take the time to explain Boone wasn't licensed yet.

"Do you two live together?" her mom asked as they passed by a group of young giggling nurses.

"We spend a lot of time with each other but don't technically live together." Piper chose not to explain that situation either.

"I really hope things work out for the two of you if it is God's will."

"At this point I have to trust Him."

"Piper, I don't think it is by accident that you and Boone are exactly where you are right now. Focus on caring for Boone like you would have if all this happened two days ago and let God handle the rest."

Piper grinned, but her smile didn't light up her face as much as normal because of her weary eyes. "That is solid motherly advice."

Piper's phone rang. "It's Dad," she announced, answering the call before her mother could respond.

He gave her the room number and directions, and then Piper and her mother sped up and followed the signs. They beat Boone to the room but not her dad.

"Where is Boone?" Piper asked, feeling anxious upon noticing the empty spot where the bed belonged. "Is he okay?" She glanced around the room as if searching for him hiding in a corner somewhere.

"Yes, sweetheart, he is fine," her dad promised. "He is being wheeled over now."

A few moments later someone rolled the bed transporting Boone through the opened door. He and Piper immediately locked eyes, and she smiled while pushing back tears. He wore a full neck brace that reminded her of one of those cone-shaped dog collars, and along with looking stiff, he appeared exhausted.

"Good evening, Dr. Luck," a nurse who walked in behind the bed greeted, and then she looked at Boone while studying his chart. "You must be a special patient if my favorite surgeon is waiting in the room for you. It usually happens the other way around."

Boone smirked like a child, and Piper could tell the anesthesia hadn't completely worn off.

"Annette, this is my wife Claire," Dr. Luck introduced, "and my daughter Piper."

"Nice to meet you both," she responded with a warm smile and a gentle wave. "Is my patient your son-in-law?"

Dr. Luck held his hands up in surrender. "That is up to these two," he replied promptly, laughing while pointing one finger at his daughter and the other at Boone.

"I might marry her," Boone announced, his voice sounding grizzly.

"That better not be the laughing gas talking," Annette chimed. "You best have a ring to put on Ms. Luck's finger if you're going to make a bold statement like that," she suggested glancing at Piper's ring finger.

"Do you have one?" Boone asked.

Everyone laughed.

"Honey, the only one I have is from my hubby," she claimed holding up her finger. "And I ain't sharing. You have to get your own."

The comment initiated another round of laughter, and Piper thanked God that she didn't have to give herself a title: friend, girlfriend, ex.

Once the staff settled Boone in and hooked up all the equipment, Piper found her way to his bedside. She reached for Boone's hand and gently kissed his forehead. "Hey, handsome."

"Hello, beautiful."

"You are looking good," Dr. Luck announced from the foot of the bed.

"Thank you."

"How do you feel?" Piper's mom asked, sitting in the chair she found upon entering the room trying to stay out of the way.

"Hungry."

Annette showed Boone and Piper the menu and explained what he could order.

"I want pizza."

"Boy, you can't be having pizza yet," Annette replied.

Once Boone figured out what he wanted from the approved list, Piper ordered for him.

Dr. Luck discussed Boone's pain level and casually reviewed the dos and don'ts. Boone needed to lie and sleep on his back for a while to keep pressure off his neck. Someone from physical therapy would come in later and help him walk a short distance in the hallway which surprised Piper; she thought he would be confined to a bed without movement for a few days.

"I wish I could relax and talk with all my patients like this," Dr. Luck stated.

"Thanks for doing my surgery," Boone mentioned.

"My pleasure, you were a good patient."

Piper eventually sat in the chair nearest Boone's bedside, and she and her mom nibbled on their salads as everyone conversed.

"All this food and talk about food has me hungry," Dr. Luck announced, "which reminds me I didn't eat lunch today." He picked up his phone and called in an order which arrived relatively quickly along with Boone's.

Once everyone finished eating, they chatted a bit longer. Mr. and Mrs. Luck then stepped out of the room to give Boone and Piper some privacy.

"Do you have everything you need?" Piper asked.

"I think so," Boone answered.

"May I stay in the hospital with you tonight?" It felt so awkward to have to ask that question.

Boone studied her eyes. "Yes, please."

Piper stuck close by Boone's bedside all night. The patient ambassador brought their bags relatively early in the evening, and Piper changed into more comfortable clothes and brushed her teeth. Her mother brought pillows from the house for her and Boone even though Piper insisted it wasn't necessary. Annette helped Boone position himself, and although the new pillow seemed comfortable, he was uncomfortable most of the time. Lying on his back and trying to keep his neck secure proved difficult.

Once the required pain medication wore off, Boone refused additional narcotics and only took prescription non-steroidal anti-inflammatory drugs for the discomfort and swelling. Piper quickly picked up on his mindset. His parents' addiction to drugs scared him tremendously, so much that he would rather deal with pain.

Boone barely slept, and neither did Piper. She did everything she could for him. They talked; she read her book aloud to occupy his mind; and she fed him gelatin and applesauce.

Things improved slowly over the next few days, but Boone experienced consistent ups and downs. He walked the hallways adding more steps each trip with the physical therapist, but his balance seemed off especially at first. Dr. Luck explained this as normal and assured everything was progressing nicely.

Having Piper's dad in and out of the room frequently and available via text at other times, primarily when random questions arose, provided comfort. However, the nurses on the floor took immaculate care of Boone, especially Annette. Her sense of humor helped keep the mood light even in tense situations.

Piper helped Boone manage the construction project from afar as he healed. She talked to the subcontractors, checked on and ordered materials, and kept in touch with Preston, who promised to stop by the site daily to look in on things. The man turned out to be a Godsend, walking through every step of the project with them. He sent pictures of the roof as it went on and had also disassembled the tent the day Piper and Boone flew to Minnesota.

The men from Boone's church group checked on him daily via texts and calls. Kelly and a couple of ladies from the church made a schedule to feed and love on Bailey, water Piper's plants, and take care of a few other loose ends she didn't have time to consider before abruptly leaving Duck.

Piper's parents tried to talk Piper into coming home for a good night's sleep, and Boone encouraged it too; however, she wouldn't leave his side other than for short trips to the cafeteria and gift shop and to stretch her legs now and then. She discovered books on the gift shop's shelves by a new author whose writing style she really liked, and she already finished two.

Boone told her she should become an audiobook narrator because of her lovely voice. Piper did a fantastic job creating a unique accent for each character, and he came to cherish the moments when she read. Sometimes her smooth tone helped him drift off to sleep if only for an hour or two.

By the time Annette wheeled Boone to Piper's mom's SUV after the hospital discharged him, he became uncomfortably comfortable in the neck brace. He stressed about being at Piper's parents' house for an undetermined amount of time although they welcomed him with open arms. Mrs. Luck even picked up pizza for him on the way home.

Boone quickly figured out Mrs. Luck was one of those people who loved hosting others. She constantly asked if he needed food, water, blankets, and a hundred other things he would have never thought about. She smiled a lot, and the resemblance between her and Piper became quite noticeable although she was lighter skinned. She was indeed a beautiful woman inside and out.

Dr. Luck wasn't home much, but when he was, he checked on Boone frequently. His bedside manner proved impeccable.

"Piper, I really like your parents," Boone reported after the newness wore off and he realized their genuine kindness.

"You know, I do too," Piper replied. "I have always loved them, but something is different on this trip. As hard as it is for me to admit this, I believe my perspective has been off all these years. I think I was judging myself through their eyes, and that wasn't wise or healthy."

When Piper wasn't in the room with Boone, she spent most of her time talking to her mother. They grew closer, and she knew she would miss her when she and Boone headed back to Duck.

"I am glad you two have been able to talk so much," Boone noted.

"Me too. I feel like I have my mom back."

"Every woman deserves her mom in her life."

"Every man does too," Piper said carefully. "I know you chose not to have a relationship with your mom, but I want you to know you still deserved a loving mother. I know you loved her, and I am so sorry she passed away."

Boone hadn't wanted to talk about his mom the night he found out about her death. Since the surgery, Piper made a few comments, but Boone previously brushed away the topic.

"Thanks. When my mom wasn't drunk or high, she was actually a decent mother."

"That counts for something."

"I guess. I wonder how my dad is doing," Boone mentioned and paused to let the thoughts in his mind settle like fresh snowflakes. "I wish I could have been at the funeral for him."

The 'for him' part of the comment surprised Piper in a good way. "I know funerals are to celebrate a person's life, but more so, I believe they are to support the family and friends who live on after the death of their loved one. It's honorable that you wanted to be there for your dad."

"I always thought I would celebrate my mom's death," Boone admitted. "My dad's too," he added. "However, they are the only family I have."

Piper touched Boone's arm. "You have me too, Boone. I know I am not your family, but I love and care about you as if you were."

"I know you do, Piper, and I appreciate you being by my side every step of the way through my neck surgery and recovery. Your parents too. They didn't even know me, yet they treated me like their own. I wish I had parents like yours."

Piper grimaced intentionally. "Don't forget that just last week I had strong feelings against my parents," she reminded him. "Maybe you should reach out to your dad and give him a second chance as an adult."

"I am not sure that is a good idea."

"He came looking for you for a reason. Maybe he wants to make things right."

"Some things can't be made right," Boone declared.

Piper let his response sink in. "My choice of words might have been poor," she admitted. "I guess I am saying that calling or seeing him might be worthwhile."

"I will think about it."

30

A couple nights later Piper went out for dinner at Victoria's, an Italian restaurant in downtown, with Leslie, her high school friend with whom she made amends. While she was away, Dr. Luck checked in on Boone, and they talked for nearly an hour.

"Piper told me about your mom," Dr. Luck mentioned. "I am sorry for your loss."

"Thank you," Boone replied, and before he realized it, he shared his life story with a man he barely knew but who made him feel more comfortable than any man other than Claude James.

Dr. Luck asked question after question with compassion and responded with love and grace. It surprised Boone when he shed tears in front of Piper's father.

"Son, anytime you need someone to talk to, you reach out to me. That offer stands regardless of what happens between you and my daughter."

Boone let the words sink in, and he sensed that Dr. Luck meant precisely what he said which carried more weight than he could explain.

A few nights later, Boone had a similar conversation with Piper's mother while Piper picked up pasta for dinner for them from The Redwood Room.

"If you ever need a mother's love or opinion, just let me know."

"Thank you. I appreciate all you have done for me."

"Having you here has been a privilege. I have come to learn why my daughter cares for you so deeply. Maybe one day we will be lucky enough to have you as part of our family although, in a way, I feel like you already are."

Piper's father came in at the tail end of the conversation. "I agree," he added.

"How did you two forgive Piper for being a stripper?" Boone asked bluntly even though calling her by that title in front of her parents felt awkward.

Piper's dad spoke first. "I don't know that we ever had to forgive Piper. We simply needed to accept her choice and let her and God handle the rest."

"Even though we didn't like the idea of our daughter dancing in a strip club, we knew her intentions were good," Piper's mom added.

Boone wondered if they knew she stripped in college for a short time, but he didn't dare bring it up. "The thought of so many people seeing her like that has been a hard pill for me to swallow."

"As a man who believes that the visual and physical pleasures of a woman's body should be solely for her husband, and vice versa, I understand your perspective," Piper's dad shared. "I think the main thing for you to remember is that this is now a thing of the past; it's not something you have to try to talk her out of in the present nor deal with regularly."

"I guess I fear Piper will decide to go back to that lifestyle, and I know I couldn't be with someone who exposes her body to other men regardless of the reasons."

"Piper may have made some choices we disagree with, but she has always been honest and transparent," her mother confirmed.

"If Piper tells you she has put that part of her life behind her, you can trust her at her word," Piper's dad verified.

"Thanks," Boone offered. "That helps me make one of the most important and difficult decisions I have ever made."

Boone came to Rochester uncertain where he and Piper would end up. Even so, they spent nearly every waking and sleeping hour together. He now believed this trial in their life—his neck and her past—brought them closer in a way he couldn't fully explain.

In some ways the trip to Minnesota seemed like it went on forever, especially during the times when Boone experienced physical pain, but the emotional support he received far outweighed his greatest expectation.

When Piper and Boone returned to Duck, they had the conversation each of them anticipated. However, it was much more cut and dry than either expected.

"I want to be with you for who you are now regardless of your past," Boone stated. "I love you, Piper Luck, and I wouldn't change a single thing about you."

"I love you too, Boone Winters, and I am all yours," Piper promised.

Boone began staying at Piper's house every night. He needed to be in a bed with solid support, and the sleeping bag in the tent wouldn't cut it.

When they went to the construction site on day one, the progress shocked them. Having the roof on the house made a world of difference. The next projects on the list included installing insulation and hanging drywall. Boone planned to help with both but knew the restrictions Dr. Luck strongly advised would keep him from lending a hand with the physical labor.

It pleased Boone and Piper to find out Beth and Derek left town after being released from the county jail with a pending trial. Boone and Piper agreed that they would rather never see either of them again, so they met with a lawyer and arranged to drop all charges under the condition that a restraining order against Beth and Derek be put in place and strictly enforced.

Members of the church brought food for weeks, and Boone's men's group prayed over him and celebrated the successful surgery. It would be months before Boone and Piper could return to their usual adventures, but the new ones they discovered relieved Boone.

Piper kept reading to him; they also watched movies and spent a lot of time in the hot tub on the patio—a surprise housewarming gift from Piper's parents. The note with the delivery read: "Relax as long as you need to, Piper and Boone. You deserve it!"

Piper jumped right back into volunteering at the dance studio. On the first day back, it warmed her heart when Kelly handed her a large envelope filled with handmade cards the dancers created for her and Boone. The drawings, many dance related, were so adorable. After she and Boone read every note and smiled at the sight of the artwork, they proudly hung them on the fridge.

The construction project continued, and although Boone hated that he could barely help physically, he enjoyed overseeing the crews and focusing on details he might have otherwise overlooked. He continued learning the material for his contractor's license. When the building project was three-fourths complete, Preston read him a note from Claude James: "Boone, I am so proud of you. I knew you would make it, and I also imagine you are trying to figure out what you will do once this project is completed. If you are interested, I would love for you to become a licensed general contractor. I have set aside money to pay for the licensing exam and for you to start a business if you choose."

Tears flooded Boone's eyes. Claude had done so much to set him up for success, and he couldn't imagine how he would pay it forward with such impact but would certainly try his best. He immediately added this goal to his journey list, and he couldn't help but think of how much this course changed Claude's life and eventually his and Piper's.

Another bonus arrived around the same time, and in October Boone and Piper used the money to fly to California to find his dad. It shocked Boone how much faster he could cross the country in an airplane than by hitchhiking, bus, and train. However, looking back Boone wouldn't have flown to Duck if he could have. The first trip turned out just as it should have, and he prayed the same would be true for this one.

When the plane landed, Boone took Piper to the location of his childhood home. They stood at the edge of the road near where the mailbox once stood as Boone looked on in disbelief.

"This is where the house used to be," Boone shared as he studied the empty lot as though the house might reappear.

"I wonder when it was torn down."

"I don't know, but I am glad someone leveled it." Visiting this place had made Boone's journey list as one of the top fears he needed to face. So many bad memories happened in that house. It being gone was probably good because he might have doused it with gasoline, tossed a match, and watched it burn like the pictures and letters. "Thanks, God," Boone whispered appreciatively.

Realizing what Boone meant, Piper smiled and reached her arm around his shoulder as he stood with his arms crossed holding his chin.

For the next thirty minutes, the two of them sat on the hood of the rental car as Boone orally painted a picture of the house and neighborhood he remembered. Nearly everything looked different now. Most of the homes had been demolished or redone and were unrecognizable.

Piper allowed Boone all the time he needed and wiped a few tears from his cheeks as the sun drifted across the sky.

"Ready for the next stop?" Boone eventually asked.

In preparation, he jotted down a list of places they might find his dad because the online search revealed nothing.

The next location Boone and Piper visited was a grocery store where his dad used to work. Boone didn't recognize a single person there, and the manager told them no one by Boone's father's name worked there during his tenure.

Boone wondered if his dad even worked anymore, and that thought led them to a dingy bar his father frequented for as long as he could recall, which he decided probably should have been the first stop. When Boone and Piper walked in, the smell of alcohol slapped them in the face. The dim lights made the place uninviting, and the dated furniture looked like he remembered. The only difference was that the smell of cigarette smoke seemed to have mostly faded after twenty-plus years.

Boone walked up to the bar but didn't sit on one of the stools. Piper stood next to him and, by nature, scouted the place like a hawk. As usual in an environment like this, the middle of the day only brought out the town drunks and a handful of others stopping by for a beer because they had nothing better to do or were avoiding somewhere they should be instead.

"I am looking for Doug Winters," Boone notified the bartender.

"I haven't seen Doug in a long time," the man cleaning a tall glass mug replied, seemingly avoiding eye contact.

It didn't surprise Boone that the bartender immediately knew his dad by name, and it also felt weird to say his father's name again. He couldn't remember the last time he spoke it before today.

"Do you have any idea where we might find him?" Piper asked.

"I wish I could help, but I don't know."

Piper didn't get the feeling the guy was covering for Boone's dad in the presence of strangers who might have motives in which he didn't want to be involved. From her experience she knew people who walked into a bar asking for someone by name were usually investigators searching for a suspect or criminals looking for revenge.

"Thank you," Boone replied, and when they turned to walk away, a man sitting a few stools down spoke up.

"Why don't you leave the lady here while you look for Doug," he remarked loudly and disrespectfully, drawing a cackle from the men sitting nearby. "I'll make sure she's smiling when you come back," he snickered.

"Frank," the bartender grumbled in the man's direction.

Piper took two steps toward the guy and jammed her fingers into her favorite pressure point. As expected, he crumbled instantly like a flaky cookie. "If he leaves me here, I will be smiling when he returns, but you won't," she guaranteed in an ordinary yet direct tone. "In fact, you will be in an ambulance on the way to the hospital and so will any of your buddies who dare to say something as stupid as what you did."

The two guys sitting next to him shook their heads east to west and, in unison, turned their attention back to the televisions that previously occupied them. The bartender looked on laughing as he put away a mug.

On the way out, Boone smirked and said, "I think I can get used to this Piper."

"Thanks. Now that you know my true identity, I feel free to be both the girly girl dancer I grew up as and the tough woman I became."

Boone pushed open the door. "Would you like a glass of wine before we leave?" he asked grinning. "The way the bartender chuckled at what you did and said to that man, I think it might be on the house."

"I don't think wine is served in this joint," Piper surmised, and the door closed behind them.

The fourth place they arrived at didn't serve wine either. Boone remembered coming to the local soup kitchen, run by a group of churches, as a child for meals. Memories flooded his mind when he walked in with Piper. Similar to the bar, this place hadn't changed a bit. Boone figured all the money brought in went to feeding the homeless rather than upgrading. His parents weren't homeless; they would just rather spend their money on drugs and alcohol than feed their family.

Nearly every table was filled, and a healthy line formed at the buffet. Out of all the people, Paul Jackson's large frame, jubilant facial features, and unmistakable voice stood out like a sore thumb. Paul ran the place, and Boone was happy to see him.

"Mr. Jackson, I am looking for Doug Winters." It still felt weird saying the name. "I was wondering if he comes here anymore."

"As a matter of fact, he is a regular these days," Mr. Jackson responded. "Is everything okay?" he asked with concern while studying Boone's and Piper's faces.

"Yes, at least I hope so," Boone replied.

"Wait a minute," Mr. Jackson noted, taking a step back while examining Boone closely. "I recognize you."

"You do?"

Boone probably hadn't seen this man in thirty years, and he knew he looked a lot different since his youth. However, Mr. Jackson didn't, other than having more gray hair and additional pounds.

"Young man, I have never forgotten your eyes. You are Boone Winters," he concluded. "I have prayed for you every day since I first met you as a wee little lad."

Boone furrowed his brow. "You have?"

"I pray for every person who comes in here, specifically for the children. There was something different about you," he mentioned. "I knew you would overcome the lifestyle you grew up in."

"How do you know how I grew up?"

"People talk, especially people here. They are reaching out for help; that's why they come."

"I think we came for the free food," Boone snickered.

"Of course, but that's not the main reason we have a soup kitchen."

"Why else would you have a soup kitchen?"

"So we can love on people."

Boone wondered if he remembered this man so vividly because he had been loved on by him throughout his childhood; he never thought of it that way. "How do you know I overcame that lifestyle?"

"I don't, I just knew you would, or you will."

"I am not sure your love worked for my parents although I appreciate you trying," Boone remarked.

"Love works for everyone," the man replied confidently.

"If my dad still comes here, it doesn't sound like it worked for him. He didn't buy his family food. We came here so he could spend the money he made at the grocery store on drugs and alcohol. I guess you didn't know that."

"People talk, Boone," he mentioned again. "Your dad doesn't come here to be loved on anymore."

"Wait, I thought you said he still comes here."

"He does, and although his purpose has changed, I can promise you he is still loved on," Paul shared. "We all are, including myself."

"What do you mean?"

"Your daddy comes here to love on other people."

Boone's eyes instantly welled with tears that his eyelids held momentarily. "What do you mean?" he asked again sniffling.

"Your daddy cooks for all these people now," Paul Jackson shared.

"He does?"

Piper smiled and felt tears forming around her own eyes.

"Has been ever since your mother passed away." He paused. "You do know your mother passed, don't you?" he asked as though he regretted mentioning it so abruptly.

"Yes."

"I didn't see you at the funeral, and last I heard, your father hadn't found you, so I wasn't sure."

"You went to the funeral?"

"I officiated the funeral."

"You are a preacher?"

"Fifty years."

"You never preached to us when we came for food."

"Sure I did. We all did. We loved on you. It usually works better than standing in a pulpit with a microphone."

Piper doubted the man needed a microphone when he preached. He already worked up a sweat during this conversation.

"Was my mom's funeral at your church?"

"It's not my church; it's God's church; and it's for the people, all people—red, yellow, black, and white, they are all precious in his sight," he said, quoting the well-known children's song. "But yes, the service was at our church, and that was the first time your daddy ever stepped in a church building."

"He told you that, huh?"

"Yes, sir. He's told me a lot of things."

"How did you talk him into having the funeral there?"

"I didn't. The day your mother died, he came here looking for me. He said he lost the two people who meant the world to him, and that left him with only two choices."

Boone waited for Paul to elaborate, but instead, the man wiped his forehead with a stained white cloth. "What choices?" Boone asked.

"Either kill himself or devote his life to this God he wasn't sure existed."

Boone didn't say anything.

"Your dad has been all hands on deck ever since. He is a new man."

Piper grinned from ear to ear. "Do you know when he will be here again?" she asked.

"Young lady, I am so sorry, I didn't introduce myself or even say hello to you yet. I got so caught up in the excitement of seeing my friend Boone Winters that I lost my manners," he apologized. "I am Paul Jackson," he announced, reaching out his hand.

"Piper Luck," she responded. "It is a pleasure to meet you."

Paul looked Boone in the eyes. "You found yourself a very lovely woman," he complimented reverently. "Men who don't overcome the past you grew up in rarely find a lady like this who will stand by their side with patience and pride," he articulated, holding his finger to his lips. "I think I was right about you."

Piper found herself hoping the man from the bar would wander in here in search of how to treat a woman properly. "Thank you," she said to Paul. "It is an honor to meet someone from Boone's past who made a positive impression in his life. I assure you Boone has overcome way more than most people could imagine."

"I show up every day and love on kids like Boone for moments like this," he responded. "And to answer your question, yes, I know exactly when and where you can find Doug Winters," he reported pointing to the end of the buffet line nearest them.

Boone's eyes followed the direction of the man's chubby finger where he spotted an old fellow who looked a lot like his dad.

Tears streamed unashamedly from the man's green eyes, each working through the wrinkles a hard life added to his face before disappearing beneath his chin.

"Boone," the man said, stepping closer.

Boone wondered how long he stood there. Boone had been so caught up in the conversation with Paul that he hadn't noticed him. "Dad," Boone replied, holding his ground. He never imagined this moment, at least not until recently.

Boone's dad wrapped his arms around him like a little child hugging a loved one, and Boone followed suit. They held one another tightly.

"I love you," Boone's dad professed.

Boone wasn't sure he could reciprocate those words. He paused for a long moment and thought about what Paul said about loving on others regardless of where they came from. He thought about how forgiving Beth freed him of so many burdens. "I love you too," Boone professed, and that's when the dam released. He couldn't hold back his emotions, and neither could Piper as she watched a reunion that warmed her heart.

"I am sorry, Boone. I am so sorry for the man I used to be," he confessed.

"Thanks," was all Boone knew to say.

"I know an apology doesn't take away the pain your mom and I caused you, but I truly am sorry for what we put you through.

Boone and Piper spent the next week getting to know Boone's dad. Although they stayed at a hotel, they spent a significant amount of time at his small apartment near the soup kitchen where they found out he walked every day because he didn't have a vehicle. It seemed odd to Boone not to see a beer bottle in one of his dad's hands and a cigarette in the other. However, his father didn't drink a single drop of alcohol, smoke a cigarette, or touch drugs during their visit.

Boone didn't think he hid it either because after eating lunch at the soup kitchen with his dad the day they found him, they went straight to his apartment. Boone couldn't help but open the fridge to look for beer. Not a single bottle occupied the shelves, and he also didn't see traces of drugs which he learned how to spot quite easily growing up in the environment in which he lived. He knew his dad's usual hiding spots in the bathroom, but nothing was there either.

Boone's dad promised him he hadn't touched drugs or alcohol since his wife died several years ago, and Boone believed him. Like

Paul Jackson claimed, his dad became a new man. Instead of being harsh and mean, he seemed gentle and patient. He repeatedly told Boone that he loved him although Boone didn't remember ever hearing those words before he showed up the other day.

On Boone's and Piper's flight home, she confirmed that she believed Boone's dad was clean. She was trained to spot signs of substance abuse which she hadn't seen the entire time they spent together.

31

When Boone and Piper returned to Duck, the home stretch of finishing the construction project began.

Inside, the walls got painted, the flooring laid, vanities and cabinets set, light fixtures, outlets, and switches put in, kitchen countertops and appliances placed, bathroom fixtures installed, mirrors hung, and the state-of-the-art alarm system completed.

Outside, the exterior finishes were installed, the trim completed, the landscaping and hardscaping finished, and the driveway poured.

All these things and other little touches turned the project into a house. To Boone's surprise, Claude put him in charge of picking out everything. He wrote that he trusted Boone's style. Boone always enjoyed helping clients with that part of the project, and this time, he was grateful for Piper's assistance.

On the morning when everything was said and done, Boone and Piper walked through the empty rooms one last time. As they talked, their echoes bounced off the freshly painted walls. Today they would hand the keys over to the owner, and it felt bittersweet. They both poured a big part of themselves into this project. They made mistakes, overcame challenges, and learned so much. Boone knew Claude would be proud, and it saddened him that his mentor couldn't be here to see the finished product.

Boone's and Piper's favorite spot was the deck on the top of the home where a hot tub and sitting area, enclosed by a glass barrier, overlooked the picturesque Atlantic Ocean.

"I could imagine relaxing with you and reading books in this hot tub for hours on end," Piper dreamed.

"We would have plenty of room for wine, candles, music, snacks, and just about anything else we wanted," Boone pointed out sitting on the marble platform surrounding the large hot tub.

After soaking in the seascape one last time, they walked down to the master bedroom where in the adjoining bathroom an enormous tub also overlooked the beach through a large window tinted from the outside.

"When the weather was cold or rainy, we could relax and read in here," Piper imagined out loud.

Boone shook his head in agreement and then they stepped out a set of French doors from the master that led to a private balcony. The wind whipped Piper's hair, and Boone sniffed the smell of sea salt as they watched the waves crash one after another. The roar of the ocean spoke to them as they stood in silence for a few moments.

"The owners are going to love waking up to this view every morning," Piper predicted as a flock of pelicans soared above the surf.

"I am jealous," Boone replied, "but I am so excited we get to meet the owners today. I hope they love their new house."

"They will, Boone," Piper guaranteed gazing proudly into his eyes. "You built an amazing home. No one would ever know this was the very first house on your resume. It's immaculate."

"I had a lot of help," Boone reminded Piper, wrapping his arms around her as he returned her gaze. "In fact, I couldn't have tackled this project without you and the team of people we put together."

"It was fun," Piper stated. "Stressful at times but rewarding to soak in the finished project." She paused to kiss Boone's lips, slowly and passionately. "I hate that we have to turn over the keys," she uttered when she pulled back.

A few minutes later, they walked through the bedroom and directly onto the indoor balcony that overlooked the living room featuring a twenty-foot vaulted ceiling.

"I hope the owners will let us see the place once it is furnished and decorated," Piper mentioned.

"That would be nice."

Hand-in-hand with fingers interlocked, Boone and Piper walked slowly down the grand staircase taking in the beauty one final time.

"A Christmas tree will look so good down there," Piper pointed out.

"A big, tall one," Boone added. "I am so glad we finished the house in time so the owners can have Christmas here if they want."

After returning from finding his dad, Boone's goal had been to finish the house by the middle of December, and that's precisely when the final home inspection was completed.

At the bottom of the steps, Boone and Piper turned into a room in the front of the house just inside the main door, where built-in bookshelves provided the feel of a library in the office.

"I would love to fill these shelves with books," Piper dreamed.

"If Claude knew you would be here to help, he probably would have given us that task, but he knew better than to ask me," Boone teased. "Anyways, you would have to buy out both of the island bookstores," Boone added.

"That's sweet of you to say," Piper replied. "And, of all the addictions in existence, a bookaholic is the best."

Boone laughed. "I can live with a bookaholic."

The last room they wandered into was the sunroom where the indoor heated swimming pool sparkled with salt-treated water.

"We should have brought our bathing suits," Boone mentioned.

"Why didn't we think of that sooner?" Piper responded in agreement.

The thought had crossed Boone's mind several times during the past few weeks while the pool company worked diligently on the final touches until the deadline.

With the certificate of occupancy granted, the last step was to close the doors, walk outside, and hand the keys to the owners who were supposed to meet them here at ten o'clock.

Piper and Boone nestled in on the front steps, appreciating the appearance of the gated circle drive as they waited. A tall cast iron fence, somewhat hidden in the trees, enclosed the entire property.

"I still remember the first time I pulled my Jeep into this lot," Piper reminisced. "The driveway was just a little gravel path with big dreams."

"That was a great day."

"Every day with you has been great."

"Right back at ya," Boone agreed.

Piper smiled. "You know, we are a lot like this house. We started fresh here in Duck and built this new life that we now share on this amazing island."

"Building us while we built a house has been fun," Boone noted.

"The Roots Beneath Us course was a Godsend."

"I agree, and I cannot wait to see what comes next."

Life really took off as soon as Piper and Boone began facing their fears with tenacity. With each one conquered they gained momentum, and their accomplishments grew rapidly.

One of the most recent fears Boone faced was removing his tent from the property, and he felt like he had left a part of his life on this lot in more ways than one. However, he looked forward to officially moving in with Piper.

A vehicle on the road slowed and turned into the driveway, moving cautiously through the opened gate before coming to a halt in front of the steps.

Recognizing the car, Boone furrowed his brow and looked at Piper. "I didn't know Preston was coming, did you?"

"No, but in our final meeting, he kept asking when we were turning over the keys to the owners. Remember, he said Claude asked him to document the date and time, so I guess he wanted to be here to meet them."

Boone glanced at his watch. "Thankfully he's a few minutes early."

"Hey guys," Preston called out as he shut his door.

"Hey, Preston," they responded in unison as if rehearsed. "We didn't know you were coming," Piper added.

"I got to looking at Claude's final wishes for the project and discovered he wanted me here to hand the keys over to the owners."

Piper and Boone turned and looked at each other. "Oh, okay," Boone replied. "I guess I figured we would get the honor," he added, trying not to sound defensive.

"This is what Claude wants, but I need you to stay because you also play an important role."

"That's a relief," Boone replied, "because we really want to meet the owners."

"Are you going to tell us if the owner is a celebrity, or do we have to wait until arrival to find out?"

"You guys are silly," he chuckled. "Hand me the keys, and I will read to you what Claude wrote, including the owner's name, which I think you will recognize."

"I hope it's a famous author," Piper mentioned excitedly.

Boone laughed. "That would explain the bookshelves."

Boone handed the keys to Preston somewhat reluctantly. Then Preston pulled a document from a manila envelope and began to read it aloud.

"Boone, I am so proud of you for building this home from the ground up. I knew you would create a masterpiece, and you deserve everything you have earned. I am even more proud that you discovered who you are and made The Roots Beneath Us journey a part of your life. You don't know this, but you saved my life. The day on the jobsite years ago when you asked if I had a few minutes to talk because you had something important to tell me, I almost said no. My life was falling apart, and when I left that home site where we had just handed the keys to the owner, I planned to end my life. Then we sat on the bed of my truck, and you told me about your past and current situation, and it was like God telling me I had more to accomplish on this earth. That was the first time in my life that I realized how much other people mattered. Our conversation that day led me to The Roots Beneath Us course." With tears in his eyes, Preston paused. He looked up at Boone and Piper whose faces were as wet as the fountain bubbling behind them. Preston smiled through his tears and handed the keys to Boone, and then his eyes returned to the document in his hands. "Boone, I have one last assignment for you. There is enough money in the budget to hire an interior decorator and fill this house to your liking. My friend, you built your own house from the roots up. Stay strong and be brave; this home is yours."

32

Boone and Piper had the time of their lives picking out the furnishings and decorations for the beach house. They visited stores in the Outer Banks and beyond, rented moving trucks to bring home large items, and ordered some stuff online. One of the first things they picked out was a Christmas tree that fit perfectly in front of the wall of windows overlooking the Atlantic Ocean. It meshed well with the layout of the room, and they added Christmas trinkets throughout the living room and trimmings on the outside of the house to celebrate the season.

Piper's wish to fill the bookshelves came true, and the local bookstores couldn't have been more delighted that she chose to purchase all the books from them. Her dream about reading in the oversized bathtub while sipping from a glass of wine, munching on fruit, and relaxing in the bubbles while glancing out the large window as the waves rolled toward the sand became a reality she cherished.

Boone and Piper set up a dance floor in the backyard similar to the one at her house, with globe lights draped amongst the live oaks. They spent a handful of the random warm December evenings out there and ate on the patio when the weather permitted.

Boone and Piper often put on swimsuits and hopped in the indoor heated pool. They swam, floated, and stared at the stars through the fully glassed enclosure. Living their lives like on a permanent vacation, they vowed never to take it for granted.

Other than moving into the new home, they went about their lives as usual. They rode bicycles, spent time at the beach, and on some cold evenings, erected the tent or simply carried the sleeping bag outside and placed it on the sandy beach or in the spot where they first kissed. Wrapped up tightly inside, just like on the night of the surprise thunderstorm, they warmed each other with body heat and let their bodies dance to the rhythm of a love that grew beautifully.

One morning after spending the whole night in the sleeping bag on the beach beneath the glow of the moon and the twinkle of millions of stars, Piper and Boone ventured into the local tattoo artist's studio with an idea that had been simmering in their minds.

They left the shop in flip flops with a vibrant live oak drawn on each side of their left ankles, the roots spiraling below their feet. The artist carved Piper's name into the tree on one side and Boone's on the other in the same spot. On the bottom of their feet, the roots of their trees bonded together, tying a beautiful knot with the initials TRBU—The Roots Beneath Us—etched masterfully.

They stared at their tattoos constantly for the first week while lying in bed talking, relaxing on the couch, sitting on the patio with Bailey, and everywhere else. Then after the suggested waiting period, they danced barefoot and couldn't quit smiling at the sight of their matching tattoos. Boone's bravery in receiving his first ink impressed Piper, and her new tattoo instantly became her favorite.

The day Piper showed her ankle to Kelly, the other dance instructors, and the kids was also when Kelly sat her down for a private conversation. Piper felt nervous but knew everything would turn out just right. Her mind wondered whether Kelly might no longer need her as a volunteer or offer her a full-time position, but she tried to think positively. Ultimately, Kelly revealed her decision to devote herself to motherhood and spend the early years with her daughter. She offered to sell the dance studio to Piper.

After discussing the decision with Boone and meeting with Preston at the bank, Piper became the proud new owner of the dance studio. As she desired, Boone upfitted the space to match her goals and dreams, and she cherished how their teamwork flourished in every aspect of their lives.

Piper and Boone celebrated with dinner at The Village Table & Tavern, one of their favorites, overlooking the Currituck Sound. They continued to frequent the Duck restaurants they loved, including Roadside Bar & Grill where Kayla waitressed. Boone told Piper about his interactions with Kayla, and the transparency helped the three of them become good friends. Boone even let Kayla continue to call him Daniel Boone.

On Christmas morning, Boone and Piper decided that rather than giving gifts to one another, they wanted to read through their journey lists and focus on being grateful for the gifts God provided.

Boone's eyes swelled with tears as he relived the fears he faced and the goals achieved: buy a car, get a phone, forgive people who hurt him including his parents, figure out God, learn to dance, seek professional counseling, forgive Beth, stand up to Beth, find a friends group, learn self-defense, live on his own, see a doctor about chronic pain, and the building the house project.

Someone reading the list who didn't understand all the intricate steps it took to reach each milestone might not appreciate the results the same. However, this journey meant the world to Boone, and he pressed through the challenges for himself, not others, allowing him to give his best to others.

After Boone and Piper read through his journey list line by line, reliving each step of the process, they read hers: buy a house, find a job/change careers, get a cat, forgive people who hurt her including her parents, ask forgiveness from Leslie, figure out God, see an eye doctor, find a friends group, own a dance studio, eat more dessert, serve the community, and find true love.

The separate notebook for the construction project included pages full of steps and notes that all came together masterfully. Reading through each one and reimagining the process and all the memories brought many happy tears.

Piper and Boone decided to make The Roots Beneath Us journey an ongoing part of their lives. They knew this course brought them together and helped build a solid foundation for their relationship; they looked forward to being each other's accountability partner indefinitely.

Boone appreciated how his wallet now had substance, including a license, debit card, and insurance cards. His safe held valuables that meant more than money, such as the title to his golf cart, vehicle, and home. With absolutely no debt, which he never imagined happening when he left Oakland, he could give generously, the way Claude James taught.

Boone pledged to send Paul Jackson money to help fund the soup kitchen. Boone and Piper decided to use her house for multiple purposes. They invited his dad and her parents to stay anytime the home was available, whether for a short vacation or an extended period. They also started a non-profit ministry to help women trapped in the strip club lifestyle. When Boone released the fear that Piper might fall back into that lifestyle, it opened his eyes to the need to help these people the same way Claude, Piper, and so many others helped him overcome abuse.

They planned to let women who agreed to walk away from stripping and take The Roots Beneath Us journey stay in the house temporarily.

Boone and Piper came to the conclusion that they couldn't imagine ever figuring out God. Still, His existence and Him playing a role in their lives and this world seemed inevitable. They reminisced about arriving in Duck at the same time and meeting, the free bicycle from the pastor that eventually led them to church, and the friends they met who stood by their side through Boone's surgery, the building project, and other ups and downs they encountered. These people accepted them for who they were, not for what they'd done.

Boone and Piper continued to feel a closeness to God through praying, meditating, fasting, and reading the Bible. Following the principles found within made sense and seemed to align with the person on their shoulder who encouraged them to follow the best path, although not always the easiest.

As the months after Christmas went by, Boone traveled back to Rochester for checkups; Piper's parents visited; Boone talked to his dad frequently on the phone; and life seemed to find a new normal. They continued building and tackling their journey lists. Boone learned CPR and earned his contractor's license; Piper met with former strippers to help them work through their journey lists; and they both officially added marriage and kids to their lists.

When Boone fully recovered from the invasive neck surgery, he agreed to ride on a horse with Piper a few more times. Eventually, he became comfortable enough to ride independently and began to love the freedom of galloping through the wind on the sandy beach.

Boone and Piper realized they didn't initially break down Boone's fear of riding a horse into small enough steps. He needed to understand the animal better and get a truer feel for how it felt to ride such a magnificent creature.

Boone jumped back into lessons with the hand-to-hand combat instructor although he previously worked with Piper slowly during his healing. One day Piper went to class with him because Boone wanted to show her a new self-defense tactic he learned for handling multiple attackers. The instructor brought in several students to perform the same feat that day, and they also provided the attackers. Boone performed his drill against two of the students near his level, and then the instructor wanted to show them how to fend off even more people. He asked Piper if she wanted to join.

At first, Piper shook her head no with a smirk on her face.

"Come on, I will go easy on you," the instructor promised. "This drill works best if I am cornered by four people."

Piper laughed. "Do I have to go easy on you?" she inquired.

Boone grinned but said nothing. He looked forward to seeing how this played out.

"Absolutely not," he replied. "Come at me as hard as you want, but realize I may meet your force with equal or greater resistance, but I won't injure you."

"Fair enough," Piper agreed, standing.

The four of them formed a square around the instructor.

"Piper, you come at me first as the initiator so I will not be distracted by the others yet. I know exactly what they can and can't handle."

Smiling through her focused eyes, Piper stepped in close and threw a punch like the average person might. However, she threw it intending to distract the instructor. When he dodged and grabbed her arm, as she imagined he would, she lowered her shoulder, thrust it into his stomach, and used his weight against him. Before he realized what happened, Piper flipped the instructor over her shoulder, and half a second later, she pinned him in a submission hold that took his breath away.

When he tapped out with cartoon-looking eyes, he asked, "Who are you?"

The others looked on with mouths gaped, even Boone. None of them moved more than a few inches.

"Boone's sidekick," she snickered.

The instructor looked at Boone from the ground. "You set me up," he laughed.

Boone shrugged his shoulders. "I didn't invite her onto the mat."

"I feel for anyone or any group who tries to mess with you two."

Piper thought Boone's instructor would want another shot at her since she caught him off guard. However, his response spoke volumes about his training intellect.

"This woman is above my pay grade," he announced to the class. "She needs to be the one standing in the middle of the square."

He talked Piper into it, and she said, "I won't go easy on you," to the instructor, "but I will on the rest of you."

They formed a square around her, and she handled things differently. She didn't wait for anyone to come at her; she took out the instructor first, even though he put up a bit more of a fight this time. Then she made quick work of Boone and the other two guys.

"You are welcome in this class anytime," the instructor acknowledged before Boone and Piper walked out sweating together yet still holding each other closely.

Boone hoped that neither he nor Piper would ever have to use their self-defense skills on another person but having the ability provided reassurance. They never heard a peep from Beth or Derek and prayed that chapter of their lives closed.

When Boone and Piper thought all the big surprises were over, the biggest happened when Boone printed a large portrait of his friend Claude James and hung it in the office.

"I want to show you something I did in honor of Claude," Boone told Piper.

When Piper walked into the office holding Boone's hand, she stared at the picture until she realized she quit breathing. Her whole body froze as hundreds of thoughts circled in her brain, connecting dots like clockwork. "You're telling me that is Claude James?" she finally uttered.

"Yes, my friend and mentor."

She glanced at Boone and then back at the large photo. "Boone, that is Hardy Turner."

Boone's brow furrowed. He looked at the picture and then at Piper. "That's Claude James," he clarified.

"Claude James and Hardy Turner are the same person," Piper revealed.

"How?" Boone asked in a daze.

"Hardy had businesses all over the country," she explained. "He also had many aliases because he wasn't always the man we came to know."

"Are you sure about all of this?"

"I am positive, Boone," Piper replied, stunned. "I am surprised I didn't connect these dots earlier," she announced, mesmerized. She remembered random thoughts crossing her mind about Hardy's and Claude's similarities. The vague ones included a close proximity in age based on loose descriptions. Each died of cancer, but the disease took far too many people in their age group. The fact Hardy and Claude both experienced The Roots Beneath Us journey and were responsible for encouraging her and Boone, respectively, to take the course was the only red flag, yet it hadn't seemed that bright. She never had a reason to connect the dots with threads. She simply accepted these incredible men as two different people, and she was glad she did. "I guess I didn't have any reason to investigate the possibility now that I am retired."

Boone smirked. "This is unbelievable," he noted. "It must have been fate, happenstance, or God."

"God."

Photo Credit: Mashal Smith

A Note from the Author

Thank you for reading THE ROOTS BENEATH US! I am grateful that you chose to invest your time in this book. If you haven't read my other novels, A BRIDGE APART, LOSING LONDON, A FIELD OF FIREFLIES, THE DATE NIGHT JAR, WHEN THE RIVERS RISE, WHERE THE RAINBOW FALLS, and ALONG THE DUSTY ROAD, I hope you will very soon. If you enjoyed the story you just experienced, please consider helping spread the novel to others in the following ways:

- REVIEW the novel online at Amazon.com, goodreads.com, bn.com, bamm.com, etc.
- RECOMMEND this book to friends (social groups, workplace, book club, church, school, etc.).

- VISIT my website: www.Joey-Jones.com
- SUBSCRIBE to my Email Newsletter for insider information on upcoming novels, behind-the-scenes looks, promotions, charities, and other exciting news.
- CONNECT with me on Social Media, and feel free to post a comment about the novel: "Like" Facebook.com/JoeyJonesWriter and "Follow" me at Instagram.com/JoeyJonesWriter. "Pin" on Pinterest. Write a blog post about the book.
- GIVE a copy of the novel to someone you know who would enjoy the story. Books make great presents (Birthday, Christmas, Teacher's Gifts, etc.).

Sincerely,
Joey Jones

About the Author

The writing style of Joey Jones has been described as a mixture of Nicholas Sparks, Richard Paul Evans, and James Patterson. The ratings and reviews of his novels A BRIDGE APART (2015), LOSING LONDON (2016), A FIELD OF FIREFLIES (2018), THE DATE NIGHT JAR (2019), WHEN THE RIVERS RISE (2020), WHERE THE RAINBOW FALLS (2022), and ALONG THE DUSTY ROAD (2023) reflect the comparison to *New York Times* bestselling authors. Prior to becoming a full-time novelist, Joey worked in the marketing field. He holds a Bachelor of Arts in Business Communications from the University of Maryland University College, where he earned a 3.8 GPA.

Fun facts: Joey Jones lives in North Carolina with his family. In 2016, he underwent successful neck surgery. Joey loves Italian food and sweet tea. While writing this novel, he traveled to the Outer Banks several times and spent most of his time in Duck.

Joey Jones is currently writing his ninth novel and working on various projects pertaining to his published works.

Book Club/Group Discussion Questions

1. Were you immediately engaged in the novel?

2. What emotions did you experience as you read the book?

3. Which character is your favorite? Why?

4. What do you like most about the story as a whole?

5. What is your favorite part/scene in the novel?

6. Do any particular passages from the book stand out to you?

7. As you read, what are some things you thought might happen but didn't?

8. Would you have liked to see anything turn out differently?

9. Is the ending satisfying? If so, why? If not, why not, and how would you change it?

10. Why might the author have chosen to tell the story the way he did?

11. If you could ask the author a question, what would you ask?

12. Have you ever read or heard a story anything like this one?

13. Have you ever experienced abuse? If so, what did you do/are you doing to overcome it?

14. In what ways does this novel relate to your own life?

15. Would you reread this novel?

Also by Joey Jones

A BRIDGE APART

A Bridge Apart, the debut novel by Joey Jones, is a remarkable love story that tests the limits of trust and forgiveness . . .

In the quaint river town of New Bern, North Carolina, at 28 years of age, the pieces of Andrew Callaway's life are all falling into place. His real estate firm is flourishing, and he's engaged to be married in less than two weeks to a beautiful banker named Meredith Hastings. But, when Meredith heads to Tampa, Florida—the wedding location—with her mother, fate, or maybe some human intervention, has it that Andrew happens upon Cooper McKay, the only other woman he's ever loved

A string of shocking emails lead Andrew to question whether he can trust his fiancée, and in the midst of trying to unravel the mystery, he finds himself spending time with Cooper. When Meredith catches wind of what's going on back at home, she's forced to consider calling off the wedding, which ultimately draws Andrew closer to Cooper. Andrew soon discovers he's making choices he might not be able, or even want, to untangle. As the story unfolds, the decisions made will drastically change the lives of everyone involved and bind them closer together than they could have ever imagined.

LOSING LONDON

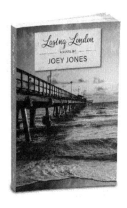

Losing London is an epic love story filled with nail-biting suspense, forbidden passion, and unexpected heartbreak.

When cancer took the life of Mitch Quinn's soulmate, London Adams, he never imagined that one year later her sister, Harper, whom he had never met before, would show up in Emerald Isle, NC. Until this point, his only reason to live, a five-year-old cancer survivor named Hannah, was his closest tie to London.

Harper, recently divorced, never imagined that work—a research project on recent shark attacks—and an unexpected package from London would take her back to the island town where her family had vacationed in her youth. Upon her arrival, she meets and is instantly swept off her feet by a local with a hidden connection that eventually causes her to question the boundaries of love.

As Mitch's and Harper's lives intertwine, they discover secrets that should have never happened. If either had known that losing London would have connected their lives in the way it did, they might have chosen different paths.

A FIELD OF FIREFLIES

Growing up, Nolan Lynch's family was unconventional by society's standards, but it was filled with love, and his parents taught him everything he needed to know about life, equality, and family. A baseball player with a bright future, Nolan is on his way to the major leagues when tragedy occurs. Six years later, he's starting over as the newest instructor at the community college in Washington, North Carolina, where he meets Emma Pate, who seems to be everything he's ever dreamed of—beautiful, assertive, and a baseball fan to boot.

Emma Pate's dreams are put on hold after her father dies, leaving her struggling to keep her family's farm. When a chance encounter with a cute new guy in town turns into an impromptu date, Emma finds herself falling for him. But, she soon realizes Nolan Lynch isn't who she thinks he is.

Drawn together by a visceral connection that defies their common sense, Emma's and Nolan's blossoming love is as romantic as it is forbidden, until secrets—both past and present—threaten to tear them apart. Now, Nolan must confront his past and make peace with his demons or risk losing everything he loves . . . again.

Emotionally complex and charged with suspense, *A Field of Fireflies* is the unforgettable story of family, love, loss, and an old baseball field where magic occurs, including the grace of forgiveness and second chances.

Also by Joey Jones

THE DATE NIGHT JAR

An unlikely friendship. An unforgettable love story.

When workaholic physician Ansley Stone writes a letter to the estranged son of a patient asking him to send the family's heirloom date night jar, she only intended to bring a little happiness to a lonely old man during his final days. Before long, she finds herself increasingly drawn to Cleve Fields' bedside, eager to hear the stories of his courtship with his beloved late wife, Violet, that were inspired by the yellowed slivers of paper in the old jar. When Cleve asks her to return the jar to his son, Ansley spontaneously decides to deliver it in person, if only to find out why no one, including his own son, visits the patient she's grown inexplicably fond of.

Mason Fields is happily single, content to spend his days running the family strawberry farm and his evenings in the company of his best friend, a seventeen-year-old collie named Callie. Then Ansley shows up at his door with the date night jar and nowhere to stay. Suddenly, she's turning his carefully ordered world upside down, upsetting his routine, and forcing him to remember things best left in the past. When she suggests *they* pull a slip of paper from the jar, their own love story begins to develop. But before long, their newfound love will be tested in ways they never imagined, as the startling truth about Mason's past is revealed...and Ansley's future is threatened.

Also by Joey Jones

WHEN THE RIVERS RISE

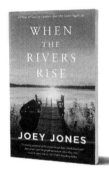

Three hearts, pushed to the limit. Can they weather another storm?

High school sweethearts Niles and Eden shared a once-in-a-lifetime kind of love until an accident—and Eden's subsequent addiction to pain medication—tore them apart. Now divorced, their son Riley is Niles's whole world, and he'll do anything to keep him safe.

In constant pain, chronically tired, and resentful of Riley's relationship with his dad, Eden is a shadow of the woman she once was. When she meets Kirk, a charismatic drummer who makes her feel alive again, she's torn between evacuating with Riley before a hurricane hits and the exciting new life that beckons.

Reese has never quite gotten over the death of her father, a cop who was shot in the line of duty. Now a detective herself and the only special operations officer on the East Ridge, Tennessee, police force without children, she volunteers to go help as a potential category five hurricane spins straight toward the North Carolina coast.

As Hurricane Florence closes in, their lives begin to intersect in ways they never imagined as each is forced to confront issues from the past that will decide the future...their own, each other's, and Riley's.

Emotions swell like the rivers in the approaching storm in this poignant story of guilt, second chances, and the lengths we'll go to protect the ones we love.

Also by Joey Jones

WHERE THE RAINBOW FALLS

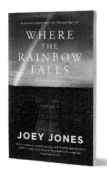

In the face of a storm, a father's love is the most powerful force.

With Hurricane Florence rapidly approaching the North Carolina coastline, all Niles North can think about is his five-year-old son Riley and how he wished he bent the law when he had the chance to evacuate him. Now, instead of being safe in Hickory with his dad, Riley is with Niles's ex-wife Eden, who's decided to ride out the storm at home with her drummer friend. Desperate to get back to his son as the storm waters rise, Niles begs Reese, an attractive police detective and rescue worker, to drive him back to New Bern.

Refusing to help Niles seems nearly impossible for Reese who quickly realizes she's in deeper than she should be—both professionally and emotionally—especially since she's drawn to almost everything about him. As the two undertake a perilous journey into the eye of the storm, Niles's worst fears come true, setting in motion a series of events that will change both of their lives forever.

Also by Joey Jones

ALONG THE DUSTY ROAD

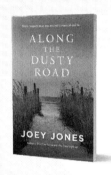

An unexpected love. A surprising second chance.

Everything Luke Bridges always wanted is in the small coastal North Carolina town where he has spent most of his twenty-six years—a fulfilling mental health therapy career, a loving family, baseball games with his dad, an adventurous beach life, and a close-knit group of friends. The only piece missing is someone to share it with, a genuine and lasting love that satisfies the soul.

He once thought Emily Beckett, the girl he dated ten years ago who has happened back into his life as his sidekick on the coed beach volleyball team, could be that someone. Emily has a seven-year-old son and an ex-husband with dangerous addictions. Although Luke enjoys spending time with Ayden, he has no interest in the challenges of being a stepfather.

Luke only dates women he can see himself marrying. With the "just friends" title firmly placed on his relationship with Emily, he agrees to a blind date with Mindy, his mentor's cousin. As he explores a connection with Mindy, the "just friends" veil with Emily is suddenly ripped away. Now he is torn between two very different women—one who might be perfectly right for him and one who doesn't seem to fit the mold but just might make his dreams of forever come true.

Fears, tragedy, love, and second chances all collide *Along the Dusty Road.*

Made in the USA
Columbia, SC
11 November 2024

45730035R00167